Missing Marie

Jo Harries

Grosvenor House
Publishing Limited

All rights reserved
Copyright © Jo Harries, 2023

The right of Jo Harries to be identified as the author of this
work has been asserted in accordance with Section 78
of the Copyright, Designs and Patents Act 1988

The book cover is copyright to Jo Harries

This book is published by
Grosvenor House Publishing Ltd
Link House
140 The Broadway, Tolworth, Surrey, KT6 7HT.
www.grosvenorhousepublishing.co.uk

This book is sold subject to the conditions that it shall not, by way of
trade or otherwise, be lent, resold, hired out or otherwise circulated
without the author's or publisher's prior consent in any form of
binding or cover other than that in which it is published and
without a similar condition including this condition being
imposed on the subsequent purchaser.

This book is a work of fiction. Any resemblance to
people or events, past or present, is purely coincidental.

A CIP record for this book
is available from the British Library

Paperback ISBN 978-1-80381-698-2
eBook ISBN 978-1-80381-699-9

To Jonathan.

Acknowledgements

My thanks to: Catharine Oldroyd and the family and friends who have helped me.

Prologue

The threat of a housing development ruining a wildlife reserve has been resolved, but many things stay the same for the residents of Merebank Bay. Bryony is still searching for her perfect husband, Sharon is striving to hold her family together, and Stuart is still an enthusiastic birdwatcher. Marie is a friend to everyone, so the local community is shocked by the news that she has bought a one-way train ticket, and disappeared.

Chapter 1

Marie slowly swizzled the remaining gin and tonic in the balloon shaped glass, before picking out a piece of the delicious alcohol infused strawberry. The heat of the day still lingered, but the wind off the sea brought a chill to the air. Shivering slightly, she wrapped a cardigan around her shoulders and watched as the garden slowly began to close down for the night, and the chorus of bird song dwindled to the single, melodic call of a blackbird in the hawthorn tree.

Gathering the crumbs from her plate, she scattered them on the lawn and entered the house just in time to watch her favourite television drama. When her phone rang, she was tempted to ignore it. She'd promised herself a leisurely week off from all her usual activities while her husband Stuart was away, and as both he and her son Damian had already phoned earlier, she wasn't expecting any more calls tonight. But with Stuart away she couldn't take the risk.

Seeing her daughter's name she hesitated, her finger hovering over the phone, but Debbie never rang her at this time. Something serious must have happened and it might mean one of the children was ill. Apprehensively she slid the accept button, pressed the loudspeaker and prepared herself for the worst. Suddenly, the room was filled with the sound of Debbie's hysterical voice, and gripping the phone tightly, Marie struggled to make sense of what she was hearing, but it was almost impossible between the racking sobs.

'Debbie, what's wrong? Are you hurt?' she asked.

'No, well yes, in a way. Oh, I'll tell you when you get here. You will come, won't you?'

Marie hesitated, hardly able to believe what she was hearing.

'Are you asking me to come to you?'

'Yes, please come as soon as you can,' she implored. 'Oh, and mum, I nearly forgot, I'm living at a different address. I've sent you a text, you must check it before you set off or you'll never get here. You will come, won't you mum?' Debbie begged.

'Of course, I will, if you need me.' Marie replied indignantly, but before she could ask what had prompted this cry for help, the call was cut off, leaving no opportunity to discuss how or when she was going to get to this unknown destination. She sat down, and tried to compose herself while she decided what to do next in this almost unheard of, situation. Checking her messages, she found the address Debbie had sent, and to her surprise it was in a town miles away from Debbie's previous home, where she had lived all her married life.

She herself, was unable to drive that distance, her son Damian would be at work and her husband Stuart was in Portugal on a birdwatching holiday she'd given him for his birthday. There was no point contacting either of them tonight, it would only worry them, so she would wait until the morning to let them know what she was planning to do.

An hour later, tired and bleary eyed from navigating many pages of online train time-tables, she'd worked out the best way to reach Debbie, but after several fruitless attempts to download the tickets, she gave up and climbed wearily into bed. Something was niggling at her, preventing her from sleeping, until it came to her in the middle of the long night. She'd sensed there was another person in the room with Debbie, someone who was interrupting when she was trying to speak to Marie. She spent a restless night trying to work out what Debbie had been trying to tell her, but it was no good, she would just have to get there as quickly as possible.

She packed enough clothes and toiletries to last a few days and dithered over what to wear for the journey. She decided navy trousers and jacket, with her pale blue blouse were practical for travelling. Now, when she was ready and waiting for the taxi to arrive, she tried to make contact with Stuart and her son Damian, but there was no reply from either of them, so she would have to try again later. She put her case in the hall and opened the cupboard under the stairs to access the safe where they kept a large amount of money, intended only to be taken out and used in an emergency. She took a wad of notes held by an elastic band, and tucked it in the bottom of her handbag, covering it with small packets of tissues and her make-up bag, and then impulsively, she removed two more twenty-pound notes, which she put in the zipped pocket of her jacket. She had no other cash in her purse and no way of knowing if Debbie would need financial help when she reached her, so she was confident Stuart would agree this was an emergency.

Expecting to be alone in the house, she'd cancelled some of the regular milk delivery, but as she returned to the kitchen, she gave a tut of annoyance at the sight of the outstanding bill lying on the worktop. When the text alert on her phone told her the taxi would arrive in five minutes, she grabbed an envelope out of a drawer and put the money and the bill inside it, which she then hurriedly pushed into the side pocket of her handbag, ready to post through Nancy's letterbox next door. They had a standing arrangement between them, when either was away, so she would know it was for the milkman.

Opening the front door, she was startled to find the taxi driver already standing on the doorstep. Flustered, and in her haste to go back inside to check the doors and windows were securely locked, she forgot all about the envelope, as she followed the driver down the path to the waiting car.

It was early morning, and a flimsy veil of grey cloud still covered the sky, but as the taxi turned onto the promenade the sun was breaking through on the horizon, and silhouetted in a single ray of sunshine was a small fishing boat surrounded by seagulls jostling and harrying each other for the easy pickings being thrown overboard. A flock of oyster catchers tried vainly to join in the feast, but lack of size and ungainly flight meant they were no match for the larger gulls, and they were quickly sent on their way, with their strident calls of pic-pic-pic filling the air. Just beyond the jetty, the shrimp boats were hauled up out of the water, and some of the oyster catchers were resting there, hoping to return to the fishing boat when the gulls had had their fill.

The roads were quiet, prior to the rush of workers and tourists who would soon be streaming into the resort, but the daily stirrings of the town were just beginning to be seen and heard, as shopkeepers swept the pavements and rolled out displays to the front of their premises. A few joggers made their way down the cobbled streets towards the sea front, and the sweeping vista of the bay with miles of open space and sky.

The journey was short and uneventful and soon they were stopping on the forecourt outside the station. The platform was almost deserted, and although her case was small and easy to handle, the taxi driver insisted on accompanying her, to make sure she was standing in the best place to board the train when it arrived. When he discovered she didn't have a ticket, he helped her to purchase one from the machine on the platform. Exactly, on time, the train to Preston drew into the station and she was on the second part of her journey.

Arriving at Preston, she was surprised to find it teeming with people even at this early hour, and most of them were walking quickly with a sense of purpose which momentarily overwhelmed her, but she quickly pulled herself together and scanned the signs leading to the different platforms. The layout of the station was familiar to her, so she had no difficulty finding the way to platform four, which was reached by descending a long flight of iron steps. Fortunately, the time she'd spent mapping out her journey the previous evening, hadn't been wasted, as it enabled her to go directly to platform four where she would be boarding her train.

Before going down the steps, she joined the queue to purchase a ticket for the rest of her journey, and in her hurry, she bought a ticket to Manchester Airport, the train's final destination, instead of Wilmslow, an earlier stop. With a sense of relief for successfully negotiating the journey so far, she decided to buy a cappuccino from the coffee shop on the platform, and seeing an empty bench, she sat down, clutching her bag in one hand and gripping the carton of coffee so tightly in the other it was in danger of spilling.

Further down the platform, two boys were fooling around playing a game of tag, but apart from sometimes getting in other people's way, they didn't give the impression they were looking for trouble. They were both wearing expensive looking trainers, and grey hoodies, which they kept pulling over their faces, but as they no doubt should be in school, they were probably hoping they wouldn't be recognised. She guessed they were between ten or twelve years old, so hopefully there would be an adult travelling with them.

When it was almost time for her train to arrive, she drank the remaining coffee and looked around for the nearest litter bin. She left her case for the short time it took her to walk quickly to the bin situated at the entrance to the café. As she turned to make her way back, she caught sight of the eldest boy moving away from near the bench where she'd been sitting. She was surprised at how quickly he'd moved, but her case was still where she'd left it, and her attention was suddenly drawn to a group of people shaking their heads, while gathering their luggage together and moving down the platform. Curious to find out what was happening, she collected her case and went to ask a man standing nearby, if he could help her.

'Excuse me,' she said. 'What are they saying? I can't quite make it out.'

'Basically, we are on the wrong platform,' he told her. 'Due to an obstruction on the line, the train to Manchester Airport will now be leaving from platform five. It's already there,' he added, raising his eyebrows.

Her heart sank as she thanked him, but glancing up at the departure board, the flashing number five confirmed what he'd just told her, so there was nothing to be done except follow the instructions and join everyone else hurrying towards platform five.

'Don't worry,' he said, seeing her concern. 'It's not due to leave yet.'

Having heard disturbing stories, about pickpockets targeting women's handbags at railway stations, she had an uneasy feeling about the large amount of money in her own bag. Deciding she couldn't take a chance, she moved to one side to open her case and put her handbag into it. She was re-arranging the contents to squeeze it in, when one of the boys she'd seen earlier, approached her. Instinctively she put the top down and securely fastened the zip.

'You dropped this,' he said, holding out an envelope. She began to explain it wasn't hers, when she recognised something familiar about it. Cautiously, she put her hand out to take it from him and saw the note and milk money folded inside.

'Thank-you,' she said. 'It must have fallen out of my handbag. Here, let me give you something.' Her words were cut short by the panic-stricken voice of the other boy.

'Adam, come on,' he yelled, 'we'll miss it and he'll kill us if we're not there.'

'Don't panic,' the boy replied, but nevertheless, he too raced away. The envelope dropped between them as he went, and Marie watched helplessly as it was caught in the blast of air from a train roaring through the station. Anxiously, she looked around her, but the only person left on the platform was the man she'd spoken to earlier. As he'd already helped her and was now absorbed in a telephone conversation, she was reluctant to disturb him. Twenty pounds wasn't worth missing the train for, so she walked as fast as she could, until she reached the steps leading back up to the bridge.

It was easier to negotiate the steps, with just one piece of luggage, but when she reached the top, she struggled to catch up with the few remaining business people who were already hurrying across the bridge. When she reached the top of the steps leading down to platform five, she was reassured to see the train waiting for the last passengers to arrive.

She paused for a moment to catch her breath, and as she was about to put her foot on the first step, she glanced round to make sure no-one was waiting to pass her. Out of nowhere the boy, Adam, appeared in front of her, but close up, he appeared older, more like a young man.

'I'll carry your case,' he said as he put an arm out towards her, but she gripped the handle tightly.

'No thank-you' she replied firmly, 'I can manage it myself.' He reached out once more, determined to pull the case from her, and as she struggled to hold on to the handle, her foot slipped over the edge of the step. For a few seconds she teetered in mid-air until she lost her balance completely and with her arms flailing in a desperate attempt to catch hold of something, she felt herself falling helplessly down the steps. Every bone in her body screamed with pain, until her head hit the ground and everything went black.

Chapter 2

Bryony took the tray from Sharon and carried it into Ralph's bedroom, where she was surprised to find him sitting in his chair, already showered and clean shaven. He was recovering remarkably quickly from the heart attack which had temporarily taken away his independence, and soon he would be able to take care of himself again. As his mobility increased, the carers who'd nursed him through the worst of the attack were gradually reducing their hours, and she began once more to believe the time was approaching when she would be free to leave, and begin the exciting new life she was planning for the future.

Just the mere thought of it, and a frisson of excitement ignited her body. She tried not to dwell on the impact it would have on Ralph's wellbeing, but there was still quite a way to go and she was determined to stay until he was fully recovered. After quickly checking the food was prepared to her satisfaction, she placed the tray on the table and swung it over his lap.

'Good morning, Father-in-law,' she said brightly, 'porridge with blueberries, toast and coffee, just as you like them.'

'Thank-you, and a very good morning to you. Hopefully, I'll soon be back to normal and I won't be a burden to you anymore.'

Bryony tapped his shoulder affectionately,

'Don't be silly, you are never a burden to me, you know that. Now, I'll leave you to enjoy your breakfast in peace, while I go down to have a word with that son of mine. I'm expecting to be faced with another of his hair-brained schemes, which I will have to turn down, due to his fanciful ideas.'

Ralph was thoughtful as he took a spoonful of the porridge and gave a sigh of appreciation when he tasted it.

'Hugh has some good ideas Bryony, don't be too hard on him. He's young and enthusiastic, so you must give him a chance to develop. You would be wise I think, to take into consideration that one day you'll be glad to hand over the reins to Hugh, and he needs to be ready.'

'I suppose you're right,' she acquiesced reluctantly 'but you must admit he is a bit headstrong.'

'I wonder who he gets that from?' Ralph chuckled, tucking into his breakfast. 'Could it be his mother?'

Bryony left the room with Ralph's comments ringing in her head. He couldn't possibly know what she was planning to do, and his allusions to her leaving the business were merely coincidental, but she was hoping to keep it that way. It was true she would be leaving her son in charge, hopefully much sooner than Ralph envisaged, and before that he needed more training, but she would prefer it if he didn't go over her head and ask his grandfather Ralph to fund one of his schemes.

If that happened, it was possible Ralph might seek the opinions of his financial advisers on the viability of Hugh's proposition, and at the moment, that was something she'd rather avoid. She would deal with it, if it happened, but for now, the foyer was alive with people waiting for attention. Bryony, acknowledged the greetings of familiar guests who returned year after year, while at the same time, she was careful not to miss out the newer clientele. The time spent talking and discussing the local attractions could prove to be invaluable, but sometimes it had to be carefully managed or time would be wasted, as Justin was sometimes inclined to do.

Unfortunately, this morning she found herself caught by a very regular visitor who always demanded her undivided attention, unavoidably making her several minutes late for her meeting with Hugh.

He was waiting in a small meeting room, but unusually, there were no papers with drawings or plans, on the table in front of him.

'Hi mum,' Hugh greeted her. How's granddad?'

'He's very well, getting stronger every day. I think he'll be able to manage without any help soon, but he'll still want to keep the physiotherapist. Ralph has a lot of faith in him and thinks the exercises are contributing to his recovery.'

'Ah, well, that's very interesting,' Hugh replied nervously, 'you see it leads me into what I want us to talk about.'

Puzzled, she took a seat opposite him.

'You want to talk about granddad?'

'No, not exactly, but about the benefits of keeping fit. I was thinking it would be a good idea to have a gym, here in the hotel.'

Bryony shook her head in despair. So, this was what it was all about. She was tired of pointing out the lack of room available in the hotel for any of his ambitious plans, and she was never going to agree to using the car-park to build something ridiculous like a swimming pool.

'Don't worry, it doesn't involve your precious car-park,' he said, as if reading her mind and she listened cautiously as he told her of his plan to turn a small conference room into a gymnasium. Bryony's thoughts were racing, as she tried to assess the size of the proposal. She needed him to see she wasn't turning it down out of hand, so she asked exactly which of the rooms he was thinking about?'

'The small conference room at the back. It isn't very well used' he added quickly. but it is just about big enough and is accessible from the rear entrance, which is good because it means people won't need to go through the hotel to reach it.'

Providing any facilities to non-residents, went against everything she believed in regarding the hotel, but when she re-iterated what she'd said many times before, he laughed and told her she was old fashioned.

'I reckon we could make it residents only,' he conceded, his shoulders sagging, 'but...'

'Go on,' she said impatiently, 'what were you going to say?'

'You are not going to like hearing it mum, but you are a bit of a snob. Dad told me how difficult you made it for him when he wanted to invite local people to come into our bar here, but despite that he made it a real go of it. And I've got to say, he and Janet have made a huge success of their new venture.'

Bryony bristled at the effrontery. This wasn't the first time she'd heard the hotel being compared unfavourably with the golf club, but she wasn't prepared to hear it from her own son.

'Are you comparing The Portland Arms with the golf club?' she demanded.

Hugh was keenly aware he'd upset his mother yet again, but this time his blood was boiling. She stamped on any idea he put to her, almost before she'd heard him out, but this time he was determined to make her listen.

'You never give dad praise for anything, do you? But you know what? He's doing really well, no matter what you say.'

Bryony stared at him. 'How dare you speak to me like that?'

He was already pushing his chair back, ready to leave. 'I'm sorry,' he replied. 'I was out of order, but I'm not taking it back. I still say dad is making a good fist of it. Anyway, I'm going to ask granddad what he thinks.'

Bryony was fuming, but she needed more time, so she told Hugh to produce a plan of what he had in mind, and that way, they could give it some serious consideration when they discussed it again.

Hugh didn't respond immediately. 'Is this a delaying tactic?' he asked dubiously.

'No, but I really don't want granddad involved in the business, so let's keep it under wraps for a while. There is no real need to involve him yet.'

'Okay,' Hugh replied. 'There isn't a problem, is there?'

'Nothing that you don't already know about. Old age, and of course he has had a heart attack. It's hard enough convincing him to follow doctor's orders to take things easy, and I could do without any extra pressure.'

Hugh nodded. 'I understand. I'll do as you ask and put it all on paper for you, before even checking granddad out.'

Breathing a sigh of relief, she promised to give his proposition some careful thought, and left Hugh looking far more optimistic about the future. She was confident she'd secured some valuable time to sort out her own financial plans, before Hugh became more impatient to make a start on his project. Young people were in so much hurry these days.

Mid-morning, she went into the office to collect the post which Justin, the reception manager, had already sifted through. There were several magazines and envelopes in different sizes in Ralph's basket, which made them tricky to hold with one hand. As she raised her free hand to knock on his door, an envelope slid from the middle of the pile onto the floor. She picked it up, and looked at it with interest. It was a square envelope, and obviously contained a card of some description, but Ralph's birthday wasn't due and the quality of the paper, and the beautiful script, didn't quite fit with a get-well card.

It would be a simple act to ease the envelope open and satisfy her curiosity, but instead she resisted and placed it on top of the pile before entering. He was sitting in his favourite chair in front of the window, where he had a panoramic view across the bay. On the small table next to him, was a pile of his favourite magazines.

'Oh, I see you've already been attended to, that's good,' she said, 'do you want your magazines nearer to you?'

'No thank-you dear, put the post on top of them if you don't mind. I'm enjoying taking in the view for now.'

'There's a very pretty envelope here,' she told him, holding it up and turning it around, 'do you want to see what it is?'

'No thank-you, I'll open it later.' Although he was unable to see her face, he could sense her disappointment at his unwillingness to share it with her. He wasn't being deliberately secretive, but he had a good idea what the envelope contained and he wasn't sure how she would react to it. He'd been hoping it would arrive on one of Bryony's days off, when his post was brought to him by a member of staff.

Bryony placed it with his magazines on the table.

'I'll see you later then.' She turned to leave the room, but stopped when Ralph put out his hand.

'No, let's do it now.' He handed it to her and watched as she slid the silver blade under the fold of the envelope and pulled out a beautiful, embossed card. She turned pale and gasped with shock.

'I'm so sorry my dear,' Ralph said as she stared at the card.

'You knew of course,' she replied, and he simply nodded his head.

It was an invitation to the wedding of Janet Bancroft and Colin Portland. He had never meant much to her, even when they were first married, and Janet Bancroft was welcome to him, but somehow, she'd found a kind of satisfaction in knowing Colin hadn't married again. But now, her boring ex-husband was marrying mousy Janet Bancroft and, of course, Ralph was being invited to his son's wedding.

Somehow the possibility had never entered her mind, but here they were, planning their wedding, and in a move which was rubbing salt in the wound it was being held at the golf club. Someone had shown initiative in having the club registered for weddings, but it was unthinkable for the son of Ralph Portland to hold his wedding there. Even if they begged her to, she would never contemplate attending their wedding, but despite that, her feelings of rejection were real.

What really hurt, was knowing it would already be the main topic of conversation in the town and yet no-one had thought to tell her. Not even Marie, her oldest friend, who would have been one of the first to know. She picked up the phone to confront her and listened with annoyance to the characterless voice of the answer machine telling her Marie wasn't available. The other place she was likely to be was the Royal National Lifeboat Institution, gift shop, where she worked as a volunteer several hours a week. Her patience was stretched even further when Marie's friend Claire answered and told her Marie had arranged to have a few days off work.

Bryony took a deep breath and, with a nonchalance she didn't feel, asked if Marie had gone away on holiday. Claire told her she had no idea where Marie was, she hadn't told her and Claire hadn't asked.

'I do know she has been feeling tired recently and she decided to have a break from her usual activities and voluntary work while Stuart was away.'

'By break, did she mean a short holiday away from Merebank?' she demanded, bristling with indignation, 'because she isn't at home. Anyway, what do you mean by saying Stuart's away? Isn't he with her?'

Claire bit her tongue and tried very hard to keep her temper in check. 'Surely you know Stuart is in Portugal on a birdwatching holiday?' In the ensuing silence, Claire couldn't resist adding. 'I presumed she'd told you that.'

'Of course, she did, I'd just forgotten,' Bryony lied. 'I still don't understand why she isn't answering her phone.'

'She did tell me she was going to have her phone switched off most of the time. So, she wouldn't be disturbed,' Claire added pointedly. 'Except of course, for the pre-arranged chats with Stuart. Do you want to leave a message or not? I've got customers waiting to be served.'

Bryony hesitated, but she didn't want to give Claire the satisfaction of having the upper hand, so she curtly declined.

'No, thank-you. I'll no doubt speak to her soon anyway.'

'Please yourself,' Claire muttered, as she replaced the phone. 'Anyway, I wouldn't tell you if I did know something.' She knew she'd rattled Bryony, but she was telling the truth, she didn't know where Marie was. For some reason, Marie had been secretive about what she was planning to do, but despite her actions being out of character, Claire had respected them. Respect was something she didn't have for Bryony Portland, in fact she'd never had any time for her, and she was well aware the feeling was mutual. For some inexplicable reason, Bryony seemed to believe she was closer to Marie than any of her other friends.

In her head, Bryony went over the brief conversation with Claire. It was obvious she knew more than she was admitting to, but why all the secrecy? Marie's behaviour was so strange and secretive, it seemed to point to one thing. Was that why she'd made sure Stuart was safely out of the way in another country? It was highly unlikely, but not impossible that Marie had another man in her life.

'Well, well,' she said to herself, 'Marie Fowler, what a dark horse you are.'

Chapter 3

Sharon watched her youngest child, Lily, run to join her friends in the middle of the playground, and waited in vain for her to turn and wave goodbye. It was a glorious June morning, and with time to spare before she was due to start work, she took the route leading towards the sea, with the intention of walking the final half mile along the promenade.

Checking her watch, she calculated there was sufficient time for her to take the short detour to where her friend Louisa lived. When time permitted and Sharon's shifts coincided with Louisa's trips to the playgroup, they took the opportunity of walking into town together and catching up on the latest family and local news.

A few years ago, following a proposal for a housing development which threatened to encroach on a wildlife sanctuary, Sharon's husband Tom, had been one of the builders involved. At the time, as newcomers to the area, they had been made unwelcome by some of the local residents. A solution to the problem had come from an unexpected source, when Ralph Portland decided to sell the family home, Portland House and the land it was built on, in the wake of his son Colin's divorce.

Portland Point, officially opened by Ralph Portland, offered starter homes for Merebank's aspiring young people, grander houses for the more prosperous of the community, and various designs in between.

Bryony Portland, who'd married into the family, was a woman people loved to hate, but in the few years Sharon had known her she'd found no reason to complain, especially as Bryony had given her a part-time job as a hotel receptionist when she first came to live in Merebank Bay with her family.

Four years ago, when Louisa and her husband Damian, after many failed IVF treatments, had been distraught to learn that Louisa would never be able to carry a child full term, Sharon had offered to be a surrogate mother, using one of the couple's own embryos.

Approaching the house Sharon could hear the childish chatter of Pearl, the successful outcome of the surrogacy, and it changed to loud shouts of joy when Sharon arrived. Pearl's face lit up and she wriggled out of her mother's grasp to throw herself headlong into Sharon's arms. While Louisa gathered the things she needed for the playgroup, Sharon put Pearl on the push-along child's tricycle which Louisa used, to speed up the process of getting anywhere on time. She felt a special bond with the child she'd carried in her womb for nine months and she would never forget the joy they'd shared when Pearl was born.

'Come along, little beauty,' she said to her now, 'let's get this show on the road, or aunty Sharon will be late for work, and we all know what that means.'

'Is Bryony still a stickler for timekeeping?' Louisa asked, as they manoeuvred the tricycle over the threshold.

'I think so, but I make sure I'm never late, so I don't really know.'

Builders working on the house opposite, called out greetings to them as they passed, and Louisa told Sharon how much she and Damian appreciated his parent's generosity, which had given them the opportunity to live on this estate.

'We are so grateful to Marie and Stuart for helping us with the deposit, and I sincerely hope we can repay them soon,' Louisa said with feeling.

'Speaking of Marie,' Sharon said, 'have you seen her recently? I haven't heard from her since Stuart went away and I've been intending to call and check she's alright. I don't believe they've ever been apart before, and if I don't go soon, she'll be thinking I've deserted her.'

'I know, I'm just the same,' Louisa replied, 'like you, I keep meaning to, and then something happens, and I forget. I know Damian has tried to ring his Mum, several times, but it just goes to the answer machine. I'll remind him again this evening. By the way, how's Tom? We used to see him around the site quite a lot, but he's rarely here anymore.'

'He's fine,' Sharon replied, 'but he's very involved in his latest project. He's just about to sign a contract to build some exclusive, executive homes in Cheshire, somewhere near Wilmslow, I think. From what I've seen of the early designs, they are not just big, they are super big and out of this world. Tom told me some of the footballers from Manchester City and Manchester United have already expressed an interest.'

'Wow,' Louisa exclaimed, 'they must be costing a fortune.'

'Yes, although I've no idea how much they will sell for. I don't think anyone knows yet.'

When they reached the town, Louisa headed for the playgroup and Sharon quickened her steps towards the hotel. She was so relieved she hadn't been tempted to confide and tell Louisa her suspicions about Tom and his business associate Fiona Campbell. It was probably all in her imagination anyway, and Louisa would think she was being foolish. The latest plans would be a very lucrative venture, and she didn't want to sound ungrateful, but even so, she would prefer less money and more Tom.

But today was a special day, and despite her suspicions she was determined to enjoy it. By a sheer stroke of good luck, Tom had secured a cancellation at the best Italian restaurant in the town, enabling them to celebrate their twentieth wedding anniversary in style. Their son Sam and his girlfriend Jodie were home from university so they'd offered to look after Lily. Sharon had bought a new dress for the occasion and arranged to have her hair done on the way home from work, in a bid to bring back some of the romance which seemed to have gone missing from their marriage recently, and as she joined the guests going up the steps to the imposing hotel entrance leading into the foyer, she felt a familiar tingle of excitement.

Reception was busy with guests, and after dropping her coat and bag in the office she joined Justin, who was handing out leaflets and advising some of the residents about the many local attractions and recommended eating places in the area. She had a meeting arranged with a young couple who were considering the options of holding their wedding at the hotel or the newly refurbished golf club. They were comparing the two venues one more time, before making their choice.

Since he'd become the events manager of the exclusive golf club, Colin Portland with his new partner Janet, had transformed the club into the hub of local entertainment and a sought-after events venue. Although it would be anathema to Bryony to provide entertainment in the hotel, Sharon knew she must hate the thought of Colin's success.

Fortunately for Sharon, today's meeting was a complete success. With very little effort from her, but a great deal of input from the father of the bride, who was paying for the whole thing, the deal was secured by a more than adequate deposit.

'They are very lucky,' she said to Justin as they watched them leaving.

'Well daddy is very rich apparently, but I wonder if they are getting the wedding they want, or the one he wants?'

'Well, it's certainly going to be wonderful,' she replied happily. 'You know I'm leaving early, don't you?' Before he had time to reply, her phone vibrated in her pocket, and after checking there was no-one around, she answered it. Justin turned and started to tidy the desk.

'It's Tom,' she said, frowning slightly. 'Hiya,' she whispered, 'Tom, please don't tell me you're running late.'

There was a silence during which her expression told Justin it wasn't good news and he moved away and busied himself straightening the leaflets on the stand.

'I'm sorry sweetheart, but I can't make it tonight. The bigwigs are having an impromptu meeting and they've asked me to join them. I promise I'll make it up to you. Sharon, are you there?'

'Yes,' she replied, but I can't believe what you are saying. Tom, we are so lucky to get this booking, please don't cancel. It's our anniversary and I'm so looking forward to it.'

'I don't think you understand,' he replied, 'this is very important.'

'And our anniversary isn't?'

'Look, I've got to go, but I'll ring you later. Don't forget, I'll make it up to you. I promise.'

She stood there deflated, all the excitement and anticipation slowly draining away. She told herself it was just one night, but it wasn't just this once. It was happening more and more, and all in the pursuit of money.

'Bad news?' Justin asked. Sharon nodded.

'He's cancelled tonight. I'm sorry, I'm behaving like a teenager. I really don't know why it's affecting me like this.'

He put his arm around her shoulder.

'You're tired. You've been doing extra hours here; and Bryony takes advantage of you because you are too soft and too flexible. You've got a husband and children to care for and something has to give. I know because it happened to me until my wife Ellie put her foot down, but now it's you who suffers. You'll have to stick up for yourself,' he said firmly.

'I know,' she replied, 'but that's enough about me. I'll go for my break and cancel my hair appointment. Looking on the bright side, at least I got an expensive new dress out of it. Now, I just need somewhere posh to go, so I can wear it.'

'That's my girl, always positive.'

Walking towards the office, she heard Bryony's voice, and not wanting to be drawn into a discussion about work, she turned quickly and made her way to the small meeting room, which she knew had no bookings. It wasn't until she'd made herself a coffee at the machine on the end of the bar and turned to take a seat, she became aware there was someone else in the room. It would be easy to walk away, but it still remained the quietest room in the busy hotel, so she sat down to drink her latte.

It wasn't just the cancellation of the restaurant which upset her, but more importantly she regretted the lost opportunity for them to spend some quality time together. She'd been looking forward to getting dressed up and having fun, something they hadn't done for what seemed like a long time. What, or who, could be so important to him he was prepared to let her down, especially on their anniversary? She became aware that the other person in the room had stood up and was walking towards her.

'Did I startle you?' he asked. 'You were very deep in thought'.

'Not at all,' she replied, recognising him as one of the business men who were resident at the hotel for a few weeks. 'I'm sorry, but I was unaware the room was booked.'

'No, I'm not here in a working capacity, I had a very early morning session and now I'm finished for the day. Do you mind if I sit down?' Sharon shook her head.

'Not at all, Mr. Philips, but I won't be very good company I'm afraid.'

'Oliver please. As I'm going to be staying here on business for some time, I think first names would be acceptable, don't you? Especially as I already call you Sharon. I must make a confession. I overheard a little of your conversation with Justin and I dived in here to get away and give you some privacy, I'm sorry it didn't work out.'

Sharon was mortified. It was totally against the hotel's code of conduct to air personal problems within hearing of the guests. Embarrassed, she apologised for putting him in a difficult situation, but he waved her apology away. 'I didn't hear anything of importance,' he assured her, 'unless of course, you count cancelling a hair appointment important. Which I guess you do.'

Beginning to relax, she smiled at the man who was sitting opposite her. There was no denying he was very good looking, and she might have commented as much to Justin, but she had never wished to be sitting chatting in a bar with him, or any other man for that matter.

They talked about the charm of Merebank, and how long it had been her home, and she told him about the problems they'd encountered following their move here, especially Tom's involvement in a contentious proposal for a housing development. She learned Oliver was divorced, had two grown- up sons, and was here doing some kind of research.

He didn't look old enough to have grown up sons, but she didn't tell him that. He'd changed from the business suit he normally wore, and the more casual clothes he was now wearing gave him a distinctly boyish look. He obviously kept himself fit as there was no evidence of middle age spread. He periodically ran his fingers through the dark blonde hair falling over his forehead and his brown eyes were alert and quizzical. Suddenly pulling herself together, Sharon looked at her watch and realised they'd been talking much longer than she'd thought. 'I must be going,' she exclaimed,

'I've got to ring the restaurant and cancel the booking. I don't suppose they will be very pleased with me.'

'I'd already decided to eat out this evening, because although the food here is excellent, I feel like a change of scene. I know one of my colleagues is thinking of eating out tonight and he might join me, if it would help you out.'

Oliver took out his phone. 'I'll just ring Tim,' he said, 'to check if he's game.' When his friend told him he'd already made other arrangements, Sharon stood up ready to leave, and was shocked when Oliver suddenly suggested they went to the restaurant together.

'That would solve the problem,' he said, but the change in her expression told him otherwise and he held his hands up, with his palms facing outwards in a gesture of surrender.

'Oh, I'm so sorry,' he said, 'I spoke out of turn. I just thought it would simply be two friends going for a meal, but understandably your husband wouldn't see it like that. Apologies again.'

'I don't honestly know,' she replied, 'he isn't the jealous type but,'

'Look, forget I said anything, I spoke without thinking.'

'No, let's do it,' she said impulsively, 'I'll tell Tom when I speak to him from home.'

'Are you sure?' Oliver asked.

'I am,' Sharon replied, suddenly picturing the smart, intelligent, Fiona Campbell who was a constant feature in Tom's conversations and who was going to be at the meeting tonight.

Chapter 4

Marie opened her eyes, and slowly moved her head to one side. A blind covered the window, but a pale orange glow framed the edges as light pushed its way into the room. Gently, she rotated her neck back again, and saw reflected in the mirror on the facing wall, a metal stand with a bag hanging from it. The fluid it contained, dripped methodically into a tube, and instinctively she moved her free hand across her body to try and locate where the canula was attached to her arm, but she cried out as sharp, splinters of pain pierced her shoulder.

She was in hospital but she had no idea why she was there. Her head was throbbing, but so was the rest of her body. She tried to pull herself into a sitting position but again cried out in pain, and although the only sound she could produce was an unintelligible croak, it had the desired effect of catching someone's attention and footsteps could be heard approaching. A few moments later, she heard the door open, and saw a nurse enter the room.

'Oh good, you're awake,' the nurse said gently. 'My name is Alice. How are you feeling?'

'Awful,' she gasped. The nurse put a band around her arm, and told Marie she was taking her blood pressure and temperature. Marie felt the familiar pressure and the whooshing sound as the air was released, but unlike previous times, this really hurt. The nurse apologised and explained it was due to all the bruising she'd sustained in the fall.

'The fall?' she asked herself. Her mind was blank and she had no idea what had happened to her. She began to panic when she realised, she didn't even know her own name or picture the house where she lived. Everything she was or knew, seemed to have been wiped from her memory. Her throat felt like she'd swallowed broken glass, and speaking was an effort, but with the help of the nurse, she managed to convey how much it hurt.

'I'll give you something to soothe it. It's nothing to be concerned about.' Alice explained, seeing her worried expression. 'It's partly due to the tubes you've had down your throat.'

'Why?' she rasped, 'what's happened to me?' The nurse paused, and pushed the trolley of instruments away. 'Don't you remember anything about the accident?' she asked gently. Marie tentatively moved her head from side to side and whispered, 'No.'

'The doctor is coming to see you soon,' the nurse told her as she lifted the notes from the end of the bed, 'and he'll explain everything, but I just need a few details. Let's start with your name and address. Do you know, we haven't even got a name for you?' She gave a little laugh as she took a pen from her pocket and stood with her hand poised over the notes. She waited patiently for Marie to speak until she saw the panic in her eyes, and quickly replacing the board on the end of the bed she moved to her side.

'Don't worry, it's only temporary. I know it's frightening but it will soon come back. Mr. Hastings, the neurologist, is the expert, and he'll explain it to you.' After adding a few comments on the record sheet, Alice made Marie more comfortable, tucking the pillows to support her arm and shoulder. 'We'll freshen you up, then you can have a light breakfast. Would you like tea or coffee?'

'I'd really love a cup of tea. Milk, no sugar.' Her voice was scratchy and almost indecipherable and the nurse advised her to rest it until it had improved a little.

'I know it's hard, but try to keep calm. I'm going to get you a bowl of water and I'll help you to wash, and then I'll bring you some breakfast.' With help from another nurse and a little assistance from the electric bed, she was soon sitting upright and feeling much fresher and brighter. Despite her sore throat she even enjoyed a slice of toast and marmalade, and the cup of tea was heavenly despite being lukewarm.

'I feel as though I haven't had a drink for days,' she said to Alice, and my throat is so dry, but it does feel a little better after that tea.'

'Well, that could be because you haven't had much to drink,' Alice replied, you've been given fluids intravenously, but you must keep drinking plenty of liquids now.'

When footsteps could be heard approaching the room, Marie asked Alice how long she'd been in the hospital, and was surprised when she was told it was three days since she'd arrived. She still had no recollection of why she was here, nor the circumstances which had caused her injuries, but one thing was uppermost in her mind, so she asked Alice if anyone had enquired about her, but she was devastated when Alice shook her head.

'Don't panic,' she said, 'it is early days yet.'

Marie watched nervously, as a doctor approached her bed, but he put her at ease when he told her he was pleased to see her awake and looking so well. He introduced himself as Mr Baines, the orthopaedic surgeon who'd operated on her arm, and after asking a few questions he carried out an examination of her injured body.

His gentle, probing fingers searched out the main sources of pain, causing her to wince when he touched the most painful places. When asked, she explained how the pain in her head and shoulder were the worst, but the most frightening thing was being unable to remember who she was and why she was in hospital.

'I don't even know where I live,' she said forlornly, putting her free hand on the front of her neck, in an effort to ease the pain which increased every time she tried to speak.

'Can you tell us anything at all, about yourself or your past?' Mr. Baines asked.

She closed her eyes, but her head was swirling in a kaleidoscope of images and colour, and no matter how much she tried, it was impossible to isolate and describe a single thing in detail. She opened her eyes, and forlornly told him how impossible it was to make any sense of it all.

'I know I'm married,' she said with a certain amount of conviction, but that may be because of this. She touched the strip of dressing on the ring finger of her left hand, which was obviously covering a wedding ring. I think I've got a husband and two children, but I don't know their names or how old they are.' Exhausted by the effort of concentrating, she rested her head back, prompting the nurse to move towards her and rearrange the pillows to make her more comfortable. The whole of her body was throbbing with pain, and she gratefully accepted the medication Alice gave to her. 'I'm sorry I'm no help to you,' she said softly.

'Don't apologise, and don't despair,' the doctor said kindly, it's very rare that a loss of memory isn't fully recovered, especially when it's due to a blow to the head. We think you may be suffering from a mild Traumatic Brain Injury, or a mild TBI as it is more commonly known, but we can't be sure at this stage.'

'A brain injury! Did someone hit me, or have I been in a car accident?'

'Neither,' Mr. Baines told her, 'You fell down the steps at Preston railway station. We don't know if it was an accident or if you were deliberately pushed. According to one eye-witness, you resisted the person who tried to snatch your case, and as he tugged it from your hand, you lost your balance and fell, banging your head as you reached the bottom of the steps. We don't know if he is a reliable witness, but the police are dealing with that.'

'The police, why are they involved?' she asked.

'It's a bit complicated,' the doctor replied, 'we'll explain when you are feeling a little better.'

Marie nodded. 'How serious are my injuries?' she dared to ask. She lay quietly and listened, while he told her she'd broken her collar bone, and cracked several ribs, for which they could do nothing except wait for them to heal naturally. He had performed surgery and put in a metal plate to keep the bones correctly aligned in the left arm, which was broken just above her wrist. Her left arm was enclosed in a plaster cast from just below her elbow to part way down her hand, and her upper arm was bound with strapping. The arm was supported by a sling. She also had extensive bruising to her body, and her face, which had taken quite a battering, was also badly bruised, and cut.

'Nothing that won't heal.' He was quick to reassure her. 'You will of course continue the pain relief you are already receiving, and we'll review it in a few hours.'

She pushed her head back into the pillows and stared at the ceiling. There was so much to take in, and so much she didn't understand.

'How do you know the injury to my brain is mild?' she asked him.

'We did a brain scan. Mr. Hastings, the neurologist, who is also looking after you, is convinced there is no serious damage'

'I can't understand how you've done all things without me knowing. Was I unconscious?'

'No, not exactly,' he replied, but we've kept you heavily sedated, and of course you were under anaesthetic for the surgery. You have been awake most of the time, but you probably don't remember. I operated on you, but Mr. Hastings is the neurologist who will be helping you with your memory. He will come to see you soon, to check everything is going according to plan. In the meantime, the best thing for mild TBI is rest and minimal stress.'

'What's mild TBI?' she asked.

'I'm sorry, it's mild Traumatic Brain Injury.'

'You've already told me that, haven't you?'

'Yes, but I gave you a lot of information. It may be easier if you just think of it as concussion. We'll be doing some cognitive tests soon, but don't worry about your loss of memory; it will come back.'

'I hope so,' she replied.

'Has your name come back to you yet?' he asked. Marie shook her head. 'I think it keeps coming, and then going.'

Mr. Baines consulted his notes.

'We've been calling you Mrs. Preston, because of the station where you had your accident. Is that okay with you?'

'No,' she replied, 'I'd prefer you to call me by my first name.'

'And that is?'

Marie thought for a moment, her forehead creased in concentration.

'Marie,' she said as last, I think my name is Marie.'

The nurse moved towards the bed to grasp Marie's hand.

'Have you made that up, or is it your real name?' she asked, with barely concealed excitement.

After some deep concentration, Marie nodded.

'Yes,' she replied confidently, 'I'm sure my name is Marie.' She looked at the nurse. 'Please will you make a note of that, so you can remind me if I forget it again. I'm sure that's right, but I don't know my surname.'

'Don't worry about that,' Mr. Baines said, 'it will come in its own good time. Is there anything else you'd like to ask?'

'Yes, one more thing. How long will it take for all my memory to return?

'That's a difficult question to answer I'm afraid, as there is no definitive way of knowing. All I can say is, it almost certainly will be restored.'

'Almost,' she said wearily, 'I suppose I'll have to be satisfied with that.'

'At this stage, yes,' he replied.

As the doctor left, a trolley was wheeled into the room by a smiling young man who asked if she wanted tea or coffee. Without thinking, Marie replied, 'coffee please, with a spot of warm milk and no sugar.'

The nurse gave her the thumbs up sign, and smiled broadly as she sat on the chair left next to the bed, by Mr. Baines.

'Well, we now know your first name, and that you like tea with milk and no sugar, and milky coffee with no sugar.'

'No,' she replied, 'coffee with warm milk, not milky coffee. They are two quite different drinks.'

'Ah,' the nurse said with a smile, 'and we can also make an educated guess that you like things just so.'

'Maybe', Marie agreed, 'but this situation is the opposite of being just so. It is a complete muddle in fact, as well as being very scary.'

Alice took her hand. 'It won't be long before your memory returns, and your family come looking for you.'

'I hope you're right. I feel as though I'm lost in no man's land.'

When she was alone again, Marie closed her eyes and waited for something to come back to her which would give a sense of who she was, but the more she tried, the more difficult it became. Images floated across her vision, but it was impossible to grasp them before they drifted away again. She couldn't even remember most of the things the doctor had said, but she vaguely recalled him telling her things would start improving in a few days. The future was scary. What on earth would happen to her if she never remembered who she was?

There were a few things which were puzzling her, and she was determined to ask some questions. She may not know who she was, but she didn't need anyone to tell her she would have been carrying a handbag, with a purse and mobile phone. When the nurse returned, she was very evasive when Marie enquired about her belongings, but instead she did tell her a policeman was coming to see her and maybe he could help.

'Don't worry, he'll be here soon, and I'm sure he'll answer all your questions.'

Marie took a deep breath, but cried out when the broken ribs reacted as the air filled her lungs. The intensity of the pain took her breath away, and she lay still, waiting for it to pass.

'I need my handbag.' She gasped. It will tell me all I need to know. It will have my purse in it, but more importantly, my mobile. I don't know why we didn't we think of that before?' But a troubled Alice was shaking her head, a look of concern on her face.

'I'm so sorry Marie,' she said, 'but we haven't found your handbag. The police have questioned the people who stayed with you until the ambulance arrived, but they all agreed there was no sign of a case or a handbag. After I was put in charge of your care, I was so certain you must have had a bag of some description, I went and checked the lost property at the station, but there was nothing remotely like that, and apparently the police had already checked anyway.'

'But I'd never go anywhere without it, I'm sure of that. Oh, I wish I could remember what happened to me. I haven't got one thing to help jog my memory, even the clothes I was wearing seem to have disappeared. Do you know where they are?'

Alice didn't know, but she promised to try and find out for her. By the time Alice had been put in charge of caring for Marie, she'd already been to theatre for her first operation and was wearing a hospital gown, and there was no sign of her clothes.

Marie yawned and rested her head back on the pillows, exhausted by all her efforts.

'I'll put the bed down, so you can have a little rest,' Alice said, and Marie agreed. It had been a very tiring session, both mentally and physically, even though the only exercise she'd had was the short journey to the bathroom.

'Can you remember my name?' the nurse asked, but Marie shook her head.

'It's Alice. I'll write it on a piece of paper and stick it on your locker where you can see it.' Marie sank into the soft, downy, pillow, already drifting into sleep. I wish I knew where I was going, and where I came from,' she whispered to herself.

Alice, paused outside the room and listened.

'You were going to the airport;' she said to no-one in particular, 'on a one-way ticket. So, it looks as if you were flying off somewhere and not intending to return. How mysterious.'

Chapter 5

Sharon looked in the mirror and could hardly recognise herself. The hairdresser had tamed her curls into a style neither formal nor casual, but which somehow made her look and feel more sophisticated and confident. She had butterflies flickering inside her, but there was still time to change her mind and pull out. The trouble was, she didn't want to. It was so long since she'd felt like this, she couldn't believe it was happening. It was only a meal after all, but it was more than that. It was an opportunity to have her hair done, buy a new dress and wear the expensive perfume Tom had bought her for Christmas, two years ago.

The memory of that happy occasion was ruined by the realisation that the bottle was unopened, still waiting for a special occasion to come along. Well, now it had, but Tom had cancelled without a thought. She hurried home to face the chaos she expected would be waiting for her, but instead she walked into an oasis of calm. Jodie had already given Lily her tea, and Sam was in the garden kicking a ball about with his younger brother Ben and two of his friends.

'Oh mum, you look so pretty!' exclaimed the ever-observant Lily. 'I love your hair.'

Jodie raised her eyebrows in surprise. 'So do I,' she said, 'that's so cool. I've never seen it like that before.'

'I've never had it like this before,' Sharon said, patting her hair gently, 'it's sort of half up and half down.'

'It suits you, it's lovely,' Jodie said, 'wait until Tom sees you.'

'He probably wouldn't even notice,' Sharon replied with a smile, 'but anyway, by the time he does see it, it certainly won't look like this.' Lily had already lost interest in the subject, but Jodie looked puzzled.

'Oh, sorry.' Sharon said, 'Of course you don't know that Tom isn't coming tonight, and I'm going with a friend.'

'That's a shame, why can't dad go?' asked Sam walking into the room, Who's the friend, do I know her?'

'Dads got an unexpected meeting, to answer your first question, and no, you don't know the friend, it's someone from work.'

'Lucky her,' Jodie piped up, 'I'd love to go to Franco's.'

Sam laughed.

'It'll be yonks before we'll be going there. Dad was really pushing the boat out, but it's way too expensive for us.'

Sharon breathed a sigh of relief as the turn of the conversation prevented her from being drawn into any further explanations. She wasn't used to all this subterfuge, and the conviction she was doing nothing wrong was steadily disappearing. Half hoping that Lily would raise an objection to being left, she was disappointed when, to the contrary, she urged Sharon to hurry up and leave them to enjoy playing a game. Anxious to avoid any return to the question of who she was going with, she opened her handbag to give Sam money for the takeaway she'd promised them, and she reminded him not to forget Ben.

'I won't,' he replied indignantly, 'Oh, and by the way, no hanky-panky tonight.' Sharon froze, hand poised over her bag. 'What do mean?' Sam shook his head good-naturedly before explaining that Friday night at the restaurant was famous or infamous, for giving everyone a free bottle of wine with their meal.

'You mean, every couple,' Sharon corrected him, but Sam shook his head. 'No mum, I mean every customer.'

'But it's a respectable restaurant with excellent food.' Sharon looked appealingly at Jodie, who, sensing Sharon's concern, interrupted Sam as he laughingly taunted his mum with stories of bawdiness and misbehaviour due to excessive consumption of alcohol.

'Stop it, don't speak to your mum like that,' she said firmly, but then turning back to Sharon, she went on to explain. 'He is right though, 'you actually do get a bottle each, so as a couple of friends, you'll get two.'

'Oh, well, I've never heard of that before; but there's nothing to say we have to drink it.'

'Yeah, but we've heard it gets quite lively. Two girls on their own? But I suppose if dad is okay with it, that's fine.'

'Don't be silly, for a start we're not exactly girls, and we won't be getting, as you so delicately put it, lively.'

Sharon went upstairs and wondered what on earth she was getting into. She took a deep breath before calling Tom. She was being ridiculous and should never even have entertained the idea of going with another man. Oliver would be able to take advantage of the table, as he'd been planning to eat out this evening anyway. He was probably regretting asking her to go with him and would breathe a sigh of relief when she cancelled.

After three unsuccessful attempts to reach Tom, she decided to have a shower. Putting on the shower-cap to protect her new hairstyle; she dialled him several more times before carefully applying her make-up, and slipping on the new dress.

She took a selfie, and dialled once more. She may as well let him see what he was missing, before she changed back into her normal clothes to go down and share the take-away with the kids. This time, he replied, but it was so noisy she could hardly hear him.

'Where are you?' she asked, 'it's very loud.'

'Sorry,' he called, 'we're in a bar in Manchester. It's owned by two ex-Manchester United players. It was Fiona's idea to come. She said lots of Manchester United and City players come here, and it would be a good opportunity to promote the development, but I'm not so sure. This isn't what was planned, but I've got no choice, I'll just have to go with the flow because I need to talk with Fiona about something important.'

'What about the meeting you're supposed to be having?'

'Exactly, I think it will be back at the hotel. Oh yes, I nearly forgot to tell you. She's booked us into a hotel for the night, because none of us will be able to drive home. Friends' rates, apparently.'

'So, you're not even coming home tonight. Tom, it's our anniversary.'

'I know, babe. I'll make it up to you, I promise.'

'Okay. Tom, I'm going tonight, I haven't cancelled the booking.'

'Brilliant,' he shouted, obviously relieved to be let of the hook.

'Do you remember me telling you about Oliver, a businessman who's staying at the hotel? I'm going with him.'

'Excellent, have a great time.'

'Don't you mind? she asked, but she was talking to herself. She knew he hadn't heard her, but she felt hurt and rejected. She looked at herself in the mirror and was pleased with what she saw. She would still prefer it if Tom were here, but he wasn't, so she had to get over it.

It was a lovely evening, so she decided to walk along the promenade to the restaurant. It would take slightly longer, but she was hoping the gentle stroll by the sea would help to calm her nerves. She had never done anything remotely like this before, and she wished she had never agreed to it.

There was a scattering of people still left on the beach, some of them young families trying to pack up at the end of a long day, and she was reminded of the times when she and Tom were too weary to squeeze a beach tent back into its bag. A young couple just below where she was standing had their valiant efforts thwarted by their two children who were taking advantage of their freedom, by jumping on the sandcastles they'd spent most of the day building. Sighing, she felt a rush of nostalgia as it brought back memories of when she and Tom visited Merebank with the children on day trips and holidays.

Tired donkeys were being led off the beach and the deckchairs were fastened against the sea wall. The sun was dropping below the horizon, but the sky was ablaze, giving the whole vista a warm, radiant glow. In the twilight, fairy lights spanning the whole length of the promenade danced and shimmered in the evening breeze and Sharon breathed the fresh, coastal air deep into her lungs. Sometimes, at moments like this, she could hardly believe they were really living here, and if Tom was sharing it with her, she knew he would feel the same.

But he wasn't, and there was no point in dwelling on what might have been, so she decided to eat her meal as quickly as possible and leave at the first opportunity.

Oliver was waiting for her when she arrived and the look on his face told her he'd been worried she may not turn up. His expression of concern was very quickly followed by a look of pleasure and he complimented her on her appearance.

'You look stunning,' he said, 'absolutely stunning.' They were shown to their table, and it very quickly became obvious that the evening was not going to be hurried.

The appetizers were tempting, and when the wine waiter brought two free bottles of wine Sharon began to protest, but she was persuaded to accept them, with the promise they could take home anything that was left at the end of the night. They were enjoying the nibbles when the head waiter came over bringing a bottle of Prosecco on ice.

'I'm sorry, I haven't ordered it,' Oliver told him, 'It must be for someone else.' The waiter laughed.

'No,' he said, 'you are the anniversary couple, and this is for you, with the compliments of the house.' He opened the bottle, filled two glasses and placed the bottle back in the ice bucket. 'There you are,' he said. 'Enjoy.'

The couple at the next table, raised their glasses, and passed on their good wishes, and Sharon blushed with embarrassment. 'I'm so sorry,' she whispered, but Oliver waved away her apology. 'It can't be helped, although it does seem wrong drinking another man's wine. Would you rather we didn't drink it?'

'Of course not, that would be a complete waste of a lovely bottle of bubbly.' But no matter how hard she tried she couldn't quell the feeling of guilt building up inside her.

As soon as she could, she excused herself and went to the ladies' room to try and contact Tom. His phone was switched off, making her angry and upset. Well, if he could forget her on their anniversary, she wasn't going to let false sentiment stop her from enjoying herself.

Making her way back between the tightly packed tables, she looked at the man waiting for her. He was incredibly good looking and very good company, but that was all it was; just good company. She told herself she may as well enjoy the evening now she was here, after all, Tom had made it very clear he was doing exactly that.

The restaurant was already buzzing, and several times their conversation was interrupted by peals of laughter or good- natured differences of opinion. There were several parties enjoying themselves and bursts of 'Happy Birthday' brought rounds of clapping from other diners. The ambience in the room was celebratory and light-hearted, and Sharon began to relax and enjoy herself. The food was varied, some of it new to her, and when they'd finished the main course, Sharon was surprised to see they'd drunk all the bubbly. After choosing a dessert, Oliver took off his linen jacket and hung it on the back of his seat.

'My goodness, it's warm in here', he said, and Sharon agreed, but as she began to slip the jacket from her shoulders she glanced at her watch and changed her mind. Turning down the offer of a liqueur to accompany the strong, black coffee, she told Oliver she would have to leave shortly.

There had been no call for help from Sam and Jodie, but even so it was already quite late.

Having walked there, she was prepared to make the journey back on foot, but Oliver insisted on calling a taxi.

'I know it isn't very far,' he said, 'but I can't let you walk back alone. I'll share until we drop you off, and then I'll walk the rest of the way. I think the fresh air will do me good, and I do enjoy being on the promenade in the evening.'

'Oh, so do I,' exclaimed Sharon, 'especially when there's no-one else around. But I can't go tonight,' she added hastily, being careful not to give the impression she was inviting herself to join him. The wine had gone to her head, and it was a lovely, tipsy sensation, but not quite enough to throw her inhibitions to the winds.

'Of course not,' he replied with a grin, and she thought she caught a hint of disappointment in his voice.

In the taxi, they sat as far away from each other as possible and when it reached her home, Oliver paid the driver and they both got out. She thanked him for a lovely evening.

'It's been an absolute pleasure, good-night Sharon,' he said. He dropped a light kiss on her cheek before turning to walk away.

As she walked up the drive, she was shocked to see Tom's car parked round the corner of the house, in front of the garage. He must have decided to come home, but why hadn't he let her know he'd changed his plans? In the light cast by the lamps on each side of the door, she checked her phone for missed calls, but there was nothing. He'd obviously tried to surprise her, and must have been disappointed to find her still out when he arrived home. She hoped he wouldn't read anything into her actions this evening.

Not quite knowing what she would find, she entered the house as quietly as possible, and was pleased to discover everyone was already in bed. Feeling like a teenager, she went into the kitchen and poured herself a large glass of milk, which she carried to the bedroom. Tom was already asleep, so she removed her make-up and hung her dress in the wardrobe before slipping into bed. She lay quietly still, but luckily, he hadn't wakened, and she sighed with the relief of knowing she didn't have to explain her actions while she was still under the influence of drink. Hopefully, by morning she would have shaken off the guilty feelings which were troubling her now.

Chapter 6

Bryony was fuming. Colin and Hugh were with Ralph, discussing Colin's wedding. Not only had he omitted to tell her about his intentions, but he also had the audacity to come here to talk about it with Ralph. He'd walked in, as bold as brass, greeted her in reception and proceeded to make his way upstairs as if he owned the place, and without even telling her where he was heading. Hugh had followed shortly afterwards, and when she asked him what was going on, he'd breezily replied for all to hear.

'Oh, we're just having a confab about dad's nuptials,' before running up the stairs two at a time. Fortunately, the only member of staff within earshot, was Justin, who watched with interest but made no comment.

Bryony busied herself at the desk until she'd calmed down.

'I hope Hugh's rearranged his schedule, I'm sure he had a meeting with a supplier this morning,' she said, glancing at the diary'

Justin was very adept at sidestepping Bryony's caustic comments, but he could also recognise the times when nothing but a straightforward reply would suffice, and this was one of them.

'He has changed it on the timetable, he's arranged for Sharon to take his place.'

Bryony raised an eyebrow quizzically. 'Has he now? I didn't realise he was in a position to order a change to Sharon's schedule simply to enable him to have time off. I must have a word with him. You'll be alright here, won't you? I've just got a few things to deal with upstairs.'

'Of course,' Justin replied. He watched her walk towards the lift, and an unexpected feeling of sympathy welled up inside him. He felt sorry for her. She was hard, no mistake. But she was human, and she was obviously hurting.

He guessed the real reason for her mood wasn't simply a matter of Colin and Hugh's behaviour today, but more to do with the fact she hadn't been invited to the wedding. He'd learned a lot about Bryony during the years he'd worked for her, and although he was certain she would have declined the invitation, she was obviously upset at being left out. It was a bit heartless to meet openly in the hotel, but Ralph still wasn't going out much, so really, they had no choice. Justin's wife Ellie, was pushing him to tell Bryony they'd received their invitations, but he was dreading it, even though he had no argument with Colin and they were entitled to go.

Bryony crept into her room and closed the door as quietly as she could. She had no privacy here, and she couldn't wait to move out, but she couldn't do anything until Ralph was fully recovered. He was responding incredibly well to the physiotherapy, and his determination to gain his independence again was in his favour, so hopefully things would soon get moving. The murmur of voices was becoming louder, and she could hear laughter and the occasional snippet of conversation. Apparently, they were now discussing who would be Colin's best man, and Hugh was trying to persuade Ralph it would be a great way for him to make his first appearance at a social event. Bryony couldn't believe what she was hearing. It would create far too much stress for him, and she was just about to let Hugh know how unreasonable he was being, when she heard him concede and accept the role himself.

When it became obvious Colin and Hugh were about to leave, she slipped out and made her way downstairs, so by the time they reached reception, she was talking to a resident and casually acknowledged Colin's wave of goodbye.

Chapter 7

The nurse had explained the need for Marie to have a chat with the police officer who was due to arrive before lunch that morning. The reason for the visit was simple and Marie had no cause to worry. She'd had a fall, which may or may not have been an accident, and it needed to be investigated. Marie couldn't accept that anyone had deliberately pushed her down the steps, but although she was remembering things from the past, the day she left home was a complete blank and it frightened her. She hoped this meeting wasn't going to turn into an interrogation which she believed could end in tears, but Alice had promised that she would be with her the whole time to ensure no such thing happened.

At the sound of people approaching, she used her good arm to try and pull herself upright and was grateful when Alice entered the room with two strangers who introduced themselves as CID officers. The senior officer was effortlessly imposing, but he had a smile on his face when he introduced himself and the young woman police officer who was with him.

'I'm Detective Sergeant Harry Pullman, and this is PC Adele Dennis. We are here to try and establish exactly what happened on the day of your accident. Do you mind if we sit down?' Without waiting for an answer, he carried two seats from the corner of the room and offered one to the young policewoman, before sitting down himself. Mr. Hastings tells me you've lost your memory, but he's hopeful you will recover it quite soon.' It was said as a statement, but after a few seconds, she realised he was waiting for her to reply.

'That's right,' she said, 'I sincerely hope so.'

'Which part of that day have you forgotten?' he asked,

'All of it,' she told him, her eyes closed in concentration. 'It's all gone.'

'Can you at least help us to locate your luggage? It's rather puzzling to us because you were caught by the security camera on platform four, carrying a handbag and pulling a suitcase, but when you fell down the steps there was no sign of them. Marie opened her eyes and looked at him steadily, but her voice was quavering.

'I don't think you understand, I have no recollection of any part of that day. I've been told I was at Preston station with a ticket to Manchester Airport, and then I fell down the steps and ended up here. I'm sorry I can't help you but I don't even know where I live or where I was going.' Her voice broke, and she tried to reach a tissue from the box left within her reach on the bed. Her right arm was free from strapping, but it was badly bruised and very painful, making it difficult to hold or pick things up. Sighing with frustration she closed her eyes while PC Adele Dennis gently wiped her face.

'We'll soon track down your family, and don't forget they will be looking for you,' she whispered.

'That's what I keep thinking,' Marie replied, 'but why haven't they found me already? I must have a phone somewhere, that would help more than anything.

DS Pullman, was listening thoughtfully, twisting a pen between his first fingers and thumbs.

'Is there a possibility, do you think, that in the time between going from one platform to the other, you gave your luggage to someone else?'

'I very much doubt it,' Marie sighed, with a quizzical look directed at the policewoman. 'Can you imagine a woman travelling without a bag of some description? 'Why would I be travelling with two bags and then suddenly have none? It doesn't make sense.'

'That is precisely what we are questioning,' DS Pullman said. 'We were hoping you might be able to help us.'

'I'm sorry, but the answer is no. I have absolutely no idea what happened to me at the station, but it is interesting to learn I had a case and a handbag and my instinct tells me I would not willingly have parted with them under any circumstances. If they are lost, or were stolen, it means I have absolutely nothing to call my own, and that doesn't make me feel good.' Her voice dropped and she glanced at the name on the small note which was stuck to the side of her bedside locker. 'Alice,' she read, and Alice took hold of her hand and suggested it was time to finish the interview. Tears were beginning to spill over and run down Marie's cheeks again and she closed her eyes.

'I am very sorry, Marie, I didn't mean to upset you,' DS Pullman, said. 'I know this must be very distressing for you, but can you try to answer a few more questions which might help us, in our search for your family?'

'Yes, I'll try. but I don't think I'll be able to help you.'

'From what little we've managed to find on the security camera, we think you were making your way to the train at platform five. Does that mean anything to you?'

Marie shook her head.

'Okay,' he said, 'if that's correct, and you were going to that platform, the first train leaving from there was destined for Manchester Airport. Does that mean anything?'

'No, sorry.'

'You've no recollection of planning to fly abroad somewhere?'

Marie shook her head, and the nurse signalled to DS Pullman, to go carefully. Marie was her patient, and she was determined to protect her. After giving the notes in his hand a quick check, DS Pullman, slipped the small pad into his pocket as if to draw the session to a close. 'One last thing. The train does stop at Wilmslow station, on route to the airport, I wonder if that may have been your destination?'

Marie frowned. 'Where did you say it was going?'

'To Manchester Airport, stopping at Styal and Wilmslow en route.'

Thoughtfully, she repeated the word 'Wilmslow.' After a few moments she shook her head.

'What is it?' the police woman asked hopefully. 'It seemed to mean something to you.'

'Nothing specific, but the mention of Wilmslow rang a bell.'

'Were you going home do you think? Maybe visiting someone?'

'I don't know, but if I live there or know someone else who does, you would imagine I'd have some recollection of it.'

'You've done very well,' DS Pullman said, as he gently shook her hand. 'When you feel strong enough and the doctor agrees, would you consider making a visit to Wilmslow with Adele? Visiting a place familiar to you, can sometimes jog the memory.'

Marie looked at the nurse, who agreed in principle.

'We'll have to check with the doctor before we can say Marie is ready for that.'

'Of course.' he agreed. 'Just keep it in mind.'

'That's enough for today,' Alice said firmly and DS Harry Pullman returned the chairs to the corner of the room and smiled at Marie.

'You did very well today, we'll be back tomorrow, and in the meantime, I promise we will do everything we can to find your case and your handbag, and of course, your family.'

'Thank-you. Mr?' Marie began, unsure of how to address him.

Sensing her dilemma, he suggested it would be simpler if she simply called him DS Pullman, and she agreed.

'You can just call me Adele,' the policewoman suggested with a smile, and Marie was pleased.

'That's fine,' she replied.

'Very well,' DS Pullman and Adele, it is.'

'That wasn't too bad, was it?' Alice asked when they'd gone. 'They'll soon be on the trail and you'll be reunited with your family before long, I just feel it.'

'I don't know,' Marie replied, 'he seemed more interested in my missing luggage than finding my family.'

'That isn't true, he's very worried about you,' Alice replied firmly.

Chapter 8

Sharon awoke, and for a few seconds she was disorientated by the sensation of a gentle thudding inside her skull, backed by the sound of Tom snoring. Slowly, she gathered her thoughts together and along with the recollections of a very pleasant evening, came the remembrance of finding Tom in bed when she arrived home. Trying not to wake him, she lay very still and feigned sleep while she decided the next course of action.

She'd told Tom she was going to the restaurant with Oliver and he didn't seem in the least bit interested, but she knew he wouldn't be very impressed to see her suffering from a hangover. What had seemed like innocent fun last night, now appeared to be slightly questionable, even in her own eyes. She'd drunk plenty of water with the pills she'd taken for her headache in the night, but the heavy weight pressing down on her head was still there. She could hear Lily's constant chattering, and the voices of Jodie and Sam in the background, with the occasional contribution from the dog. Rusty, never liked to be ignored. 'A bit like Lily,' Sharon thought to herself, and satisfied that everything seemed to be running smoothly, and being careful not to disturb Tom, she buried deeper under the duvet.

When the phone rang, she ignored it, until moments later when Sam entered the bedroom and gently rocked her body.

'Mum, it's Louisa, she wants to talk to you.'

'I'll call her later; what time is it?'

'Mum, I think she means now, it sounds important. She's been trying your mobile, but it must be turned off.'

'Tell her I'll be down in a minute, and I'll call her back.'

Dragging herself out of bed, she pulled on her housecoat and went downstairs. Her heart was pounding with dread. Had something happened to Pearl? She patted the top of Lily's head as she passed her sitting at the table eating a bowl of cereal. 'Morning sweetheart, Good morning, Jodie,' she said brightly, and nodding at Sam, she picked up the phone and walked back out of the room.

'Oh, hi', Louisa said, 'sorry, did we get you out of bed?'

'It doesn't matter,' Sharon replied, 'Louisa, is there something wrong with Pearl?'

'Oh, no, she's fine. It's Marie we're worried about.'

Sharon sagged with relief, which was instantly replaced by a strong sense of guilt. 'What's wrong with her?' she asked fearfully.

'We don't exactly know if there is anything wrong, but no-one knows where she is. When was the last time you saw Marie?'

Sharon tried to think when she'd last spoken to her, but with her head still throbbing it wasn't easy.

'I can't honestly remember, but I'm pretty sure it hasn't been since you and I walked into town together and discussed it. We both said we would be getting in touch with her,' she added lamely.

'I know, and I feel so guilty now. I promised Stuart I'd keep an eye on her, and I've seen her less than usual.'

'Has something happened to her? Is she poorly?'

'No. She's missing. We don't know where she is.'

'What do you mean, she's missing?'

'It's hard to explain, but it seems that she told Claire she was having a few days doing nothing, except relaxing and taking things easy. That meant she wouldn't be doing her voluntary work in the RNLI gift shop and Claire would need to get one of the other girls in to cover for her. She didn't mention what she was planning to do, and it wasn't until a few of her friends found they couldn't get in touch with her, and by comparing notes they realised she hasn't been seen for days.

'How about Bryony?' Sharon asked, 'does she know anything?'

'Same response, she hasn't seen her either.'

Sharon listened with dismay, and promising Louisa she would be with her as soon as possible she ran upstairs and tried to wake Tom, who grumbled as he pulled the duvet over his head. She ignored his plea to be left alone, and told him he had to get up to organise Lily, who was having her friend over and Ben who was going to play football.

'Freddie's dad is taking them,' she told him. 'So, Ben must be ready when they come. Oh, and he'll need some money.'

'Why can't Sam and Jodie look after them?' he mumbled.

'Because they've made plans with their friends.' She didn't add they'd already looked after them the previous evening and were still doing so now. It wasn't the time to be going into why she was suffering the after effects of the night before. There would be time enough for that later.

She began to shake him.

'Come on Tom please, I'll get you something for your hangover while you get dressed.'

'I wish you'd stop banging on about my hangover, I haven't got a hangover, I'm just tired that's all. I left before everyone else and drove home, and I wouldn't have done that if I'd been drunk, would I?'

'I'm sorry,' she replied, 'but I must be going, Damian and Louisa are waiting for me.'

'What's all the panic?' Tom asked, pulling on his jeans.

'It's Marie, she's gone missing, at least we think she has.'

She kissed him and he put his arms around her.

'Don't worry sweetheart, I'm sure there will be a perfectly good explanation. Keep me posted.'

'I hope so, and of course I'll be in touch.'

By the time she reached Marie's house, she'd sifted through numerous reasons why Marie might have gone away without telling Damian and Louisa, but none of them made sense. Louisa was speaking to someone on her phone and Damian was pacing the room when she arrived.

'Is there any news?' she asked, but he shook his head. 'No, there are signs that mum hasn't been here for at least a few days. Louisa's going through mum's address book, but no luck so far.' Louisa finished the call and shook her head.

'I think we should ring dad,' Damian said, 'he's the one person who we can be sure will know where mum is.'

Louisa shook her head.

'I think we should wait before we do that. If, and I know it's a big if,' she said, 'he doesn't know where she is, what can he do? He's abroad, and we'll have achieved nothing except frighten him.'

'You're right I suppose,' mumbled Damian, 'but we can't just sit here doing nothing. Personally, I think we are wasting time. We ought to be ringing the police now.'

'I agree,' Sharon said, 'but it won't do any harm to try and find out if Marie told anyone of her plans. Let's make a list of people she may have contacted in the last week or so and if that doesn't help, we'll have to contact the police. We'll start with you Damian, did your mum give any clues about going away for a few days?'

Damian tried to remember when he'd last spoken to his mum.

'I saw her when I picked dad up, to take him to the station, but I don't think I've spoken to her since then. I can't believe it; I always have more contact than that, and I promised dad I'd look after her. I have tried several times to get her on the phone, and she didn't get back to me, but that's no excuse.'

'You have been very busy at work,' Louisa said in his defence, and you had that life-boat incident.'

'We're not here to apportion blame,' Sharon said firmly. She was becoming increasingly aware she was as much to blame as anyone for not keeping an eye on her friend.

She and Louisa went over their own attempts to contact Marie, before concluding, that since Stuart went away none of them had been successful.

'Right, that's us done,' Sharon declared, 'now what about the neighbours, have you asked them?'

'I had a word with Nancy next door, but she couldn't help. She did say mum hadn't left the money to pay the milkman, which she always does when mum and dad go away.'

'She probably just forgot,' Sharon said. 'It was probably a last-minute decision.'

'Apparently, Claire told Bryony that mum had asked her to get someone to cover for her shifts at the Lifeboat gift shop this week. So, I suppose she must have been planning something,' Damian added thoughtfully.

Sharon laughed.

'I didn't realise she'd done that. There you are, we're worrying unnecessarily.'

'But that doesn't explain why she hasn't told us,' Louisa said thoughtfully.

'She probably thought one of us would tell dad,' Damian said, 'and she didn't want him to know, because he would have worried about her.'

They all nodded at the simple explanation, and there was a collective sigh of relief. Louisa took a deep breath and grinned, looking at Damian.

'Your mum is having a prearranged holiday, so whatever her reasons for not telling anyone, there is nothing for us to worry about. Can you imagine her reaction if you reported her missing just because she's chosen to have a little break?'

He grinned.

'She'd have my guts for garters. When you put it like that, it does seem a bit of an overreaction.'

Louisa clapped her hands over her face. 'I think I can guess where she is,' she exclaimed, 'I don't know why we didn't think of it before. She'll be with Stuart. She'll be surprising him on his birdwatching holiday.'

'That's impossible,' Damian replied, 'she's never travelled abroad on her own.' Louisa and Sharon groaned.

'There you go again,' Louisa chided, 'that doesn't mean she can't. Give your mum a bit of credit, Damian. Don't forget, your mum arranged that holiday, she would be able to fix herself a few days at the end, to join Stuart.'

'But why would she suddenly do that?' Damian asked.

'I don't think it was a sudden idea, I believe she planned it all along. She must have decided they'd have a few days together at the end of his birdwatching trip. You must admit it makes sense.' They all agreed it made perfect sense, and after contacting both local taxi firms, the second one of which confirmed taking a lady from that address to Preston station to pick up a train destined for Manchester Airport, they almost fell about laughing.

'Well mum, you are amazing, but if you were here now, I'd want to strangle you,' Damian said. After many hugs and a few tears of relief, they locked up the house and said their goodbyes. Thanks for coming Sharon,' Damian said, but she waved the words away. 'I did nothing,' she replied.

Sharon walked down the street towards the promenade and went to sit in the Japanese styled shelter which was Marie and Stuart's favourite. Today, there was a clear view over the estuary, and the windows of moving cars and the buildings of the resort on the coast opposite reflected the sun's rays like mirrors. Etched on the horizon, the wind turbines were visible, reaching upwards like giant windmills in the sky.

Pondering the events of the morning, she considered all the things they'd discussed before reaching the conclusion that Marie had joined Stuart in Portugal. Although she'd agreed with them at the time, the more she thought about it, the more she doubted it. Something just didn't ring true.

From what she knew of Marie, it was impossible to believe she would risk worrying her family and friends by disappearing like this. It was understandable to want to surprise Stuart, but it was illogical to keep everyone at home in the dark. She was sure Damian and Louisa would quickly come to the same conclusion, but hopefully by then they would have worked out what had really happened.

A breeze was coming over with the incoming tide, and a shiver chilled her spine.

Something was very wrong, but she had no idea what it might be.

Chapter 9

The hotel was busy, and it was mid-morning before Bryony had an opportunity to speak to Hugh, but before going down to see him she phoned Louisa, who told her they still didn't know where Marie was. Bryony told her if no-one else contacted Stuart in the next few hours then she most certainly would, pointing out it would either solve the mystery or prove something serious had happened, in which case Stuart had every right to know. 'I can't understand why you don't just do it.'

'It's not as simple as that,' Louisa replied, 'she might be annoyed and think we're interfering.'

'Rubbish, if she reacts like that, tell her it's her own fault for being so secretive and stupid.'

'We've got to find her first, and what if she isn't with Stuart, where could she be?'

'If we knew that, there wouldn't be a problem. All this dithering is getting us nowhere,'

'Please don't do anything yet,' Louisa begged, 'I'll tell Damian how you feel, and I'll get back to you.'

'Make sure you do. She's my friend, and I'm not prepared to hang around much longer.'

Bryony was genuinely concerned. Marie was her oldest friend and despite many ups and downs including a long-lasting rift, thankfully now healed, they were still close. Bryony had a very uneasy feeling which wouldn't go away.

Joe was at nursery, giving his mum Lucy the opportunity to spend a few hours working in the hotel. She was settling in well and gaining experience, and Bryony was confident of her ability to support Hugh when it was time for them to take over the running of the hotel, but they were also saving for a deposit on a house, especially as there was now a second child on the way. To keep the Portland family's image intact, she was prepared to give them some help with the mortgage, so they could buy a more upmarket property than they could afford, but she wasn't going to tell them that until the time was right. She could have given Hugh a pay rise instead, but they might have spent that on other things, instead of saving for a house.

The houses on the new estate were proving very popular, but she'd heard there was a shortage of starter homes for first time buyers. Witnessing her home and land being demolished, had been heart-breaking, but even that had been preferable to keeping it in the family, with the risk of Colin and his fancy woman benefitting from it. Her acceptance of the situation had been helped by the unexpected arrival of Ross Holmes into her life.

She'd joined the 'Exclusive Dating Service for Discerning People', hoping to meet someone special with whom she could form a relationship, but for a while she'd been very disappointed. When she eventually met Ross, although he was ridiculously handsome and sexy, there was no spark between them, but their mutual interest in the holiday industry gave them a reason to let their friendship grow. He admired her business and management skills, and she was very impressed with the way he'd started and built up a successful travel agency, dealing in lettings for people who required a touch of extravagance in their holiday home. Home from Holmes Holidays with its instantly recognisable signature logo of three gold aitches intertwined together, was a very successful and lucrative operation.

Running one hotel, even one as large as The Portland Arms, seemed to pale into insignificance against his business, but he was impressed by her acumen and they found they had much to talk about and discuss. They both continued to meet partners through the agency, until one night when everything changed. Instead of the usual parting with a swift air kiss between them, he lifted her chin and placed his lips on hers. They kissed with a passion neither had known was there, but they recognised the feeling was mutual, and soon they were seeing each other exclusively. When their need to be together grew stronger, he told her he loved her and wanted them to spend the rest of their lives together, and her future was suddenly much brighter.

As they saw more of each other, the edges between personal and business interests became blurred, as they discussed their hopes and aspirations. Ross was determined to expand his business to include exclusive hotels and she was touched when he confided in her and shared the details of the first suitable property he'd found.

After keeping a close eye on the market, the perfect opportunity had presented itself at last. It was the kind of property he was aiming for, and it would be an ideal investment. Unfortunately, the purchase price, which was higher than he'd hoped to pay, was not up for negotiation, and the seller's implacable stance meant there was no room for manoeuvre. With reluctance, Ross was having to find a partner who would invest some cash into it.

Bryony said nothing, but the thought of a third person in the partnership was not to be taken lightly, and she was kept awake, night after night, as she searched for a way to help him.

After reviewing her own financial situation, and with some trepidation, she told him she was able to help, if he wanted her to. She was overjoyed by his response.

'It will be the perfect solution,' he told her, my business partner at work, and my partner at home. What more could I wish for?'

She was slightly concerned about the amount of money she would be putting in, but she had never enjoyed such a satisfying and exciting relationship, and she was determined to hold onto it at any price. She'd consulted with her accountant and solicitor, who both advised caution, but after reading the terms and conditions of the agreement they'd agreed it covered most eventualities and wished her well. 'It is a reputable concern, and your money should be quite safe,' her accountant told her, 'Of course, there is never a guarantee,' he added with a smile.

She didn't mention her relationship with Ross, she didn't feel a need to. A lot of her money was tied up in the house on the promenade which she'd bought with part of her divorce settlement, and was originally meant to be invested to form a large part of her pension. But now her plans had changed, and she would be living with Ross, so when the house was finished, she would sell it and invest the money in their joint business.

When Ross asked her to move in with him, she reluctantly declined. Ralph was recovering from a heart attack, and when he'd been discharged from hospital, she'd promised to look after him in his own apartment until he was fully recovered. Carers were employed to tend to his medical needs but Bryony supervised his day to day living.

Ross was agreeable to the temporary arrangement, as it suited him to keep his new relationship out of the public eye, following his acrimonious divorce.

While the solicitor was dealing with the formalities of the hotel purchase, Ross was told by his accountant, that there would be very little money left over when all the costs of the transaction were paid. Unless he could find some extra funds, the improvements would have to wait until they'd recouped some of their outlay. Ross reluctantly accepted the news, but by this time Bryony was totally caught up in the excitement of the venture, and she was determined not to let this golden opportunity slip away. Out of the blue, an idea began to form.

Chapter 10

Marie eyed the clean nightgown laid out on the bed and sighed with disappointment. She'd asked them to give her the clothes she was wearing at the time of the accident, but the nurse had mumbled something about them being blood-stained and being sent to the cleaners. It was an acceptable reason for the delay, but enough days had passed for it to have been done and she was getting impatient. Having to wear the hospital nightwear, only added to her sense of anonymity, and she shuddered with disappointment at the thought of another day passing with no progress made.

Reluctantly, she showered and put the gown on, and was standing in front of the full-length mirror when Alice entered the room carrying a bag.

'Mm, I think you could do with something a little more stylish, why not try these for size?' Putting the bag on the chair, she invited Marie to look inside. Tentatively, Marie walked to the chair and peeped into the bag. Dipping her hand in, she took out a blouse in a soft shade of blue, and hardly daring to breath, she awkwardly held it up to her body and looked in the mirror, willing herself to recognise it.

'Very suitable for travelling in,' she said with a weak smile, 'is it mine?'

'Yes, those are the clothes you were wearing on the day of your accident. They've been cleaned obviously.'

Marie smiled. 'Yes, I appreciate that, thank-you so much.' She hesitated, almost afraid to ask. 'Do the police know about this?'

'They do,' she replied, 'they've taken all the DNA they require.'

Marie held the blouse close to her body and watched Alice take out a pair of dark blue trousers and matching jacket. Marie reluctantly told her she didn't recognise the clothes, but she did feel something, 'a kind of familiarity.'

Alice helped her to get dressed and Marie smiled at her image. 'I don't know how to describe it, but I feel as though I've found a small part of myself today. Slipping a hand into a pocket, she pulled out two twenty-pound notes and Alice told her they'd been found and taken out of the jacket before it was cleaned, and replaced afterwards, so they were rightfully hers. Marie put them back and zipped up the pocket. She felt like a child she was so delighted to have some money of her own, and she couldn't wait to spend it. Maybe, if she went to Wilmslow, she would be able to buy herself some underwear, or maybe a new handbag. The possibilities seemed endless.

'Will it buy very much?' she asked Alice, who shook her head.

'You may get both, if you shop around.'

'Then I'll shop around.'

'That's the spirit,' Alice said, 'I think that's a little bit of the real you coming out.'

Despite everything, she was feeling physically stronger and able to walk about without assistance. The dizzy spells were less frequent and the pain from her injuries was easing a little, so she was aware the

MISSING MARIE

time for her discharge was getting nearer. Having no idea where she would be sent next was frightening. She'd been informed about a meeting, which was due to take place soon, where the next phase of her treatment and care would be discussed. Trying to calm her fears, Mr. Hastings reassured her she would not be transferred or discharged without including her in the discussions, but despite his best efforts it didn't make her feel any better. When she was discharged, where would she go? She had no idea where she lived, or even if her children were close by. If they were, they didn't seem to be making much effort to find her, which added to her feelings of not belonging.

You will simply stay with us,' Mr. Hastings, the neurologist, assured her when she reluctantly voiced her fears to him. 'We'll transfer you to another part of the hospital, where you'll have more freedom and the opportunity to move about. But Marie, you mustn't worry too much about the future. We have already established there is no serious injury to the brain, so I am quite confident the main part of your memory loss will be restored quite quickly. It may take a little longer for everything else to be restored but come back it will.'

Marie sighed. 'It doesn't feel like it, at the moment.'

'I understand, but it's early days yet, and symptoms are worse during the first week or two after the injury. You'll see a big improvement over the next two weeks, and in a few months, you'll have forgotten all about it.' He laughed at his own, unintended joke, and Marie found herself joining in.

'Sorry' he said, but she shrugged away his apology.

'Don't be,' she told him 'That is the first laugh I've had since I came here.'

The feeling of optimism lasted until mid-afternoon, when she groaned with disappointment at the sight of Alice approaching with DS Pullman and Adele. DS Pullman was in a happier mood than normal, and she was pleasantly surprised when he commented on her state of mind and told her she looked much perkier than when he last saw her.

'I do feel slightly better today,' she told him, but that's only because I've got my clothes back at last.'

'Ah yes,' he said, 'that will help of course. Now, down to business.' Marie closed her eyes and remained very still, trying to bring back images of the incident that day at the station. She'd found that sometimes it helped to jog her memory into action if she could conjure up areas which were familiar to her, but today there was nothing happening.

D S Pullman coughed, breaking her concentration.

'I want you to take your time,' he said, 'to tell me everything you can remember about the day in question, no matter how small or insignificant. From the moment you woke up, until you arrived here, at the hospital.'

Marie shook her head in frustration, and no matter how hard she tried, she could only visualise the usual vague, unconnected pictures, so she opened her eyes and shook her head.

'It is strange that Mr. Hastings, the neurologist, predicted you would be able to help us by now, but I suppose every case is different. Have you had any more thoughts about your missing bag or case?' Marie shook her head. 'Or where you were going to, especially if you have any ideas about Wilmslow?'

No', she replied, 'but I do still have the feeling Wilmslow is somehow relevant. I feel better within myself, and I want to go, but I have to wait until the doctors give their approval.'

'Of course. I'll have a word with him.' Flicking over the pages of his small notepad, DS Pullman turned to Marie' 'I believe, you went to platform four where a boy approached you. It looks as if you gave or took something from him, before making your way to platform five, which is when the attack happened. Do you have any recollection of seeing or talking to two boys on the platforms or on the bridge when you were crossing over from one side to the other? I want you to think very carefully, because it could be very important.'

'No matter what she did, the time of her accident was a complete blank. Concentrating on images of Preston station, which she knew well, only sparked memories of earlier visits, but nothing which related to the day she fell. Hearing the urgency in DS Pullman's voice, she tried to dig deep into her mind to find something relevant buried there, but the harder she tried the more stressed she became. That particular day was completely lost to her, no matter what she did.

'Mr. Hastings, told me it's quite normal for the time surrounding the trauma to be the last memory to be recovered, but that doesn't mean it won't come back. I'm hoping he's right.'

'Will you tell me as soon as it happens?' he asked.

'Of course, she replied, impatiently.

'I was hoping, that you might be able to explain something to me. You see, we have reason to believe that those two boys were involved in the theft of your bags, and in their determination to get their hands on it, one of them pushed you down the steps. That poses the question we are now faced with. What were you carrying in your handbag, or case, that the two boys were so desperate to get their hands on. Whatever it was, how did they know it was there?'

Seeing the distress on Marie's expression, Alice stood up.

'I'm sorry, but that will have to wait for another day, my patient is very tired and needs some rest.' DS Pullman agreed, but as he was preparing to leave, he casually asked if the boys could have known what she was carrying in her bag. She shook her head.

'No,' she said firmly, 'there is no way they could have known I had a lot of money in my handbag.'

The room fell silent. Marie knew she'd said something very significant, but she was unable to explain the meaning behind her words. She felt his eyes lock onto hers. 'I've no idea, where that popped up from, but I think it's true that I was carrying a lot of money in my handbag. I suppose that's another complication,' she added wearily.

'It could be, on the other hand it might help us if we can find out what the money was for. Do you think it's possible someone had just paid you in exchange for something you'd obtained for them?' DS Pullman asked.

'If it was, I have no idea what it could be,' she replied, 'but I have a feeling you might. Are you going to tell me?'

DS Pullman hesitated, conscious that he was dealing with a very vulnerable person, but because of her memory loss and the fact she was so much at risk, he felt he had no choice. The hospital was buzzing with gossip, some of which was detrimental to Marie and she was bound to hear it soon.

'The boys in question are experienced drug dealers,' he said quietly, 'and we believe they were using your luggage to carry drugs onto the train to Manchester Airport.'

Marie leaned her head onto the back of her chair.

'I knew there was something you were all keeping from me,' she murmured, 'but I had no idea it was anything like this.' She looked directly at DS Pullman. 'Do you believe I'm a drug dealer?' she asked.

'I think you were being used by drug dealers,' he replied, 'I suspect the cancellation of the train threw them into a panic and they saw a golden opportunity to hide the drugs in your bag.'

'Oh, my goodness,' she sighed, 'I never in a million years imagined this could happen.' Alice decided the time had come for her to intervene, and she asked the officers to draw the interview to a close. They offered no resistance, but before they left Adele said she hoped Marie would soon feel well enough to make the trip to Wilmslow.

'It will be soon, I hope,' Marie said wearily. She couldn't help feeling it would prove to be a big disappointment if nothing relevant came out of the visit.

'Oh dear,' she sighed, when she was alone at last, 'when is someone going to come and claim me?'

Chapter 11

Sharon watched Tom from an upstairs window. Always in a hurry, he strode down the drive to where he'd left the car the previous evening. Unusually, he'd left the sunroof down when he'd parked it, which hadn't proved to be a problem, as the weather was still warm and dry. When she'd casually remarked on it, during the normal school day breakfast time, his reaction had been sharp, and when she responded by saying she was only passing a comment, he retorted crossly.

'Oh, for goodness' sake Sharon, stop wittering.'

She was just turning away from the window, when she caught sight of him listening very intently to his phone, and without his customary wave, he drove onto the road and sped away.

A tear pricked her eye. This behaviour was of no real significance, but it was very uncharacteristic of Tom, and for days his moods had been erratic. Even Lily had expressed surprise when dad said he didn't have time to read with her before she went to bed. At first, Sharon had welcomed his lack of interest in the normal family activities, as it had meant he hadn't brought up the subject of her night out, but now it was upsetting her because she was almost certain he was having an affair. She told herself it was unlikely he would have come back early from Manchester, on the night of their anniversary if he was having an affair with Fiona Campbell, but when her imagination took flight, logic didn't come into it. Maybe they'd quarrelled because he hadn't kept his promise to tell his wife he wanted a divorce.

Persuaded by Bryony to use some of the many hours she had owing, she found herself with an empty day stretching before her, and she was determined to enjoy it despite everything. First of all, she was meeting Louisa, Bryony and Damian, to discuss what they were going to do about finding Marie. There was still no news of her, and if she wasn't with Stuart, they had no time to lose. They'd arranged to meet at Marie's house as before, but unlike last time, they'd invited neighbours, who they hoped would be able to throw some light on the situation. The room was already full when she arrived, and there was a general feeling of disbelief in response to a suggestion that Marie might have gone away without telling a soul. They made no secret of their genuine concern for their friend and neighbour, and everyone agreed enough time had been wasted already, so Damian told them he was going to ring his father. The police wouldn't treat Marie's disappearance seriously, until they'd eliminated the obvious possibility of her being with her husband Stuart. He went into the lounge with Louisa, while the rest either went home or stayed behind with Bryony and Sharon in the kitchen.

After a few minutes, Louisa came to join them, her face pale and drawn. It was obvious there was nothing good to report.

'I presume Marie isn't with him?' Bryony said. Louisa shook her head.

'He has absolutely no idea where she might be.'

'How did Stuart take it?' Sharon asked, leading Louisa to a chair.

'He couldn't believe it. I suppose he's in shock. Fortunately, he's with a friend from our local birdwatcher's group who's promised to help. Damian has promised dad he'll get in touch with the holiday representative, and between them they're going to try and arrange for dad to fly home as soon as possible.'

Everyone turned towards the door when Damian returned, and seeing the fear etched on his face upset them all. The reality, that this was only the beginning of a nightmare, wasn't lost on anyone.

'I can't believe I've wasted so much time,' Damian said, 'we need to contact the police as soon as possible.'

'Before you do,' Bryony replied, 'let me ring Claire at the gift shop again. I only spoke to her briefly, and that was before we realised Marie was missing. It was a casual enquiry and Claire could have been protecting Marie's privacy, but when I tell her how serious the situation is now, I'm sure she will tell us all there is to know.

'Thanks, Bryony,' Louisa said, putting her hand on Damian's arm as he reached for his phone.

'A few minutes won't make any difference,' she told him gently.

They all listened on speaker, and if anyone noticed the initial coolness in Claire's voice when she answered Bryony's call, they didn't comment on it. Claire was quiet while Bryony explained the situation and they all listened with a deepening sense of concern as Claire told them that she too, had no idea where her friend was.

Bryony and Sharon left Damian and Louisa waiting for the police to arrive, and they walked together in silence as far as the Portland Arms, where they parted with an awkward embrace. Bryony walked slowly up the steps and Sharon continued on her way home, but when she arrived at the empty house, she was restless and afraid. She couldn't believe she was losing her husband and friend at the same time and she felt helpless, not knowing what to do. Reluctant to stay at home, but unwilling to meet people asking about Marie, she decided to take her own advice to Oliver, and she grabbed her bag and library book and set off to drive along the coast, to find somewhere peaceful. A respite, from all her problems.

Eventually, she came to a sign pointing to a narrow, winding road, leading to a small town she'd visited a few times with Tom and the children when they were younger. It was a quiet little cove which would suit her very well today, so she parked in a small car park on the front, and wandered round the town, which in fact was no bigger than a village. The variety of shops was intriguing in an old-fashioned kind of way, where beach paraphernalia and gifts proliferated, but there were some quality clothes shops and several cafés and restaurants. She headed towards the beach, choosing to sit on the bottom step of what looked like a newly built sea defence, which hadn't been there when they'd last visited.

She wriggled her toes in the sand and looked out towards the water. There was an aura of tranquillity, which slowly, but gently, relaxed the tense knots of stress in her body. In the distance, she could make out the figure of a man walking way out on the sand. Gradually she realised he was throwing a ball into the sea and his dog was chasing after it to retrieve and return to his master. She hoped the man was aware of the rip tides which were synonymous with this bay, and sometimes trapped people who were unaware of the danger. It was easy to become marooned on the island of sand which formed in the centre of the sea's pincer-like grip.

A few years ago, before they lived on the coast, Tom's brother and his friend almost lost their lives in Merebank Bay. Totally inexperienced, they'd taken Tom's poorly equipped dinghy to join the cockle pickers in the newly opened cockle beds. It had been a time of austerity when they'd all, including Tom, been made redundant. The memory of their reliance on food and clothes banks was embedded in Sharon's heart, and she would never forget it. Their luck had changed that night of the near-disaster, when many lives had been saved, and the move to live in Merebank had been the fulfilment of their dreams. She couldn't believe Tom was putting everything they had at risk, by having an affair, but what other explanation could there be for his change in behaviour? Something had gone terribly wrong

Keeping her eyes on the horizon, she tried to ignore the sound of someone coming down the steps. She wasn't in the mood for making small talk with a stranger, so she opened her book and pretended to read. Moments later, a shadow fell across her, accompanied by a familiar voice.

'I don't want to disturb you if you'd rather be alone. So, if you want me to go away, just tell me and I will.'

'I don't wish to be rude, but I'd rather be alone,' she replied, without looking up.

Immediately, he began to retrace his steps and she turned to watch him leave.

'Oliver,' she called, 'I'm sorry, don't leave.'

He turned. 'Are you sure?'

'Yes, I didn't realise it was you, and actually, some company would be nice.'

They sat in companiable silence for a while, each deep in their own thoughts, until Sharon began to tell him about the disappearance of Marie.

'I received a text from Louisa, just before you arrived. Apparently, the police are reluctant to start looking for Marie because she'd obviously planned to go away.'

'I can understand that' Oliver said, 'just imagine how she'll feel if she's just enjoying a little break, and she finds herself on the missing person's register.'

'I know, but it's so out of character.'

'We all do things occasionally, which are a bit out of the ordinary to us, but it doesn't mean there's something wrong. Look at us, who would guess we'd be here today?' Anyway, it's lunch-time, do you fancy a bite to eat?'

She glanced at her watch, unable to believe time had passed so quickly. She was feeling peckish, and after a short battle with her conscience, she decided there was nothing wrong with an impromptu lunch with a friend. After all, Tom was doing it all the time. Checking the time, she told Oliver she would have to be back in time to pick Lily up from school and they went back up the steps together. When they reached the top, she turned and with her hand shading her eyes, she searched for a sight of the man with his dog. After a few moments she picked him out close to the edge of the water, and satisfied he was out of danger, she joined Oliver, who was waiting patiently nearby.

'I noticed on the way in, the pub next door to the car-park has a light-lunch menu, how about going there?'

'That's fine by me,' she replied. It was relaxing, talking with someone who wasn't a part of the stresses of her work and family life and time seemed to slip away. When she checked the time, it was later than she thought, and she told him she would have to leave. Intrigued to know how he had found out where she was, she smiled when he told her he had found himself with a free day and decided to take her advice to explore the surrounding areas. It was by a stroke of luck; he'd turned off the main road and found himself in this interesting little place.

'What a coincidence.' Sharon smiled, 'I'm sorry about my rudeness when you arrived, 'but I'm glad you stayed.'

'So am I,' he replied.

She gave Oliver a few more suggestions for places to visit, before reluctantly walking back to her car.

'Goodbye, Oliver,' she said, 'thanks for lunch.'

'It was my pleasure.' He replied, 'Have a safe journey home.'

Momentarily, her vision was blurred, as she took the road back to Merebank Bay. In her mirror, she watched him waving, until he was lost from view.

Chapter 12

Bryony was going through agonies of indecision. Having temporarily reached the limit of drawing money from her own funds, she needed to find another way to keep her promise to Ross, but the idea which had taken root was potentially a dangerous one. A few years ago, following his first heart attack, Ralph had opened a new business account, which could only be accessed by himself and Bryony.

'It makes sense,' he'd said, 'this attack has been a wake-up call, and if anything like it happens again and I'm incapacitated or even worse, something major might go wrong with the hotel, and you may need money urgently. I'm sorry to say, but with Colin's track record I can't yet trust him to be in charge of it. No-one else needs to know of its existence.' She was so upset at the suggestion of him dying, she put all the documents at the back of the safe and tried to forget about it. But now she was desperate.

She waited until Justin had left the hotel for his lunch-break, before going into the office. Ellie was in charge of reception, so she gave her strict instructions she was not to be disturbed. Her hands were trembling as she opened the safe and took the file out. She glanced at the contents before placing it in her bag and carrying it to her room to read. Still shaking, her eyes skimmed the legal jargon until she came to the part where it clearly stipulated the bank was to honour any request for funds, by Mr. Ralph Portland or Mrs. Bryony Portland, for the running or development of the business.

It should be a simple procedure, but the repercussions didn't bear thinking about. She strove to push the image of Ross to the back of her mind as she tried to resolve what to do, but the thought of him, and the reason they needed the money, helped her to come to a decision. She hoped and prayed her request would raise no questions. Before she lost her nerve, she made an application for five hundred thousand pounds to be transferred from the special account to one of the business current accounts to which she had instant access. She returned the documents to the safe and nervously waited for the phone call telling her they'd received it.

She didn't have long to wait and when it came, the voice was verging on being apologetic. Graham Hollinsworth, the Business Manager, had received her request and would be in touch again, shortly, after he'd made one or two checks. Bryony took a deep breath and tried to stop her voice from trembling as she described the reasons for needing the money, until she almost believed they were undertaking some radical changes to Merebank's favourite hotel, the Portland Arms.

'Yes, that's right,' she replied, 'we are going to have a lot of work done on the premises, and possibly an extension. It will simplify matters if the money is accessible as and when we require it. Also, I feel I will have better control of the outgoings if I can keep a check on them as we go along.'

'Very sensible. I suppose that son of yours has got big ideas for the future.'

'Yes, something like that,' she replied, anxious to end the call.

'Of course, it is important to keep some resources in reserve, but I have no doubt that both you and Mr. Portland have considered this very carefully.' Bryony's heart beat faster at the mention of Ralph, but the banker appeared to take his agreement as given.

'I'll make sure everything is completed as soon as possible. It's lovely doing business with you, Mrs. Portland, as always.'

In the past she'd taken his subservient manner for granted, but today it seemed to conceal an unnerving hint of sarcasm. Nervously, she replaced the phone, as the enormity of what she had done hit her with force. She wouldn't rest until the transfer had been completed, and then she would transfer it into the two accounts she had control of, and from there, straight into her own account. She would do all in her power to pay it back before Ralph knew it was missing. The only way she was able to curb the unsettling sense of guilt, was to hold on to the fact that it was only a loan.

All her fears were swept away that night, when Ross left her in no doubt about how grateful he was.

Chapter 13

The following day, when DS Pullman came to see Marie, he was accompanied by a young woman, who introduced herself as Lydia Symonds, the FLO assigned to Marie's case. Marie had no idea what that meant and in response to her puzzled expression, Lydia smiled apologetically.

'Sorry for the jargon, I'm your Family Liaison Officer.'

'But I don't have any family,' Marie told her.

'Yes, you do,' Lydia replied firmly, 'we just have to find them.'

'We're working on it,' DS Pullman said, 'but we thought you might be more comfortable talking to Lydia, as and when your memory returns. Mr. Hastings has assured me, that should be quite soon.'

The visit to Wilmslow was due to take place the next day. Alice promised she would not give permission for it to go ahead if Marie was having second thoughts, and advised her to think it over. Marie had no intention of thinking it over again if there was the slimmest chance of it triggering her memory. She had too much time to worry and the possibility of never regaining her memory really scared her. She'd asked Dr. Hastings if it was possible for her family to walk into her room without her recognising them, but he would only say it was most unlikely, which did nothing to calm her fears.

The following morning, Alice helped her to dress, ready for her outing. Turning her to face the mirror, she tucked in the empty sleeve of her jacket.

'With that hidden away, nobody would guess there was anything wrong. At least,' she added with a smile, 'not from a distance, and in a crowd.'

They were both laughing when there was a knock on the door, and thinking it was Adele, they replied simultaneously, 'come in,' followed by a shocked exclamation when, instead of Adele, a man opened the door and stood just inside the room. He told them he was George Harding, and he was ready to stand in for Adele, who was unexpectedly unavailable for personal reasons. Marie was ready to call the whole thing off, but she listened when he explained he was a family liaison officer who had experience of dealing with similar circumstances to the one Marie had found herself in. Nevertheless, he told her he would fully understand if Marie preferred to wait until Adele was available, and Marie looked to Alice for guidance.

'It's entirely up to you,' Alice said, 'but we don't know how long it might be. It may be better to go today.'

'We'll go now,' Marie said, and within minutes he was leading her down the corridor towards the lift which took them to the ground floor. Approaching the exit she hesitated, her body shaking with nerves and apprehension. She was about to leave the building where she'd been safe, and the thought of venturing outside into the real world, was daunting.

George took her arm and suggested they sat in the foyer until she felt ready to continue, but she shook her head and insisted they carried on.

'It just feels a bit strange.' she told him, 'All these people who know who they are and where they are going, and why. My head, on the other hand, is a very scary place to inhabit.'

'Well. for a start, you know you are Marie, I am George, and we are in Preston, but about to go for a visit to Wilmslow. How's that for starters?'

'It'll have to do for starters, I suppose,' Marie replied ungraciously, 'I don't have any choice, do I?'

George burst out laughing.

'Well, you don't mince your words, I'll say that for you, but at least I know where I stand.'

Marie was mortified. Words just seemed to pop up from nowhere sometimes, leaving her feeling as if she'd taken on a new personality, and what was even worse, not a very pleasant one. Dr. Hastings had tried to reassure her it was a good sign she was feeling that way, as it meant she had a sense of who she really was. At the moment she had no idea what was real and what was fantasy, but when George stopped at a car and opened the front door, she accepted his assistance with a smile, especially when she found herself struggling with the seat.

'You've made a mess of this arm and shoulder,' he said sympathetically, 'let us hope they catch the perpetrator soon.'

They travelled in silence for a while, giving Marie time to enjoy the passing scenery and reflect on the situation she was in. She was desperate for this visit to trigger a memory of where she was travelling to before the accident cut her journey short. It was a long shot, but worth a try.

After a while, she noticed they were pulling into a railway station car-park.

'Why are we stopping here?' she asked.

'This is the start of our journey; this is Wilmslow and one of the destinations on the train ticket found in your pocket.'

She looked around thoughtfully. 'I don't know this place,' she sighed, 'it doesn't look familiar at all.'

George told her to give it time. Don't try to force it,' he advised, it will come back to you more readily if you're relaxed. Come along,' he suggested, 'let's just have a wander round.' They walked slowly around the station, where the platforms were easily reached by gentle slopes, in stark comparison to the steep and difficult steps at Preston. George was almost tempted to point out the obvious, that Marie wouldn't have suffered the catastrophic fall had she been at this station, but he refrained and said nothing. It may have proved more constructive if they'd made the journey by rail, but Marie's doctor had suggested travelling by car would give them more flexibility, if Marie needed to call a halt at any-time and return to the hospital. It was quite daunting for her first outing since the accident.

When it became obvious Wilmslow station wasn't stirring any memories, they returned to the car and George drove them into the middle of town.

'We are here to relax and do whatever takes your fancy; a bit of shopping, have a bite to eat, anything you wish. Of course, you may not have been here before and so you have no memories to recollect.'

'In which case, we will have completely wasted our time,' she muttered.

'Not at all.' he replied, we will have eliminated Wilmslow from our list of possibilities, and had a nice trip out.'

It certainly was a lovely place, with its tree-lined high street and lots of interesting, small individual shops, and she could imagine herself having a good shopping-spree here, but try as she might, she couldn't remember actually doing it. 'Is that a Marks and Spencer, down there? I think that's where we'll make a start.'

'Oh, no,' he groaned, 'I'm having a sense of deja vu.'

Marie felt a great weight lifting off her shoulders, and for the first time since she'd wakened up in hospital, she felt light-hearted. 'Come on George,' she urged, 'if you take me there, I'll treat you to lunch. You have brought my purse, haven't you?' She stopped abruptly, and stood looking at him. 'How stupid of me. I can't buy lunch for myself, never mind you. Oh, this is awful, what's the point of coming here. I need some clothes but I have very little money to spend. It's so annoying because I know I must have had money when I was attacked, but they won't give me my belongings back.'

Torn between anger and frustration, she didn't know whether to laugh or cry, but George told her not to get upset as he'd been given some money to cover their lunches.

'You are my business lunch,' he said, and Marie reluctantly agreed to join him. 'There is a very good chance the things you have lost will be covered by your insurance,' he told her, so I've also been given some money for you to use until such time you can repay it.'

'I may not have insurance.'

'I very much doubt that, so let's make a start.'

'Can I go and have a quick look,' she asked sheepishly, pointing up the high street, and he took her arm and carefully led her between oncoming shoppers.

As soon as they walked into the store, she looked around and exclaimed with pleasure.

'Now, this does look familiar,' she cried as she began to walk towards a rail of sale items. 'Does that mean I've been here before?' she asked excitedly, but George shook his head.

'They all look alike to me,' he said, 'and I don't think we can read anything into the fact they look similar to you.'

Knowing it would be impossible for her to try on any of the clothes she liked, she was quite happy to choose some items which she knew would suit her. Picking out two tops, she held them up in front of a mirror to compare them. 'I don't know which to choose,' she murmured, looking at her reflection and then at the tops she was holding in her hand.

'Have them both,' George said, 'you can afford it.'

She burst out laughing. 'You sound like Stuart, he says that.'

She stood still, looking at George. 'Did I really say that?' she asked, and he nodded his head slowly.

Repeating it, she tried it out for sound. And it sounded right. Stuart sounded right.

Allowing him to guide her towards the check-out, she was relieved when he told her to sit down while he joined the queue to pay for the clothes she'd chosen. 'This is all very emotional for you,' he said thoughtfully as they were leaving, 'I think we'll go and have some lunch.'

Marie peeped into the bag, and touching one of the tops, she told him it was her favourite colour.

'Stuart says it suits me, especially this shade of blue.'

'Stuart,' George said, 'he's popped up again.'

'My husband,' she said under her breath, "I'm sure that's what he's called, and I feel I can almost visualise him.'

Deep in thought, they made their way to a wine bar recommended by George, but Marie was tense, her eyes flitting over shops and buildings they were passing, desperately hoping for something to jolt her memory. Reaching the wine bar, she forced a smile but cried out as a man pushed past her and banged her arm against the door. Wincing with pain, she grabbed George for support and he instinctively put his arm round her shoulder to protect it. A waiter led them to a table and pulled out a chair for her, but her mood had changed leaving her deflated and sad.

'The sparkle has left your eyes. Is it because you are in pain?' George asked thoughtfully as he helped her to remove her jacket. He put his hand over hers and squeezed it gently, when she told him how remembering her husband's name had affected her. She smiled weakly when he tried to reassure her it wouldn't be long before she was reunited with him, especially now she knew his name.

'What was it again?' she asked.

'Stuart,' he replied.

'Oh, yes, Stuart.'

The food was tasty, and to her delight she could actually taste it. Ever since her accident everything had been so bland, and despite Mr. Hasting's reassurances, she'd begun to suspect her sense of taste and smell were lost forever. But things were definitely looking up, and she was determined to enjoy it. They laughed together as he cut up her food, and occasionally when she was really struggling, he held a fork to her mouth, but when she stood up to go to the toilet, he told her he drew the line at taking her there, but he watched her attentively as she walked slowly towards the ladies' toilets.

They were enjoying a leisurely coffee at the end of the meal, when Marie suddenly cried out.

'Tom. There's Tom, over there.' She stood up and was about to go after him, when she slumped back, 'oh no he's leaving, and he's walking so quickly I can't possibly reach him.'

George moved swiftly.

'Stay there, I'll see if I can catch him.' She watched him hurry towards the door, where he stood looking both ways before running down one side of the street and then coming back to go down the other side. Worried about leaving Marie he quickly gave up and came back to where she was anxiously waiting. She wanted to urge him to carry on searching, but he shrugged his shoulders and sat down again. His body language was relaxed, giving off no signals, but his eyes were alert and watchful.

'He must have moved very quickly, there was no sign of anyone who looked as though they were leaving the restaurant.'

'I wonder why he didn't say "hello", I'm sure he recognised me.'

'Who was it? Who did you see?' When she didn't reply he prompted her. 'You called him Tom. Does that mean anything to you?'

'Yes,' she replied slowly, 'he's a friend and he's married to Sharon, and they have three children, Sam, Ben and Lily. But I don't know where they live.'

'Never mind, it doesn't matter,' George told her, 'That was quite significant progress. It proves your memory is coming back.

George topped up their coffee from the cafetiere, before pulling out his phone and keying in a quick description of the man he'd glimpsed running out of the door. If he was a friend of Marie's, it was puzzling why he hadn't come over to see her. He must know she was missing, but his actions demonstrated he didn't wish to talk to her.

He'd certainly moved quickly in an attempt to avoid being seen.

Tom parked the car and checked his watch. He had some time to spare, so he took a walk around the town. It was the sort of place he'd always aspired to, with its upmarket shops and posh restaurants, but he was happy with their new home in Merebank Bay, which was where he and Sharon had always longed to live. When his fortunes had turned around, bringing with it the opportunity to buy a piece of land near the sea, they'd designed their perfect home and watched it rise from the ground to its completion.

There'd been a few hiccups along the way, but everything had settled down now, and that's the way he was determined to keep it. Sam, the eldest son, was settled at university. Ben the middle one, was doing well at school, and was in the local, under fifteen, football team. Lily, at nine years old, was the boss of them all. Sharon loved life and was happy in her job at the hotel, although he believed she was underpaid, but now she seemed pre-occupied and out of sorts. When he'd mentioned it, she denied there was anything wrong. He knew she was concerned about the whereabouts of Marie, but that had only come to light a few days ago.

He was having to tread very carefully, because when he'd made a joke the previous day about his belief that

Marie was making the most of Stuart being away by having a few days with her fancy man, Sharon had burst into tears and called him heartless.

Today was proving to be to be even more stressful than he'd expected, but after checking the time, he decided to go straight to the restaurant and calm his nerves with a beer. Tom, had arranged to meet Fiona at two, and she didn't take kindly to being kept waiting, but hopefully this meeting would mark the end of their relationship. He would be glad when it was over, but he'd made his mind up and he wasn't going to change it, no matter how upset she was. This was to be the end of the line.

He went into the restaurant where they were going to eat, followed the waitress to an empty table and ordered a drink. He'd gathered himself together by the time Fiona arrived, but when he stood up to greet her, he gasped with shock. Sitting at a table which was partly hidden by a pillar, was Marie, but even more shocking was the presence of a man who seemed to be paying her a lot of attention. Marie, if it was indeed her, was behaving in a way he'd never seen before.

Fiona sat down and picked up the menu.

'Don't mind me,' she said, petulantly, when she saw his attention was occupied by something or someone out of her sight. Tom apologised but leaned his seat to one side so he could see and observe the couple. Marie, was clearly upset about something, and the man took hold of her hand, before giving her a napkin which she used to dab her eyes. When she gave him a weak smile in return, it was obvious she was very close to the man she was with. There was no danger of her looking over here in his direction, her eyes were fixed on the person in front of her, and as he watched, the man stabbed something on her plate with a fork and fed it to her. Marie smiled coyly at him.

'Bloody hell,' Tom muttered under his breath, there could be no doubt now. When he'd joked about the possibility of Marie having an affair, it was because it was such an outrageous suggestion it was laughable. No-one would believe him, but he couldn't think of any other explanation for her being with another man and behaving as she was. It may have been because she'd sensed someone watching her, but suddenly she looked up and stared back at him. He knew instantly she'd recognised him, and in the shelter of the pillar he stood up.

'I've got to go,' he said, and almost ran out of the restaurant with no explanation.

'What the hell is going on?' Fiona demanded when she caught him up in a shop doorway, but she laughed at his brief explanation. 'So, a middle-aged woman is having an affair. Good luck to her I say. Now what about that lunch you promised me? I'm hungry.'

For the rest of the day, his mind was occupied with what he'd seen, and the planned discussion was rearranged for another time. He couldn't decide what to do. It was obvious Marie was here by choice, and feeling so sorry for Stuart, he didn't want to be the one to blow his world apart. Was it his place to tell anyone what he'd seen? There had been something strange about Marie's behaviour; he couldn't imagine her letting Stuart feed her like that in public, she'd be more likely to laugh at him and push his hand away. But maybe the opposite was true, and she wished Stuart was more romantic. His mind went round in circles, but the more he thought about it the more certain he became, that it wasn't his place to give away her secret.

He couldn't help Stuart to find his wife on the flimsy evidence he had, so it would be better if he said nothing. With a sigh of relief, he walked back to his car. It also meant he wouldn't have to explain to Sharon why he'd been in Wilmslow, meeting Fiona Campbell.

Chapter 14

Justin was alone and having a busy spell at the counter, so when the phone rang, he took the opportunity to hand it to Bryony as she tried to pass by without even looking in his direction.

'I think it may be a personal call,' he told her under his breath, and as she took it from him, she told him she would take it in the office. Convinced it was Ross, she closed the door and left him in no doubt how pleased she was to hear from him. To her astonishment, it was received with great hilarity by the person on the line.

'Sorry to disappoint you Bryony, but don't you keep that kind of talk for your lover?' She recognised the voice immediately and cursed Justin for his stupid blunder. 'Sorry to disappoint, but this is Bill Jackson.'

'Yes, I know who you are,' she replied, her cheeks burning from what she'd just said to him. Of all the people in Merebank, it had to be him and no doubt it would be in the local paper at the week-end. 'What do you want?' she asked, 'and make it quick.'

'I suppose you know it's the three hundred years anniversary of Merebank Bay next year.' He hesitated, waiting for a response, but Bryony was silent, unsure how to respond. If she'd known, she'd forgotten, but it would be unwise to admit that.

'I knew it was coming up, but I'm not sure about the details.'

'It's going to be massive, and of course the Portland Arms, although it came much later than that, must be featured. The original village is celebrating three hundred years of its existence, which is no mean feat in anyone's imagination, and there's going to be one hell of a party.'

It wasn't until next summer, he explained, but he was ringing to tell her they were planning a series of supplements to be printed in the run-up to the celebrations and he was sure they would want to take part. It was a perfect opportunity to help ensure the success of the event and at the same time advertise all the amenities the hotel had to offer.

'The Golf Club is very keen to be involved, and all the shops located within the square and the streets leading into it are joining together to represent traders of bygone times. I did think your son would enjoy getting involved and maybe even become a member of the committee. We badly need some young blood.'

'I can't speak for Hugh, but I'll tell him what you've said, and I'm sure he'll want to be involved. He's very keen to see Merebank thrive and he's got all sorts of ideas for the hotel in the future, but like you said, he's young and not afraid of change. He would be invaluable as a member of your committee, I'm sure.'

'If you could ask him to ring me, that would be good. We're hoping to get Damian Fowler representing the RNLI, but I heard his mother is missing so we are giving him some space. Just as a matter of interest, you're a friend of hers, aren't you? What's the latest news on that?'

'Nothing, as far as I know.'

'It's just that it's a quiet time here, on the news front, and an exclusive story like that would bump up our sales. We're lagging behind our rivals at the moment and we could do with a boost.'

'I will see what I can do.' Bryony curbed her excitement for the remainder of the call. This could prove to be the answer to her prayers. All she had to do was make sure Hugh was on a decision-making committee which would keep him busy for months to come. She was confident he would put his heart and soul into the town's celebrations, and any improvements to the hotel would be put on the back-burner, giving her time to implement her plan.

Leaving the office, she passed Justin who no longer had anyone waiting at the desk.

'Next time you answer the phone for me, make sure you know who is calling before you say anything. That was very embarrassing.' Justin nodded, although he had no idea what she was talking about.

'I've got to go out,' she called over her shoulder, walking quickly to the swing door, 'I'll be back as soon as I can.'

'Take your time,' he called good-naturedly, but Bryony didn't even acknowledge him.

'Oh dear,' Justin said to himself, 'there's something amiss. I wonder if its anything to do with that phone call I put through to her?'

Chapter 15

DS Pullman seemed to be in a strange mood, and she could feel an air of suspense within the room, so she prepared herself for news of some kind. The door was open, with no sign of people waiting to come in, only the poor man who seemed to spend all his time in the corridor outside her room. DS Pullman, looked at his watch and with a look of determination he went to close the door. Marie was certain she saw a nod of recognition pass between him and the man outside the door, but she was more interested in what he was going to tell her.

'Have you got something important to tell me?' she asked, after he closed the door.

'I have, but we must wait until the nurse and the liaison officer arrive,' he said. As if on cue, Alice and Lydia came into the room together, and went to stand by Marie.'

There's been a development, DS Pullman told her. 'Your luggage and handbag have been found.'

'Oh, that's fantastic.' She glanced round the room but she could see no sign of them. 'Where are they, haven't you brought them?'

Her heart sank, as he explained they couldn't be returned to her for some time, as they were being examined by forensics as possible items of evidence.

Marie turned her head away.

'Why do you make me feel like a criminal, when you keep telling me I've done nothing wrong?'

Lydia, stood by Marie's side and gently stroked her back. 'Try not to get upset, there's some good news coming.'

DS Pullman, cleared his throat. 'The few things you thought were in your case are there, together with several other items you didn't mention. Lydia will have a chat with you later to compare her list of contents and whatever you can remember. Your handbag was found containing a purse and some cards, which you will have to describe, but the two items which are missing, are the money, which you say you were carrying, and your phone.'

'Oh no,' she cried, 'that was my only chance of contacting my family.'

DS Pullman flicked over the pages of the small ring bound pad which he kept in his top pocket. Marie was caught in a dilemma and didn't know which way to turn. In the middle of the night, images of her bag filled with wads of money flooded her mind, but despite what DS Pullman thought, she still had no idea what it was for.

'Have you been able to put a figure on the money in your bag?' he asked, catching her off-guard.

She took a deep breath, and then gasping with pain, she held her chest and waited a few moments for it to subside.

'Take your time,' DS Pullman, said with feeling, 'there's no hurry.'

'A thousand pounds,' she whispered.

D S Pullman whistled between his teeth. 'That's an awful lot of money for a lady travelling alone, to be carrying around.'

She nodded in agreement, but cried out in frustration, when he asked her again if she knew what it was for. Hearing the distress in her voice, the liaison officer stepped forward and said she would call a halt to the meeting if Marie continued to become upset. Marie agreed to carry on the discussion, but told DS Pullman she had absolutely no idea what the money was for, but she denied any possibility of it being a payment she'd been given, for something she had sold to someone. She wasn't surprised he found that puzzling, but she became angry when he failed to understand how jumbled her memory was. He seemed to be implying it was selective, and she suggested he ask the doctor why she was able to remember some things but not others, with no sense of rhyme or reason.

'And let me know if you find out,' she said crossly, 'because I would be as interested as you are, to find out why some things come back very clearly and others are completely lost.'

'I'm sorry, I didn't mean to upset you again, but you see, there has been a very significant development. Your case was checked by a sniffer dog trained to find drugs. Although there were none in your case when it was found, there is strong evidence it has been used to carry them.'

Marie was stunned. Until now, it had been worrying, but this was too horrendous to contemplate. Lydia, gripped her hand, and Marie summoned up the strength to ask him which drugs he was talking about, although it was completely irrelevant as she had no idea of the difference between one drug and another. Even so her grip on Lydia's hand instinctively tightened, when he told her it was probably heroin and cocaine.

'I'm going to ask you again Marie, so please try to remember. Did you have any contact with two boys on the platform at Preston station?'

Stunned, by what he'd told her, she remained silent, concentrating her thoughts as much as she was able, but with little success.

'The most I ever get is a blurred image of two youths messing about at the station. My first impression was they were young lads, but when they came closer, I realised they were older than I'd first thought.'

'But you didn't talk to them?'

'Of course, I didn't talk to them. Why do you say that?'

'Because you were caught on the security camera on platform four, not only speaking to one of them, but also taking something from him. Can you remember that?'

The colour faded from her face, at the thought of what he was suggesting.

'You can't seriously believe I'm involved in drug dealing?' she cried.

'Why did you immediately think I was suggesting you are involved in drug dealing?' he asked, 'I never suggested that.'

Marie's voice was low.

'You as good as did, and I could hear it in your voice,' she said.

'We have to keep an open mind,' he told her, 'But no, I don't believe you are a drug dealer. That doesn't rule out the possibility of you being drawn into carrying something without your knowledge. Obviously, it would help if you could tell us what he was giving you, or what you believed he was giving you, because no doubt he didn't tell the truth about what it really was. I do understand how difficult this is for you, but if they were trying to get you to carry heroin, even if it was only from one platform to another, you must tell us, because we need to find it.'

'I wasn't carrying drugs,' she exclaimed, 'I had nothing to do with those boys. I'm just a middle-aged woman who wouldn't recognise heroin if I fell over it, so why would anyone trust me enough to give me their drugs, let alone recruit me into dealing in them?'

'That's just where you're wrong.' he said. 'They deliberately use the kind of people you wouldn't expect, from young, vulnerable children, to older people and those who've fallen on hard times. Nobody is ruled out. I don't want to be rude, but if you give the impression of being the last person to sell drugs, to them you are the perfect specimen.'

'But I don't understand why you think they chose me, out of all the other people there. What possible use was I to them?'

'You were an easy target, it's as simple as that. On one side they'd discovered we were after them, and on the other, they were afraid of what would happen to them if their boss discovered they hadn't delivered the goods as arranged. They were feeling cornered, when luckily for them, you came along with a case, preparing to take the train they were under instructions to catch. It was a perfect answer to the problem.'

Alice raised a questioning eyebrow at Lydia Symonds, who, to Marie's relief, indicated the meeting had gone on long enough, and not wishing to overstay his welcome, he stood up ready to leave.

'I'll leave you now Marie,' he said, 'Thanks again, it's been a very interesting morning.'

'I wonder what he meant by that,' Marie said when he'd gone.

'Don't worry, he's just doing his job,' Alice replied, 'he has to ask all these questions, and every time he does, you seem to remember things in more detail. I suppose it's the way they have of talking and asking questions.'

The more her physical injuries continued to improve, the longer the time stretched into hours of nothingness. Lacking the concentration to read a book, she was left with magazines and newspapers, neither of which kept her occupied for very long. Her mind still kept playing tricks as she tried desperately to bring back memories of her past life, but she clung to Dr. Hasting's promise that everything would eventually surface. The daily physiotherapy was a welcome diversion each day, and she decided to take the therapist's advice to go a little walk down the corridor to the ward and meet some of the other patients.

Feeling apprehensive, she opened the door and took a few steps outside the safety of her room and smiled at the man who was sitting there alone. She'd caught glimpses of him occasionally when someone had entered her room and she'd thought he must be waiting to visit one of the patients. She began to walk towards the main ward, but she was surprised to hear him stand up and begin to walk behind her. She stopped to let him pass, but he declined and stood looking at one of the paintings on the wall. When she'd almost reached the ward, she sensed he'd caught up with her, and she guessed he'd been measuring his steps to hers so that he didn't overtake her despite her slow progress.

When she reached the main ward, she stopped to speak to some of the women who seemed happy to pass the time with her. It transpired she'd become a minor celebrity within the confines of the hospital and there was a great deal of interest in the mystery woman with no identity. The sympathy they showed her seemed genuine, but it only served to set her apart from them. Everyone here had someone who cared enough to visit, while Marie was an object of pity due to her lack of friends and family.

On the way back, there was no mistaking the actions of the same man who mysteriously appeared as soon as she turned into the corridor. It was so obvious, she was tempted to ask him if he was lost, but it was possible he was suffering a lapse of memory similar to hers. Realising she couldn't help him to find his way to anywhere, she decided against doing anything and moved as quickly as she could to the peace and quiet of her own room. Her brief excursion had tired her both mentally and physically, so she lay on the bed and quickly fell asleep, and the next thing she knew, Alice was coming into her room.

'I'm so sorry to disturb you,' she said, 'but it's time for your medication.'

Putting the tablets into a small container, she handed them to Marie with a glass of water. 'You were calling out when I popped in earlier,' she said, 'were you dreaming?'

'I did have a dream,' Marie said, 'I can't remember it all, but there was a man and lots of birds.'

'Did you recognise him?' Alice asked gently.

'I don't know,' she sighed, 'I think I did while I was dreaming, but I can't see him now. At least it was a pleasant dream and not a nightmare, so I suppose that might mean something.' They both laughed, but this time, Marie automatically placed her arm across her ribcage to try and prevent the sudden, sharp pain.

'Oh dear,' she sighed, 'I'll be glad when these ribs knit together.'

The following morning, she was surprised to hear the voice of DS Pullman outside her door, and tilting her head in that direction, she looked at Alice and frowned. With the memory of the gruelling session Marie had experienced the previous day, Alice suggested she asked him to come back later, but Marie declined and told her she would prefer to get it over and done with.

DS Pullman, accompanied by Lydia, politely knocked before entering and greeted them both. Alice, who'd just started her shift, suggested the session ought to be shorter than the previous day, and less stressful. DS Pullman agreed to keep it shorter, but judging by his demeanour he wasn't promising to keep it light. Marie shuddered at the prospect of another serious conversation while being asked questions she was unable to answer. His first one shocked her, and she asked him to repeat it.

'I was asking if you know what the term county lines, means?'

'Yes, of course, I do. It's been on the local news many times. People, mainly young people, are forced to carry drugs from one place to another, on trains of course. Stuart and I were appalled at what goes on, especially as they target areas and small towns where there aren't many drugs to be found.' Suddenly, she realised the implications behind his words. 'Oh, my goodness,' she exclaimed, 'you really do think I was dealing drugs, despite what you said yesterday.'

Lydia jumped up and put her arms round her.

'It's not that,' she said, 'they believe you may have been used by the traffickers, to carry drugs in your bag without your knowledge.' Marie lifted her head and looked directly at DS Pullman.

'You don't think that, do you?'

'We have to keep an open mind at this stage,' he said, 'but don't worry, you're not being accused of anything. We just want to establish what happened on the day you were attacked.'

'That's enough for today,' Alice said, 'my patient is very tired.'

Tired didn't come anywhere near how she felt, and she was grateful to Alice for bringing the discussion to an end. If they really believed she was a drug dealer, she had no way of proving she wasn't. She didn't even know who or what she was. Fortunately, Alice was becoming impatient with DS Pullman, pointing out it was an impromptu visit, so, apologising for the intrusion, he agreed to leave. He walked towards the door and turned to look at Marie.

'There's just one more thing,' he said thoughtfully, 'I believe you walked around the hospital earlier today, unaccompanied. I must ask you not to do that again, you must always have a security guard with you in future.'

'Why?' she asked, and his expression softened.

'It isn't safe. Believe me, it's for your own good. The drugs are still missing and until they are found the dealers will leave no stone unturned in their efforts to find them. It's likely, they believe you are still in possession of the drugs, and will be putting pressure on the lads to retrieve them. They, in turn, will be terrified and desperate to get the drugs back. Until then, we have to make sure you are safe, so no more wandering about the hospital without telling some-one first. Maybe now,' he added, 'you can understand why it is so important for us to find the drugs, wherever they are.

Lydia tried to calm Marie, and explained things hadn't got any worse, it was simply that she was becoming more aware of everything. 'Security, has been in place all the time you've been here, and will keep you safe until the police catch the men who were using you. Isn't that so?' she said to the DS Pullman. He nodded and apologised for upsetting Marie.

'There is some good news on the horizon,' he said. 'I believe we are getting very close to finding your family, but I'm under instructions not to say anything more at the moment. I'll come and see you tomorrow. I may have more news then.'

'Oh dear,' Marie sighed. 'I've thought about nothing else, for days, but now I'm scared. I know it sounds ridiculous, but I was half hoping you wouldn't find them until this dreadful business with drugs is sorted out. How can I explain it to them?'

'That is what I'm here for, I'll do that for you,' Lydia told her, 'Don't you worry about a thing.'

Hearing voices outside the door, Marie asked if there really was a guard outside her room.

'There is, but he's only there to make sure you are safe.'

'I thought he'd lost his memory like me,' she said with a smile, 'I was feeling sorry for him. Well, I suppose I still do, it must be a very boring job.'

'It has its moments of excitement,' DS Pullman laughed. 'But I know what you mean.'

'Oh, dear. What have I got myself into,' Marie asked herself.

Chapter 16

There was an air of expectancy throughout the town, as friends and family awaited the return of Stuart Fowler from his trip to Portugal. Both he and Marie were well known and well liked, and the general opinion was that Marie would not have gone away without telling her family. As soon as Damian had contacted his father in Portugal and found out he had no idea where Marie was, he'd contacted the police to notify them of her disappearance. After the initial enquiries were made, it became obvious no-one in her family or circle of friends knew where she was.

Gossip was rife, and Sharon's nerves were at breaking point. For the first time since she started work at the hotel, she found herself putting on a false smile while listening to casual discussions surrounding her friend's disappearance. Justin, did his best to relieve the pressure, and when her lunch break was imminent, he urged her to go immediately. Thanking him, she went to get her bag from the office, before hurrying outside to look for somewhere on the promenade where she could eat her lunch in peace. Deliberately avoiding Marie's favourite place, she chose a shelter opposite the hotel, and sat down.

She could almost see the house where Marie and Stuart lived, and she knew Louisa would be there waiting for Stuart to return, so she decided to phone.

Louisa's voice was shaky when she answered, but she told Sharon that Damian was on his way back from the airport with his dad.

'I'm dreading meeting Stuart,' she said, 'I just don't know what to say to him.'

'Oh Sugar,' Sharon exclaimed. 'What a mess. Has Damian been able to tell you how his dad is?'

'Just briefly,' Louisa said. 'We spoke while he was driving the car from the car-park, to pick his dad up. He said Stuart was in shock and angry with the family for not telling him sooner. Sharon, I don't suppose you could come over? I feel completely out of my depth here.'

Sharon was tempted to go but decided against it. Apart from having to be back at work soon she didn't want to intrude on what would be an emotional family reunion. Her mind had wandered, but when she heard Louisa talking about the house being under siege by journalists waiting outside for Stuart's return, she became alert.

'I don't know what to do,' Louisa was saying, 'there's even one from the local radio. You'd expect him to have a bit more respect for Stuart's privacy.'

Sharon made no attempt to hide her disgust. 'I can't believe that. Look, I'm going to go back and tell Bryony what's happening. She'll understand when I tell her I need to be there to support you.'

Before Louisa had time to respond, Sharon was halfway across the road. She was panting when she bumped into Bryony in the foyer, but in between her gasps she described the chaotic welcome awaiting Stuart's arrival home. Before Sharon had chance to catch her breath, Bryony took control and stated her intention to go and sort them out.

'You stay here,' she said firmly, 'I'll go. I'm sorry Sharon, but they won't take any notice of you. I've got a couple of favours I can call in, and I'm sure they'll oblige. I know they have to do their job, but I'm sure I can arrange for them to give Stuart some breathing space.' She looked at Sharon and shook her head. 'Keep your eye on things here. This shouldn't take long,' she called over her shoulder as she wheeled her way through the group of people waiting to enter the revolving door.

Sharon went into the office and caught up with some paperwork which demanded little concentration, and waited. It all seemed so scary now that Stuart was coming home, but the reality couldn't be denied. Damian was driving down the motorway with his father Stuart, but there would be no happy reunion while Marie was still missing.

She breathed a sigh of relief when Bryony returned and told her she was confident the problem with the journalists had been resolved. As the hotel was running smoothly under the capable hands of Justin and Hugh, Sharon left the hotel a few minutes early and set off for home. When she was almost at the bottom of the steps, she met Oliver coming up.

'I gather there's no news concerning your friend,' he said, gently taking her arm to lead her away from the crush of people on the steps.

'I guess there's nothing I can do to help, but I hope you hear something positive soon.'

'Thank-you,' she replied, 'that's very kind.'

She slipped away and hurried home.

His thoughtfulness was touching, and soothed her raw nerves. He seemed to be the only one who really understood how she was feeling. It was somehow reassuring, to know that Stuart was coming home, but he had never been in any danger. Meanwhile, Marie had disappeared without trace, and they had no idea what had happened to her. Until Marie was on her way home, no-one involved would feel like celebrating.

It was still on her mind, when they were getting ready for bed, so she mentioned it to Tom, hoping for some reassurance, but she was shocked by his reaction.

'Why does everyone assume Marie has come to harm? It's perfectly possible she's left home by choice,' he said indignantly.

'Why on earth would she do that?'

'I've no idea, but like I said before, maybe she's having an affair.'

The idea was so outrageous, Sharon burst out laughing.

'This is Marie we're talking about,' she gasped, 'that would never happen.' For once Tom didn't respond with a smile.

'I wouldn't be too sure,' was all he said. Sharon went quiet. Either he knew something he wasn't telling her, or he was simply being obtuse, but that wasn't the first time he'd talked casually about people having affairs. It was as if the idea of it was on his mind.

'Whatever you do, please don't say that to Stuart,' she said, 'but he was barely listening. 'I don't suppose you're interested,' she persisted, 'but apparently he looked awful when Damian picked him up.'

'Of course, I'm interested, he's my friend,' Tom said, climbing into bed. 'I'm sorry love, I was miles away.'

Tom lay awake, his mind going over and over the images of Marie and the man she'd been flirting with, in

Wilmslow. He could think of no legitimate reason for her doing what he'd seen with his own eyes, other than she must be having an affair. He'd tried to tell Sharon several times, but she'd become so upset, he'd given up trying. She flatly refused to believe Marie was capable of such deceitful behaviour. He decided it was better not to say anything to anyone. Now, Sharon seemed to be annoyed with him anyway, so he couldn't win whatever he did. He reached out to her but she'd turned away from him, so he closed his eyes and went to sleep.

Chapter 17

When DS Pullman and Mr. Hastings entered the room the following day, she guessed by their expressions, they had something to tell her. Her heart was beating fast and her hand was clammy, but when Lydia came in and sat next to her, she began to calm down. DS Pullman waited patiently, but he was obviously eager to impart his news.

'You have something to tell me?' Marie asked anxiously.

'Yes,' he told her with a smile. 'We have traced your family.'

Marie cupped her face in her hands. This was the moment she'd longed for, but also the thing she'd feared the most. If she was a suspected drug dealer, where did that leave the rest of her family? Maybe they were involved and her accident had exposed them, or even worse, they were a lovely, respectable family who wouldn't want to be associated with her. All these things had been going round in her head and now, there was nothing she could do to change things.

'Oh dear,' she said, 'what will happen now?'

Lydia took Marie's hand.

'This is good news,' she said. 'I know it's a bit scary, but I'll be here to support you as long as you need me. It will be lovely seeing your family again, try to focus on that.'

'I wish I could,' she replied. 'But they are not going to welcome a drug dealer with open arms, are they?'

'You are not accused of doing anything.' DS Pullman told her. 'It is other people who've implicated you. Marie nodded and told him she understood what he was trying to tell her, but something didn't seem to add up, leaving her full of doubts about her supposed innocence.

Mr. Hastings reiterated what DS Pullman had already told her. It was good news and with the help and support of her family, the rate of her recovery would probably be improved.

'Have you met my family?' she asked DS Pullman., and his serious expression, broke into a smile.

'I've met your son Damian and his wife Louisa,' he replied, 'and they are very friendly people who obviously love you very much. It goes without saying, they have been very, very, worried about you. We haven't met your husband yet because he was out of the country when he was told about your disappearance. I'm going to leave you now, to give you some time with Lydia, I'll call in tomorrow.'

Her emotions were like a roller coaster, one minute she was longing to be home again, and the next she was dreading being rejected by members of her own family, especially when they discovered what she may have done. She couldn't bear to imagine what would happen if she didn't recognise them.

'Oh dear,' Lydia said, in response to Marie's mounting list of concerns, I believe you are overthinking this. No more "what ifs," let us concentrate on the positives. A good place to start, would be to draw up a list of family and friends you can remember.'

After they'd finished the growing list, to her satisfaction, Marie asked Lydia if she'd been with DS Pullman when he'd met members of her family.

'I was,' she replied with a smile. 'They are lovely people, and I think I'm correct in saying, it will be very difficult keeping them away from visiting you very soon. Which reminds me, I bought you this.' Taking a small bag out of her pocket, she handed it to Marie. 'I thought it might make you feel a bit more special when your husband comes to visit.'

Marie was delighted at the sight of a lipstick in a lovely shade of coral.

'Thank-you so much, that is so thoughtful of you.'

'Well, I always say there is nothing like a touch of lipstick, for giving a boost of confidence. Sounds silly I know, but there we are.'

The following day, Marie asked Lydia to test her knowledge of the members of her family and the friends she'd written down.

Lydia read them out one by one and waited for Marie say who they were and describe them, but they were both shocked to find she couldn't put a face to any of them.

'I know my husband is called Stuart, but why can't I picture his face?' Marie asked Lydia.

'That's a normal part of the healing process', Alice said, as she entered the room.

After Lydia had left, Alice asked Marie if she was aware that her husband Stuart was on holiday at the time of her accident.

Marie concentrated hard.

'Yes,' she said, 'he's gone to Portugal, bird watching. It's a birthday present from me.'

'Wow,' said Alice, 'some birthday present. Are you always so generous?'

'No, of course not. It's something he's always wanted to do, and I'm not interested, so I decided to treat him. Is he still there?'

Alice told her he was on his way home, and for the first time since the accident, Marie relaxed in the comfy chair with the newspaper and settled down to find out what had been happening in the world, while she'd been lost.

Chapter 18

Stuart was pacing the room like a caged tiger, which did nothing to calm Damian's nerves. His mother had been located in a local hospital and DS Pullman, who'd helped to track her down, had visited Damian and was now coming to meet his father, Stuart. She was being treated for injuries sustained during a fall while waiting for a train at Preston railway station. A hard bump on her head had caused a temporary loss of memory, which explained why they'd had trouble identifying her sooner

They were both impatient to go and see her, but DS Pullman advised against acting on impulse, as the hospital were following instructions from the police to allow prearranged visits only. Twice, his father had gone into the hall and come back with his coat, saying he wasn't waiting for anyone to give him permission, he was going to the hospital.

'If your mother is in hospital, I'm going to see her,' he said, thrusting his arms in the sleeves, 'and nobody can stop me. She needs me and she'll be wondering why I'm not with her.'

Damian went to take the coat from him, as he gently reiterated what they'd been advised to do.

'I know it is frustrating Dad, but it won't be long now, and we don't want to upset the people who've been looking after mum.'

Stuart reluctantly agreed.

'No, I suppose you're right. Your mum wouldn't thank us for that.'

'Let's wait to hear what they have to say, and then we'll go,' Damian replied.

'Alright son. But nothing will stop me then. Nobody can prevent me from seeing her. I'm her husband after all. What I can't understand,' he added, 'is what your mother was doing on Preston station in the first place. She didn't mention she was going anywhere to me, and she never does anything like this without us discussing it first. Neither of us do,' he added forlornly.

Damian didn't know what to say to make his dad feel better, because it was the truth. While his parents were both independent people, his father was right; it was very unlike his mum to undertake a journey of any kind without telling his dad or another family member. 'I shouldn't have gone,' Stuart said. 'I should never have gone to Portugal leaving your mother here on her own.'

'That's rubbish,' exclaimed Damian, 'Mum bought you that trip as a birthday present, you had no choice but to go.'

'I can't help wondering if it was nothing more than a ploy to get me out of the way, so she could go cavorting off somewhere. Maybe,' he said thoughtfully, 'they're right.'

Damian was appalled to hear his father refer to the gossip which was spreading through the town. Even some people who'd known Marie all their lives couldn't resist speculating on why she'd embarked on a journey she'd kept secret from her family and closest friends. He'd been hoping his father hadn't been privy to the gossip, but with social media in full swing it was a hopeless expectation.

'Dad don't say that,' he said calmly, although his stomach was churning, 'you know mum would never do such a thing, Anyway, she wouldn't even know how to cavort.'

'Don't you believe it,' Stuart replied with a secretive grin, and for the first time since his mother went missing, Damian's face cracked into a smile.

Hopefully it wouldn't be long before they would learn the truth, but a knot of fear was tightening with every passing second. Damian sensed an undercurrent in the words the sergeant had used on the phone, but he couldn't even begin to imagine his mother having broken the law. Fortunately, they didn't have long to wait before the imposing figure of DS Pullman was dominating the room. He was accompanied by a young woman he introduced to them as Lydia Symonds, and Stuart visibly started to relax, when she told him she was the Family Liaison Officer who had been supporting Marie throughout her ordeal. He was pleased to meet someone who'd been in close contact with her, who was telling him that Marie was doing fine. Lydia explained her role was now to help Marie and Stuart adapt to their new situation, and to be a conduit between themselves and the police. Damian silently questioned why his parents would need a conduit between themselves and the police, but he didn't want to voice his fears when his dad looked so reassured.

D S Pullman, insisted they addressed him simply as Harry, but he did admit it was something he'd failed to persuade Marie to do. 'She's a very charming lady, but determined,' he said with a smile.

'Tell me about it.' Stuart returned the smile, but Damian sensed the light-hearted camaraderie wasn't due to last. What felt like hours later, Stuart and Damian stared at each other in shock.

Damian was the first to speak.

'I can't believe you can think for one second, that my mother is a drug trafficker,' he said. 'She is the last person on earth to do anything like that.'

'I'm not saying she is,' DS Pullman said, 'or that we think she is, but we are in the middle of one of the most comprehensive crackdowns on the local network of county lines, and somehow Marie has become caught up in it. We don't know if she innocently agreed to carry something from one platform to another, or if the stuff was planted in her case when she got a bit flustered at the prospect of changing platforms. We think she bought a coffee while she was waiting, and the boys could have had access to her case, but this is all speculation.'

'I can imagine mum being naive enough to fall for an appeal for help, she's a sucker for helping people in a tight spot, but never in a million years would she knowingly get involved in carrying drugs.'

'Unless she didn't know the contents of the package,' DS Pullman replied. 'It would help a lot if she could remember what she took from him, but unfortunately her memory isn't fully recovered.'

Damian looked at his father. This was beyond their worst nightmare, but with a typical response, Stuart showed more concern for Marie's health than the antics of two boys, even though one of them was responsible for Marie's injuries. No matter what happened, she was his top priority.

'When can I see her?' Stuart asked. 'Is she well enough to come home?'

Lydia looked at him with sympathy, as she shook her head and explained why Marie was not quite ready to leave hospital. 'But we are going to arrange for you to visit her. I'll give you a ring later this afternoon, when she's been seen by her consultant.'

Reluctantly he agreed, but before he saw Marie, he wanted the answers to some questions concerning her health. Lydia told him he would have to save those questions for when he met the doctor. 'Marie is very bright and much more cheerful now, especially at the prospect of seeing her family again. Meeting you may jog her memory.'

'Hopefully,' DS Pullman added under his breath, and Damian had to stop himself from saying something he might regret, but he was increasingly getting the impression the detective did in fact suspect his mother of some kind of involvement in drug carrying, and he obviously had doubts about her loss of memory. For his father's sake he had to keep quiet until they'd been to the hospital and found out for themselves, what was happening

Damian went to open the front door to see DS Pullman out, and just as he was about to close it again, he was ambushed by Bryony Portland, thrusting a bouquet into his hand.

'I believe the police are here,' she declared 'Is Marie in trouble?'

'No, it's nothing like that, she's fine.' Damian said angrily.

'She can't be fine if the police are here, she called. Damian, tell me what's happened. Has she done something wrong? Is it drugs?'

'No, of course not,' he shouted. It's the boys who tried to kill her for drugs, who are in trouble. Now go away Bryony.'

Exasperation and fear were fuelling his anger, and he stood in the hall for a few seconds before going back into the lounge.

'Was that Bryony Portland?' Stuart asked.

'It was,' he replied. 'I'm afraid I was very rude. I hope I haven't offended her, for Mum's sake.'

'It will take more than a few words to offend her. She's too thick skinned for that, I tell you.'

'Well, maybe. But I've got a feeling Mum is going to need all the friends she can get, when she comes out of hospital.'

'Don't you worry, she's going to be alright. She's got me now.'

Chapter 19

Mr. Baines, the surgeon who'd operated on Marie's arm, was satisfied with the x-ray results, which showed the bones were healing well and, as he so nicely described it, 'all in the right places.' As far as he was concerned, her physical injuries no longer required her to be hospitalised, and he would arrange for her to receive a course of physiotherapy at her local hospital, once she was safely back home.

Mr. Hastings was more cautious. Her memory wasn't fully restored and the reunion with the rest of her family would be emotional and stressful, but there was no real reason to keep her in, so he too gave his consent for her to be discharged. She would be carefully monitored for some time to check that everything was going according to plan, but he wasn't envisaging any set-back.

Damian and Stuart had already visited her in hospital, and although there were many questions still to be answered, they had been advised to leave them until another time.

'Take it slowly,' was Mr. Baines advice. 'Baby steps,' he added, and demonstrated by walking his fingers along the top of his desk.

Marie left the hospital to the sound of clapping from the patients and staff on the ward, but she was aware of the gossip concerning her connection with drugs, which was circulating through the hospital. Hopefully, she was leaving all that behind her. The parting from Alice was emotional, and they made a promise to keep in touch in the future.

Stuart stayed with her while Damian went to bring the car to the entrance, and after Alice had helped Stuart by demonstrating the intricacies of assisting Marie in and out of the car, he went round to sit next to her and take her hand in his. He was visibly shaking but raised his free hand in a gesture of thanks to all the people who'd taken care of Marie while she'd been lost to him. Marie relaxed at last. She was safely back with the two most important men in her life. As they pulled away, she glanced in the mirror and caught a glimpse of a vaguely familiar man getting into a car behind. Suddenly, she recognised him. The man who'd spent so much time outside her room was now following them in his car. The seriousness of the position she was in, was becoming ever more evident as time went on.

When Damian drew up in front of the house, they were greeted by a small group of friends and acquaintances, some of whom handed bunches of flowers to Stuart and Damian.

Marie walked unsteadily along the path, and when Louisa opened the front door and took her inside, she gave a deep sigh of relief and burst into tears. Emotionally, she'd been to a very dark place, but now she was home. Stuart's arms were around her, and it felt like he'd never let her go, as tears of relief and happiness mingled on their faces. 'It seems like I've been away such a long time,' she told him, and he agreed.

'Not knowing where you were, was the hardest thing,' he said gruffly.

Slowly, she eased herself away from him and Louisa went to embrace her. 'Oh, we've missed you so much,' she said, 'and we were so worried.'

'I know, and I'm sorry,' Marie replied, 'let's sit down and I'll try to explain everything.'

'I still don't understand why you were at Preston station?' Stuart said with a tremor in his voice.

'Why I was there is easy to explain,' she replied, 'but what happened while I was there is still a bit hazy.'

'Look,' Damian said, 'you don't have to do this. It's between the two of you, and I think we should give you some privacy to sort it out.' Marie looked at Stuart, and they simultaneously shook their heads.

'Thanks, son,' Stuart said, 'but you have a right to know what happened, and I'd rather you hear it from your mother.'

'It all seems so silly now,' Marie said, taking a deep breath, 'but the truth is, I was on my way to visit Debbie.' Stuart gasped, his expression a picture of confusion. 'You were going to see Debbie,' he said, 'is that it? Why didn't you tell me what you were planning to do? You would have saved us all this trouble.'

Marie was still feeling disorientated, and all the questions were making her head spin, but she had to give them an explanation, she owed them that much. So, she went through it with them, how she'd planned to have a quiet time at home, until she received the totally unexpected phone call from Debbie, who was very distressed and begging Marie to go and help her. She looked at each of the puzzled faces in turn.

'So, you see, I had no plans for the following week which you believe I should have told you about. Her phone call came out of the blue. It was so out of character, I believed it must be serious and I had no choice but to go.'

Stuart remained silent while Marie explained how she'd tried to contact him and Damian before she left home the next morning, but there was no reply from either of them. It was too complicated to leave a voicemail, so she decided to contact them both later. Of course, she never managed to make the calls later.

'I never reached there, that's why,' she said, quietly.

'I still can't understand why our Debbie asked you to visit her.' Stuart said, shaking his head in disbelief. 'She rarely invites us, that's why I never want to go, because I've seen you get hurt too many times.' Marie agreed it had been difficult in the past, but this time was different because Debbie needed her.

'What's wrong Mum. Is she ill?' Damian asked.

'I've told you all I know,' Marie replied, 'but she sounded very depressed.'

'What I really don't understand,' he replied, 'is why you were apparently on your way to either Wilmslow or the Airport.'

'I told you. I was going to Debbie's.'

'But she lives in Bolton,' he pointed out, and Marie shook her head. 'That's what I thought, but they must have moved to Wilmslow. Don't ask me why or even when, because I'm in the dark as much as you are. She was going to explain everything when I got there.' The room was unusually quiet while everyone mulled over what they'd heard, when Marie suddenly tried to jump to her feet.

'What are we thinking?' she exclaimed. 'Debbie doesn't know what happened to me, she'll think I didn't bother to go. I must ring her.'

'I'll do it,' Damian said, 'I'll explain you had an accident on your way, and I'll tell her you'll get in touch later.'

'Thank-you son,' she said, as Damian took his phone out of his pocket and left the room.

Marie turned to Stuart.

'Do you understand why I had to go?' she asked

Scratching his forehead, he gave it some thought before replying. 'Of course, I do, it goes without saying, but I'll never understand why you felt you couldn't tell me.'

'I thought I'd already explained,' she said wearily. 'You were away, and I couldn't contact you. I would have tried the emergency number you'd given me, but there wasn't time. But anyway, I'm sorry.'

Stuart nodded and looked up anxiously as Damian came back into the room. 'How is she?' he asked.

'I'm ashamed to admit, that is the first time I've spoken to my sister in quite a while, and I was shocked. She is very down, and yes, Mum, she is depressed. She's certainly not the confident person I knew, but then who would be with all the problems she's faced.'

'Like what?' asked Stuart.

Reluctantly, Damian told them how Debbie's husband Eddie, has been a controlling, sometimes abusive husband and father. He paused, as they grasped the enormity of what he was saying. 'It was so bad,' he added reluctantly, 'the kids couldn't wait to get away and go to university. Quite recently he sold the house and moved them to Wilmslow, hoping to continue his long running affair with his secretary, but Debbie found out and went to see a solicitor to start divorce proceedings. Due to moving away, she'd had to give up her job and leave all her friends behind. That was when she became desperate and rang mum.'

'So that's why they never visited us or invited us to go and see them,' Marie said.

'Yes,' agreed Damian, 'he's been controlling them.'

'Is he there now?' Stuart asked and Damian shook his head. 'He's with his girlfriend.'

'He'd better stay there,' Stuart said, 'or I won't be responsible for my actions.'

'I must go to her,' Marie cried, but Damian stopped her.

'Don't be silly Mum, you are not well enough, but anyway, you don't have to go. Debbie wants to come here, and I've said that I will go to pick her up when arrangements are made.'

'My God,' Stuart gasped. 'She must be desperate if she's enlisting our help.'

Chapter 20

The carnival was in full swing and Lily's excitement knew no bounds. Ever since it had been announced she was to be crowned the Rosebud Princess of the year; she had talked of nothing else. Second only in status to The Rose Queen, she followed behind her on a beautifully decorated truck, attended by her own retinue of ladies-in-waiting.

She and her attendants carried baskets filled with rose petals, which they were to scatter at intervals along the way. Unfortunately, it didn't go according to plan when Lily and her best friend Zoe spied some of their friends standing at the front of the crowd. Their enthusiasm carried them away, as they showered them with the full contents of the baskets, causing a fit of giggles throughout the retinue.

Sharon, who was carrying a spare bag of petals rushed over and gave it to the adult accompanying the children along the processional route. 'Don't be silly now,' she called to them. 'There are no more left.'

'We won't,' Lily replied, as Sharon moved away. She walked at the side of the procession, but it sometimes meant weaving between the throngs who were enthusiastically cheering and calling to the people dressed up in different guises on the vibrant floats as they passed by.

As the procession entered the park, Sharon heard Tom's voice calling her name. Pushing her way through the melee of people, she found him on the edge of the crowd, standing with Ben by his side. Out of breath after her effort to keep abreast of the procession, and now pushing her way through to them, she asked if they'd seen Lily.

'Of course, we did,' Tom said, 'we wouldn't have missed it for the world.'

Ben's face was beaming. 'We saw her throw all her petals on her friends, and then you tried to walk backwards, giving them some more. It was so funny.'

'Well, thanks a lot,' Sharon retorted, 'you just try and do it.' But as much as she tried to keep a straight face, she couldn't stop grinning at them.

'How did you go on in the football tournament?' she asked Ben.

'Great,' he replied. 'We're straight through to the next round.'

'He played really well,' Tom said, 'I must say the organisers have done a great job. Considering it's the first time they've held a football competition at the carnival, it was pretty good. You've just got to make sure you win the cup in its first year, haven't you son?'

'No pressure there then,' Ben replied with a grin. 'Some of the men were asking dad to join the club and be a coach or referee or something,' he added, looking at his mum. 'I think he should, don't you?'

'It sounds like a good idea,' Sharon replied, 'do you fancy it, Tom?'

'I don't know, I'll think about it. It would mean a lot of commitment. I'm not sure I've got the time.'

Sharon scanned the edge of the crowd until she picked out Lily and her entourage ready to be disbanded. 'I've got to collect Lily,' she told them. 'Do you want to come and have lunch with us, I imagine she'll be hungry?'

'I've just had an energy drink and a banana,' Ben said, 'because I'm in the races now. I think I'll have a quick lunch after that and before the football.'

'And you?' Sharon asked Tom.

'I said I'd meet Damian in the pie and pint marquee.'

'Okay,' Sharon said, 'I'll see you later.'

Tom kissed her cheek.

'Are you okay with that? I'll come with you and Lily if you want me to.'

'No, it's fine,' Sharon replied, 'she'll probably want to be with her attendants, and you wouldn't enjoy that.'

'Oh no. Good luck with that.'

Sharon watched him walk away with Ben striding proudly at his side, and a wave of love washed over her. Pulling herself together, she hurried over to where the floats were discharging their medley of characters. She was just in time to take charge of Lily, and as she'd thought, arrangements were already being made for the girls and mums to meet in the burger and fried chicken tent. Although Sharon wasn't in the mood for incessant chatter, she accepted there was no alternative when her daughter was about to be crowned the Rosebud Princess.

Lily didn't very much resemble a rosebud after she'd finished eating her cheeseburger and chips, with the addition of a few sachets of ketchup, but by the time Sharon had used half a packet of wipes on her, she looked presentable enough. Her behaviour during the crowning ceremony was impeccable, and she received the compliments of the Mayoress with a shy modesty. Sharon's thoughts flew back to the year when her boss, Bryony Portland had been the Mayoress, and how seriously she'd taken the role. In contrast, this one seemed to be enjoying herself, and the children were very relaxed in her company.

How quickly things had changed since then. It was three years since Lily had been on the colourful Rainbows' float, and afterwards listened to the brass band with Marie. Louisa had been recovering from a hysterectomy, so Sharon had invited her and Damian to share the evening with them. This year was significantly different. Marie was resting at home following her ordeal, and Damian and Louisa were being host to Bryony's daughter Amelia and her husband Piers for the weekend. They were all friends from their time at university, and when Bryony had introduced Sharon to her daughter Amelia yesterday, she'd proudly stated the obvious, that her daughter was pregnant. Bryony was positively glowing with pride, but Sharon couldn't help noticing a touch of sadness behind her smile.

At the end of the crowning ceremony, Lily was presented with a book and a voucher entitling her to several free visits to the local zoo, which she asked her mum to take care of, but she was more excited about an invitation to stay with Zoe.

'Do you mean tonight?' Sharon asked, and both girls simultaneously started grinning and replying 'yes' at the top of their voices.

'For a sleepover!' Lily said.

'Hi,' Sharon, Cora said, as she caught up with the girls, 'shall we grab a couple of chairs in the marquee? My feet are killing me and I'm gasping for a cup of tea.'

Sharon laughed. 'Cora, you don't know how welcome those words are. I was just trying to figure out how I could tempt Lily to sit down while I rest my feet.'

They found some empty chairs at a table and sat down.

'Where do they get all their energy from?' Cora asked, slipping off her sandals, to massage her aching feet. 'I have no idea,' Sharon replied, 'but I'd like to bottle it, we'd make a fortune. Are you sure you want to do this? The girls are very excited and I know Lily won't settle for ages after she goes to bed.'

'The thing is,' Cora said to Sharon, 'My brother Phil, and his family are staying the weekend. They always come for the carnival weekend. They've got two boys, similar age to our son Julian, but no girls, and Zoe always gets left out. So, when she asked if Lily could stay, I thought it was a good idea. But, of course it's up to you. To be honest with you, Sharon, it will be easier for me, because Zoe will be occupied with Lily instead of constantly coming down with one excuse or another. I'll tell you another thing, the boys will be pleased, because they get fed up with her, which always causes arguments.

'Please, mum,' implored Lily.

'Okay,' laughed Sharon, 'as long as Cora doesn't mind.'

'Not in the least.' Cora said.

'You must be very good for Cora,' Sharon told Lily, 'And when she says it's time to go to sleep, you must do as she says.'

'I will,' Lily said, holding out her little finger, 'pinkie promise.' Sharon hooked her finger with Lily's before giving her a hug.

'I love you,' she whispered, but Lily wriggled free, more interested in being with her friend.

'I must go,' Cora said, looking at her watch, Julian is in the knock-out tournament, and I promised to watch.'

'Well, we can go together,' Sharon said, 'because Ben is playing too, and I said I'd go and support them, especially as they've got through to the second round.'

'Oh, I don't know if Julian has, I never even thought of that. Oh well, fingers crossed. Come on girls, we're off to watch football.'

'Oh no,' they groaned.

After promising to drop Lily's overnight bag at Cora's, Sharon made her way to where the tug-of-war was about to take place. When an almighty roar filled the air, she quickened her step to make sure she was there for the start. This year, a significant change was about to take place and she didn't want to miss it. Historically, the most popular adult event of the carnival was the tug-of-war competition and as regular participants grew older and less able to take part, they made way for the younger generation coming up. But this year was different, because for the first time, the veterans had formed a team and thrown down the gauntlet to challenge the losers of the main event.

Slowly, interest in it grew and the two legitimate teams began taunting the older men; suggesting they were only doing it because it meant they would be taking on a team who'd used all their energy on the main contest.

She'd seen the first round and was just in time to see the formation of the runners-up and the newly formed veterans' team. They stood facing each other, listening to the referee reading out the rules and regulations, but their impatience to get started was obvious. While they were preparing themselves, Sharon looked at the two teams. Tom was first in line, followed by Greg, Bryony's ex- lover, Ralph Portland's son Colin and the rest of the team made up of several local men who'd been coerced into taking part. There was no doubt Greg had spent some time in a gym; his body was firm and muscular, and Colin had definitely improved his fitness in the last few years. Maybe his impending marriage had given him the impetus to get fitter. Tom, who'd been a member of the first team, was still smarting from being demoted to the veterans' team, as he was years younger than the rest of them. There was no denying his fitness and strength, making him an asset to any team. Stuart had understandably pulled out and was at home with Marie.

She felt someone pushing their way to the front and turned to see Bryony standing beside her.

'Hello,' she said, with surprise. 'I didn't expect to see you here.'

'No,' Bryony replied, I didn't expect to be here, but old habits die hard I suppose.'

Further conversation proved impossible, as the crowd cheered for their favourite team. They were so evenly matched, the advantage moved from side to side, with support building to a frenzy. Sharon was cheering Tom's success and as she made a sideways glance at Bryony, she was surprised to catch her with eyes riveted on her ex-boyfriend Greg. She stood transfixed until a mighty cheer greeted the winning side, and when the prize went to the challengers, a whole swell of movement carried the victors towards the beer tent.

Sharon laughed as she stood on tiptoe to wave to Sam, who was with Jodie, and a group of friends from Benton, where they had lived before moving to the coast.

'Is that your son?' Bryony asked, and Sharon nodded proudly. Bryony's eyebrows lifted with approval. 'He's a very good-looking young man, I suppose he takes after his father, who was definitely the best of that bunch. By a mile.'

'I don't know,' Sharon couldn't resist saying. It was obvious Bryony was still carrying a torch for her ex-lover, and she couldn't wait to tell Marie what she'd seen. 'Greg's still looking good for his age. He must go to the gym regularly.'

'Well, apparently my ex-husband has also taken to doing that. Less successfully, I'm inclined to think. It's a shame Stuart isn't taking part; he's always been a member of the team. Is he alright?'

'Yes, I think so,' Sharon replied, 'but the whole thing has been a shock to them.'

'Have they learned any more about what happened to Marie?' Bryony asked 'It all seems very mysterious.'

'Not really,' Sharon said, 'but I know Marie is anxious because the police want to interview her again, I think it's about the person who stole her bag.'

'Have they found out who he is?'

'I'm not sure, but I think he might have been caught on the security cameras.'

'Oh, really, and was Marie caught by the security camera?'

There was something in her voice which alerted Sharon and caused her to hesitate before replying.

Marie and the policeman had asked her not to repeat anything she was told and here she was, almost letting things slip. She niftily side-stepped the question and suggested they went for a drink together. There was no way she'd be seeing Tom for some time, and with Lily being cared for, she may as well enjoy her unexpected freedom.

'We won't go to the beer tent', Bryony said, 'but we could go and have a gin and tonic.'

'That would be lovely. They've got some of the fruity, locally made ones, I think I'll have one of those.'

Bryony insisted on joining the queue to buy the drinks, and if she was put-out with Sharon, she was hiding it very well. It was difficult for Sharon to pinpoint exactly why she was feeling this way, but it made her more determined to keep everything to herself.

Chapter 21

After leaving Sharon, Bryony made a quick dash to her room, to collect her bag, before setting off to meet Ross at their usual meeting place, the Windmill Inn. It was located a few miles along the coast from Merebank Bay, and from there, he would drive them to the luxurious hotel in Windermere, where he'd booked a room with a four-poster bed, and a view overlooking the lake.

She sped along the coastal road, and as she pulled into the carpark, she saw he was already there, leaning on the side of his open top car, and her heart beat faster at the sight of him. When he turned and saw her, his face lit up, and she ran and fell into his arms. He kissed her passionately, and when he suggested taking a room at The Windmill Inn, she was almost tempted, but the luxurious Regal was waiting for them. As a car entered the carpark, she gently eased herself away.

'No, she whispered, 'but I'll make it up to you when we get there. I promise.'

'You're a hard woman, but I'll keep you to that promise,' he laughed, taking her overnight case to put in his car, while she parked hers at the back of the building, pre-arranged with the very accommodating landlord.

The hotel in the Lake District, was set in the trees at the end of a long, winding driveway, but Ross drove past the imposing doorway to pull onto the carpark at the side of the building.

'It's very impressive,' she said, as they approached the steps leading to the entrance, 'I've been aware of it of course, but never stayed.' She watched with interest as the girl behind the desk raised her eyes from the screen in front of her, and smiled in recognition at the sight of Ross.

'Good evening, Mr. Holmes,' she said, placing a single slip of paper in front of Ross for him to sign, before handing him a card. 'Would you like an extra key?'

Ross shook his head.

'No, thank-you,' he replied, 'we'll be together wherever we go.'

'Very well. Your suite is ready, but would you like a drink in the bar before you go up?'

Ross smiled his thanks and shook his head again.

'We'll have one in our room.'

He led Bryony to the lift and the moment the doors slid closed, he took her in his arms and kissed her. 'I thought we'd never get away,' he said, as he opened the door to the landing and led her into the most luxurious suite she had ever seen. It was tastefully decorated and furnished, with a large balcony which ran the whole of one side of the room, giving a panoramic view of the surrounding hills and down towards the lake.

Captivated by the stunning view, they sat on the balcony with their drinks, but when room service delivered their meal, the air was becoming cooler, so they chose to eat indoors. The waiter closed the large windows against the chilly air and set up the meal on a small table, with a second one close by for the wine.

Bryony, confident now of their future together, held no feelings of jealousy towards Ross and his ex-wife, but she was curious, and couldn't resist asking him how many times he'd stayed at this hotel. He gave a little laugh between tasting the delicious duck parfait and the smooth red wine and asked her how she'd figured out it wasn't his first visit.

'The classic giveaway. The receptionist and other members of the staff obviously know you.'

'Ah, yes. Well, I'm not certain exactly, but a few.'

'With your wife?'

'No, Mandy's never been here, at least, not with me.'

'With a lover then?'

'No, never with a lover. You are the only person I've brought here; I promise.'

She had to be satisfied with that, and what did it matter anyway, their pasts were exactly that, in the past. So, she didn't ask if he'd stayed in the luxurious suite they were now occupying, but she couldn't help noticing he seemed very familiar with the layout when they arrived.

'I was going to leave telling you this until later,' he said with a grin, 'but I thought you'd already guessed. This is the hotel we're buying; this is what you and I are investing in.' He reached over the table and touched her cheek.

'The staff know me as a customer, but that is as far as it goes. They have no idea of our status as potential buyers.'

Looking around the room and taking in the stunning view, made it very easy to imagine living here, but more importantly, she could see herself as his partner and co-owner of this magnificent property. Her heart was pounding at the prospect, but with supreme effort she maintained an outward composure. 'Where will we live?' she asked.

'There's a penthouse suite I think you will like. Until we find our own place' he added quickly.

'Will we be viewing it tomorrow?' As prospective buyers, I mean?'

'No, of course not, we are here for a little break and to give me the opportunity to do this.' He took her hand across the table and kissed it gently.

I was also going to leave this until later,' he said with a grin, 'and I'm not going down on bended knee, but Bryony, will you do me the great honour of saying you'll be my wife?' Utterly shocked, she stared at him, until he opened a small box and placed it on the table in front of her. Bryony gasped. It contained a ring set with a beautiful solitaire diamond. When he slipped it on her finger she was overcome.

'Do you like it?' he asked, but for once, she was lost for words and Ross grinned with delight. 'I think the waiter will be calling on us soon to remove the trolley and ask if we'd like a dessert. Would you like something sweet?'

'Are you having something?' she asked.

'Would I like something? Now let me see. I would love something to end this lovely meal, but I won't find it on the dessert trolley. How about you?' She simply smiled her reply.

Chapter 22

Sharon was at a bit of a loose end, now that her plans had changed. Originally, she'd expected to have a quiet night in with Lily, so when Sam asked if some of his friends could come round after the carnival, she'd agreed provided it didn't turn into a full-blown party. He told her it wasn't a party; it was simply intended as a place to meet at the end of the afternoon sports before they went to the funfair on the downs. Those who'd taken part in the afternoon activities also needed a place to change their clothes.

As some of his friends had come all the way from Benton, she asked him where they were staying, but when he told her she wouldn't want to know, she guessed it was probably in the sand dunes or on the beach as usual. If ever a torrential storm tore through the bay, as it had few years ago, she would offer them all somewhere to sleep, but otherwise they had their own tents which were stored in Sharon's garden shed during the day.

Tom had somehow become involved in yet another macho competition later in the evening, and she wasn't in the mood for going to the disco by herself, even though some of her friends would be there. She decided to have a stroll through the town and call to see Marie. She was still feeling guilty about not checking on her when Stuart was away, and she was determined to help now if she possibly could.

The town square was buzzing with activity, and as it was a balmy evening, all the cafés and restaurants had tables outside. Residents and visitors were enjoying meals and a glass of wine, and when she saw a group of friends, she was almost tempted to stop and join them. But she was anxious to see Marie and no doubt she would be offered a drink while she was there.

The cobbled street where Marie and Stuart lived was always well kept, but during the summer months it was a blaze of colour. The window boxes and the hanging baskets on the Victorian streetlights were spilling over with an abundance of beautiful flowers. This evening, with the streetlights already lit, it was worthy of its success in the N.W. Britain in Bloom competition.

The light was on when she arrived, and as she opened the gate, she saw Marie and Stuart sitting close together on the settee, and she hesitated, reluctant to disturb their peace. As if on cue, Stuart stood up and walked out of the room, and as soon as she rang the bell, he opened the door and invited her in.

'Look who's here,' he said, and she was touched to see Marie's face light up at the sight of her.

'Will you have a drink with us?' Stuart asked 'We were just about to have one.'

'I'd love a coffee,' she replied, but when he pointed out it was supposed to be a toast to Marie for her safe return, she changed her mind and said she would join them and have a gin and tonic. She gasped at the generous measure but it slipped down easily, and before she knew it, she'd been persuaded to have a top-up.

'I'll get some more ice-cubes and lemon slices from the fridge,' Stuart said cheerfully. 'I'm glad you popped round, we needed a bit of company, didn't we love?'

He seemed oblivious to the weakness of Marie's smile, but Sharon knew it wasn't because he was unconcerned about her, he was just so relieved to have her back.

'I don't know what we are supposed to be celebrating,' Marie whispered, when he was out of the room. 'I feel so angry with myself for acting so stupidly. I spoiled his holiday, worried my family and friends, and wasted the time of the police and the people who cared for me in hospital.'

'We've all done things we regret, and any way, you were only going to help your daughter, you were not to know it would end up like it did. It's all over now, and everyone is just pleased to have you safely back home.'

'That's just the point,' Marie explained, 'it is very far from being over.' Glancing towards the door she hurriedly told Sharon about DS Pullman's impending visit to talk about something they'd found on the security camera, which might help them to find the young man who'd pushed her down the steps, and stolen her bag. Sharon only had time to whisper her opinion that 'surely it was good news,' before Stuart came back whistling cheerfully. The tray was full, including a glassful of crackling ice-cubes and a small bottle of tonic.

'I think this is the only time we've ever missed the carnival, isn't it love?' Stuart said, giving Marie her drink. Marie gave him an affectionate smile.

'One year, we were away the week before, do you remember? We went to South Wales, but the kids were desperate to be here, so we came back on the Friday.'

'So, we did,' he laughed, 'I'd almost forgotten that.'

'There's obviously nothing wrong with your memory now,' Sharon commented, but Marie gently disagreed.

'My long-term memory seems to be okay, and I can remember things that are happening now or years ago, but everything around the day I left home and whatever happened at the station draws a blank. I hope it all comes back, because I have the distinct feeling the police don't believe me when I tell them I can't remember anything about it.'

Stuart was obviously in no mood to be glum, so he quietly but firmly told Marie she had no reason to believe that, and the doctor at the hospital had told her the road to recovery was rest and no stress, which also included not worrying about the future.

'That's easier said than done,' Marie replied.

'I'm going to leave you in peace now,' Sharon said, going over to embrace Marie, 'I hope you get some sleep tonight, the noise from the funfair is so loud.'

'Yes, it is,' agreed Stuart, 'it's strange, but when you are there, in the middle of it, you adapt, despite how loud everything is, but when you need a bit of quiet, it sounds horrendous.'

'I know Lily wants to come and show you her Rosebud Princess outfit tomorrow,' Sharon said to Marie, but I'll ring first, to see if you feel up to it. We can always come another time.'

'Oh, but that wouldn't be the same. You, must come while the carnival is still on. You could ring before you set off, just to make sure I'm awake.'

'As long as you're sure,' Sharon asked. 'I know Lily is so excited about seeing you.'

'Actually, you'd be doing me a favour,' Stuart said to Sharon. 'We had planned a little party before all this happened, and Marie ordered food from that new bakery in the square. Of course, with all the excitement, we'd completely forgotten all about it, and it's too late now to cancel. Damian and Louise, and Pearl are coming, so it will be a nice little welcome home party.'

Sharon hesitated. 'Lily is anxious to see you, but you might get overtired.'

'I can't wait to see her,' Marie insisted. 'Oh, and please make sure you bring Tom, I want to ask him why he didn't let on when he saw me in Wilmslow. It definitely helped to jog my memory. I knew his name straight away.'

Puzzled, Sharon looked to Stuart, to see if he could enlighten her, but it was obvious he was as perplexed she was, and Marie seemed totally unaware of the impact she was having. 'This is news to me,' Sharon said, 'how did he jog your memory, Marie?'

'I only saw him for a few seconds, while we were in a wine bar having lunch, but they left suddenly, and by the time George reached the doorway they'd disappeared. It was a shame really,' she sighed,' because he could have helped to identify me. I think George thought I'd imagined it, but I knew I hadn't.'

Stuart and Sharon stared at her, both worried her mind was playing tricks, but she gave what seemed to be a very clear account of the day she went to Wilmslow with George, the family liaison officer. They'd been to M & S and she'd bought some clothes, and then they'd gone to have lunch in a wine bar where she saw Tom. She called to him but he mustn't have heard because they ran out and were nowhere to be seen when George went after them.

'You said 'they', Sharon continued, 'was Tom with someone?' Marie nodded

'He was with a young woman, well, not that young, but she looked very smart and business-like. I only got a glimpse of her as they left, but they were in a hurry. From what I could see, she wasn't very pleased, in fact I'd say she was quite cross.'

'It would be Fiona Campbell,' Sharon told them 'He's having dealings with her about the development in Wilmslow. So, you can tell your policeman you are not imagining things.'

Sharon could see Marie was getting tired and a little agitated, trying to recall the day she'd seen Tom, so she kissed them both and promised to see them the following day.

'It was Tuesday, yes I'm sure it was,' Marie said suddenly. I saw Tom on Tues.' Stuart warned Sharon against taking much notice, as Marie's memory was very unreliable.

Sharon left them, and stood for a moment, undecided which way to go. The funfair was in full swing, and Ben would be there with his friend Toby. She'd been reluctant to let him go on his own, despite his argument that at fourteen he was old enough to take care of himself. She phoned him to check he was safe, before walking through the square and then onto the promenade.

She was as sure as she could be, without checking Tom's work calendar, that he hadn't been scheduled to go to Wilmslow on that Tuesday, but Marie's memory couldn't be trusted, and Tom's plans were often changed. But why hadn't he told her he'd seen Marie when he knew how worried everyone was? It didn't make sense, unless he'd chosen to remain silent to save himself the embarrassment of having to explain why he was there. And that could only mean one thing; he had a very guilty conscience.

'Well, look who we have here,' a voice called out behind her, and she turned to see Oliver in the middle of a group of people, walking, or stumbling together. Oliver broke away and walked beside her.

'Why are you alone?' he asked, 'I thought you loved the carnival?'

'I usually do,' she said, 'but this year is a bit different. I'd ignore me if I were you,' she said with an attempt at a smile, but it didn't work.

'Well, I'm not you, so, tell me where you're going, and I'll escort you there.'

'I'm going home, hoping that my son and his friends have already left, and the house will be empty.'

'You can't go home until you've had a drink with us. Now, come along and I'll try to put a smile on that lovely face.

Despite all her resistance, she found herself swept along by the gregarious group, until they reached the row of beach huts facing the sea. One of the men searched his pockets to find a key and opened the door with a flourish. Inside, the table and worktops were covered with bottles of alcohol and jumbo packets of various snacks. In no time, the music was playing, and the party began. Against her better judgement, Sharon accepted the drink being thrust into her hand, and before she knew it, she was joining in the fun, dancing and whirling around with abandon. She felt as if she'd always known this band of revellers who were effortlessly helping her to enjoy herself instead of wallowing in self-pity.

'Where do these people come from?' she asked Oliver. 'They aren't all staying at the Portland Arms, I know that'

'No,' he replied, moving to the rhythm of the music, 'they are here for a conference and some of our guys hooked up with them at the golf-club.'

'Oh, I see.' Although the beach huts weren't officially open during the carnival weekend, the rules were obviously being broken, as it was obvious there was another party taking place at the far end of the row of huts. Whistles and greetings were exchanged, and Sharon laughed when she found herself dancing on the promenade with Oliver.

'Just listen to that racket,' he laughed, 'our music is much more my era.'

'I know,' she shouted back, 'but I'm used to that as well, it's Sam's favourite group.'

The surface of the promenade was rough, and the livelier she danced the more her shoes were pulled from her feet, and one serious stumble catapulted her into Oliver's arms. Suddenly, she froze, as a group from the other party approached, singing and dancing their way along the promenade.

'I recognise this,' a familiar voice called out, 'it's my mum's favourite.' Pulling herself free, she ran into the hut and began to rummage amongst the things piled up on the bench seats lining the walls.

Oliver followed her; his face full of concern.

'Sharon, are you alright?' he asked. 'Have I done something wrong? It was very nice when you threw yourself at me, but honestly...' Her body began to tremble.

'Oh Oliver, stop it,' she cried, 'what am I doing here? I'm so sorry but I've got to leave.'

'I thought you were enjoying yourself? It's just a bit of fun.'

She rummaged amongst the pile of things on the bench until she found her bag and turned to go, but he stood blocking her way. 'Aren't you going to tell me why you are so upset?'

'I just heard my son and his girlfriend Jodie. They're in the group down there, and now they've joined yours. I had no idea they were going to be here, and I can't let them see me.'

Needing no more explanation, he told her he would walk by her side and after plonking a wide brimmed hat on her head, which she pulled over her face, they walked away from the party. When they were safely out of sight, she apologised and thanked him for being so understanding, and she persuaded him to let her make her own way home.

'I feel so stupid,' she said, but he waved her apology away.

'Goodnight, Sharon,' he said, 'take care.'

He turned to go and walked unsteadily down the path. When he stumbled, she couldn't repress the laughter that burst out of her and, as he regained his balance, he turned and joined in, before blowing her a kiss.

'Oh, we've forgotten this,' she called, waving the hat in the air, and when she gave it him, he put it on his own head with an exaggerated flourish.

Chapter 23

There were a few sleeping bodies strewn around Sam's bedroom, and a couple of girls in what was now known as Jodie's room, but Sharon ignored them on her way to wake Tom up. She guessed he would be a bit worse for wear, so she placed a large mug of coffee on his bedside table.

'A good evening, was it?' she asked, opening the blinds by the smallest margin in deference to his probably delicate condition.

'It was great actually,' he said, running fingers through his hair until it was sticking up in all directions 'what did you get up to?'

'Nothing special,' she replied, picking up the clothes he'd left on the floor, 'I did call at Marie's, to see how she is.'

'And, how was she?'

'She seems to be doing fine. We are going round soon, for Lily to show Marie her Rosebud Princess outfit. I've been trying to make it presentable as it took quite a hammering yesterday.'

'Oh, that'll be nice. What time are you going?'

'I'm picking Lily up from Zoe's and bringing her back here, because actually you're coming too. Marie and Stuart have invited us to a picnic lunch in their garden. Apparently, they'd planned it before Stuart went away and all the food is already ordered.'

MISSING MARIE

Tom groaned. 'Sharon, do I have to? I love them to bits, and normally I'd look forward to it, but not today. I'll maybe wander along later.'

'They're expecting us, and I've already made excuses for the boys, so you must come. Drink your coffee, that might help.' She put it on his bedside cabinet but he had other ideas.

'Oh, you're a bossy one,' he said, stretching out his arm to grab and pull her onto the bed. 'How about a bit of...' but she wriggled free from his grasp. 'Tom Lester, save your energy for going out later.'

Lily chattered all the way home from Zoe's. She'd had a very exciting time with her friend, and now she was looking forward to seeing nana Marie.

Sharon reminded Lily she must not expect Marie to play games or dance as she still wasn't completely well again. But Lily puffed up with indignation, saying she already knew that and didn't need to be reminded.

'I'm not a baby' she said indignantly. Sharon apologised, hiding a smile.

'It's okay', Lily said airily, 'I've decided to take Rusty instead.'

'Oh, Lily, that's the last thing we can do. You know what's he's like. He'll trample all over the flower beds.'

Lily giggled. 'Joked you! Oh mum, you're so easy to trick.'

'Come on, you little monkey. Let's go and see if dad's nearly ready.'

The house was slowly waking up, with teenagers taking over the kitchen and bathrooms, but as Lily had showered at Zoe's house, Sharon sent her straight to her bedroom to change into her costume, and pack some more suitable clothes for playing in later. The tiara was a little wonky, but with the help of a few hair grips, Lily looked almost the perfect Rose Petal Queen of the day before.

Tom emerged from the bathroom bright-eyed, with a clear head and not for the first time Sharon envied him his ability to shake off the effects of too much alcohol.

'You look good,' she said, a little grudgingly. 'It's surprising what a shower will do. Will you have a quick word with Sam, before we leave, to make sure they all clean up after themselves. I don't want to come home to the house littered with dirty pots and pans.'

'Will do,' he replied. 'I'll catch you up.'

Sharon was already regretting her decision to leave Tom unaware of Marie's claim she'd seen him in Wilmslow, but she was hoping a chance would present itself before Marie dropped her bombshell. When Louisa and Damian approached from the other end of the road, Lily ran as fast as her glitter shoes would allow.

'What an elegant princess,' Tom said affectionately. 'She loves Pearl, doesn't she?'

Sharon agreed. 'Yes, she does, and it's good for both of them to have someone to play with when we adults get together. Do you remember when Pearl was born, and Lily wasn't happy when we told her Marie was Pearl's nana too?

'Will I ever forget? Tom laughed, 'thankfully, she soon got over it.' He took Sharon's hand and squeezed it. 'We're a nice little family, aren't we?'

Sharon returned his smile. 'Yes, we are. Tom, there's something I want to tell you before we go in,' but before she had time to speak, Pearl hurtled herself at him and another opportunity was missed. Watching Tom greeting Damian, she found it hard to understand how he'd kept such important information to himself.

Every worktop in the kitchen held trays of food or drink, which caused an intake of breath at its variety and appetizing appearance.

'You've done yourself proud Dad,' Damian said, as he poured Sharon and Louisa a glass of wine. I can't believe you've done all this yourself.'

Stuart beamed. Gone was the haunted look, which had aged him overnight when Marie was missing, and back was his healthy complexion gained from the outdoor activities he enjoyed during the summer months. Sharon's sympathy with Tom began to ebb away. If he had seen Marie in Wilmslow, his failure to tell anyone had dragged out Stuart's agony; It was unforgivable.

'Oh, I'll have to confess, this wasn't my doing,' Stuart replied. 'It's courtesy of our new local bakers. Anyway, let's go through and see the person who is the reason for this celebration.'

Marie was pointing out to Lily and Pearl the place where the bees had made a home in the Virginia creeper which covered the roof of the shed. Lily was totally absorbed, but Pearl was too young to appreciate the wonders of nature and was more interested in the bowls of crisps on the garden table and the fascinating array of food in the kitchen.

It was late in the afternoon, when Marie and Sharon were sitting watching the rest of the group playing croquet on the lawn, when Sharon noticed Marie's troubled expression. She suspected Marie wasn't as relaxed as she would have them believe, but it was a tricky situation and Sharon didn't know how to handle it. Would Marie welcome an opportunity to talk about what was worrying her, or would it spoil what had been a lovely day. Deciding to leave it to a more suitable time, she sipped her drink and concentrated on the activity taking place on the lawn.

Her eyes were drawn towards Tom, who seemed totally relaxed and as competitive as usual. Louisa had been drawn into the game to make up the two teams, and, with her as his partner they were on course to be the winners of the best of three games.

'When I see what a happy little family, they are now they've got a child, I'm filled with gratitude towards you,' Marie said quietly. What you did for them is beyond belief.' Turning towards Sharon she added, 'I want you to know, we will never forget it.'

Sharon shook her head. 'I do know that' she replied, 'but all the thanks I could wish for are there, seeing them so happy together.'

We are all one big happy family now,' Marie said. 'It enriched our lives when your children adopted us to be nana and granddad to them, when you first came to live here.'

'And ours,' Sharon said. 'I don't know what we would do without you.'

'Talking of being happy, how are things with you and Tom? Tell me to mind my own business if you like, but I sensed a bit of tension the other day, and it would break my heart if anything went wrong between you.'

'We're fine Marie, it's nothing more than Tom taking too much work on; he gets tired, and I get fed up when he's never at home. He's absolutely driven, ever since the time he had no work he feels he has to prove something, but the sad thing is, all I want is to have him spending more time with the family.'

'Have you told him how you feel?'

'Yes, but he pretends to listen and then the next thing is, he's planning another project.'

'I suppose he's doing it for the family.'

'That's what Tom says, but we're comfortable now and he could ease off a little.' Marie made no comment, and when Sharon turned to look at her, she was surprised to see her staring into the distance. Sharon was mortified.

'Oh Marie, I'm so sorry. Here I am going on about me and Tom, and really there's no problem at all. Forget what I was just jabbering on about, we're fine.'

'It isn't that' Marie replied, 'it's all this about me and what happened at the station, I honestly can't remember, but the police believe I accepted a package of heroin, or maybe cocaine, from the boy who attacked me.'

'*What*? That's outrageous. How can they possibly believe you are capable of doing that?'

'Well, they say they think he was passing it to me to avoid being caught in possession of it, but I don't believe they really mean that. The awful thing is, I can't remember.'

Sharon hugged Marie and felt the tension in her body. 'Oh, Marie I'm sure you've got nothing to worry about, and everything will be alright.'

'I hope so. You won't say anything will you? I'm supposed to keep it to myself.'

'Of course not, I won't tell anyone. Oh look, here come the little horrors. Lily is absolutely shattered, it was a very busy and exciting day yesterday, and I don't think she got much sleep at Zoe's. Lily made straight for Sharon, and together they began to watch the climax of the croquet match. As Tom was about to take the winning shot, Pearl ran across the lawn and kicked the ball away seconds before Tom's mallet made contact. Much to his annoyance, a draw had to be declared.

There was so much food left over most of it was put back in the original packaging and handed to the visitors as they left. Sharon was particularly grateful, as it would be well received by the boys and Jodie, and whoever of their friends were still around. She kissed Stuart and thanked him for a lovely day, quickly followed by Lily's. 'Love you, grandad Stuart.'

'And I love you,' Stuart replied with a smile and a high five.

Sharon turned to Marie who was being held in a bear hug by Tom. Although Marie didn't complain, Sharon saw her grimace with pain and Tom, sensing what was happening, quickly released his hold. 'I'm sorry.' he said, 'I keep forgetting about your ribs, but it's great to have you home safe and sound. You gave us quite a scare.'

'It's lovely to be home, especially with all my family around me. She paused. 'Oh, that reminds me Damian, have you arranged a time go and collect your sister yet?'

Damian shrugged. 'No, I haven't, because every time I ring and suggest a time, she puts me off. There's always something she has to do first.'

'Typical.' Stuart said, but Marie stopped him from saying anything else. 'She'll come when she's ready. You can't just up and leave a place, without telling anyone.' Her voice petered out when she realised what she was saying.

To cover her embarrassment, she said the first thing that came into her head. 'It was an odd experience when they took me to Wilmslow because it meant nothing to me, and yet I instantly recognised Tom when I saw him.' Completely unaware of the effect she was having on Tom, she went on, 'I recognised you, and I was certain you'd seen me, but I must have been mistaken because you ran off as fast as your legs could carry you. The lady with you, struggled to catch up.'

Damian shook his head in disbelief. 'What must the odds be, of you two being in the same place at the same time, like that? It's such a shame, because if you'd seen mum we would have been reunited so much sooner.'

'I wasn't in Wilmslow that day, so Marie must have been mistaken.' Tom said.

'Oh well, my head was all over the place at the time, and it's very likely I imagined it. All I know is, if you had seen me, you'd have come over before you rushed off. And that's all that matters.'

'Exactly,' Tom said. As she listened to the exchange, Sharon could feel his sense of relief. It was obvious Tom had been in Wilmslow that day, and he had seen Marie, so why was he lying about it? Obviously, the attractive, woman in the wine bar with him was Fiona Campbell. Hopefully, everyone else believed what he was saying, because the thought of them finding out that Tom had seen Marie and not told anyone would be unbearable.

She would have to ask him for the truth, even if it confirmed her fears about Fiona Campbell, but first she must eradicate the picture in her head of herself and Oliver dancing around on the promenade.

Chapter 24

Marie tried to make out the voice on the other end of the phone, but Stuart deliberately moved away so she couldn't hear what was being said. She was watching his expressions very carefully and knew it wasn't good news. Thoughtfully, he replaced the receiver and returned to his chair, where he'd been sitting doing his crossword. Marie waited patiently while he folded the newspaper and placed it, with his reading glasses, on the coffee table by the side of his chair.

'So, are you going to tell me what that was all about?' she asked. 'I presume it concerned me?'

'There isn't a lot to tell, but it was DS Pullman, or Harry as we're supposed to call him.'

'What did he want? I suppose it's too much to hope he isn't coming this morning.'

Stuart shook his head. 'No, he isn't coming, but don't get too excited, he was calling to tell us to expect someone else instead. I believe it's a detective inspector. Yes, here it is.' He glanced at the scribbled note by the side of the telephone. Detective Inspector Longridge.'

Marie's face turned pale.

'A detective inspector? That sounds very serious. Oh, Stuart what have I done?

'You've done nothing wrong, absolutely nothing, but for some reason, DS Pullman wouldn't tell me what it's about. He just said the detective will explain when he gets here.'

'It's because they've found out what I've done wrong, and they are probably going to arrest me, otherwise why do they want to talk to me again? What time is this inspector coming?'

'Not until this afternoon, so we'll have a bit of lunch first. You may as well enjoy your last few hours of freedom.'

'Stop it. Stuart that isn't funny.'

'It is to me; the very idea of you dealing in drugs is laughable.' Despite his attempts to make light of the situation, she knew he was as worried as she was. It was simply his way of coping with the situation while trying to keep her spirits up.

'Let's sit in the garden,' she suggested. 'It looks lovely out there.'

He followed her outside, doing his best to hide the panic threatening to overtake him. He could tell Marie was anxious and well she might be, but he was clinging on to his belief, that there was absolutely no way she would have knowingly carried those drugs anywhere, but it wasn't looking good.

'There's a bit needs doing,' he said, joining her on the lawn, 'but it won't take long to get it back into shape.'

The garden was showing a few signs of neglect after Stuart's holiday, followed by the anxious days of Marie's disappearance. Since then, all his time had been spent looking after her, but she was feeling stronger and he hoped to get back into his routine as soon as possible. The lawn was in dire need of cutting and the weeds were fighting with some of the flowers for prominence. Despite this, the borders were still looking good, with the roses even better than ever.

'I'll try to do some dead heading and cut some sweet peas after the detective has been.' Marie said brightly, and Stuart burst out laughing.

'I'm sorry,' he said, but the thought of you with a pair of secateurs in your hand doesn't bear thinking about. I'm sorry love, but you'll have to leave everything to me for a while.'

'I wish I could leave all the questioning to you, I'm sick and tired of it. They keep telling me I'm not a suspect, so why do I feel like a criminal every time they say they have a few more questions to ask me?'

Stuart had no ready answer, so he threw some bits of cheese on the grass and watched a family of blackbirds enjoying their meal. He glanced at Marie as he took the tray of crockery into the house and put them in the dishwasher. It was the last thing he would admit to her, but he couldn't help being concerned at this latest turn of events.

Marie put the newspaper in the magazine holder for the fourth time that day and moved the vase of flowers slightly to the left on top of the sideboard.

'For goodness's sake relax,' Stuart said impatiently. 'I thought the newspaper had grown legs; every time I put it down for a minute it finds its way back to the rack.' She flopped into the sofa, her face crumbling, and cursing himself inside, he went to console her.

'It's only another interview love,' he said, 'you should be used to them by now.'

'But it isn't just another interview,' she sobbed, 'this is an inspector, don't you understand? It means they've uncovered something serious.'

MISSING MARIE

'Listen to me,' he said firmly, 'even if it is something serious it doesn't mean you've done anything wrong, just keep telling yourself that.'

'I'll try.

'Good, and I'll be with you, so there's nothing for you to worry about.' Marie was afraid this time, they would insist on speaking to her alone, but she was underestimating her husband's determination.

'I presume it's alright if I stay,' Stuart said in a tone which broached no argument.

'Of course,' DI Longridge replied.

Despite his title, he was a personable young man, who tried to put Marie at ease the minute he walked through the door. The trouble was, her nerves were like a coiled spring, and she was convinced he was going to be the bearer of bad news.

It was only when Lydia Symonds arrived, that Marie began to relax a little.

'My name is Grant, and you are welcome to call me that,' the detective said. 'I know you are Marie and Stuart, is it alright for me to use your first names?'

'Of course,' Marie replied. 'But I struggle to call policemen by their first name.'

'DI Longridge it is then. That's fine with me.'

'I'm sorry to interrupt,' Stuart said, 'but is this an official visit, I mean, do we need a solicitor here?'

DI Longridge smiled at them both. 'No, it's just an informal chat.'

Turning to Marie, he told her there was nothing worry about, he was just hoping she might be able to help him with a couple of things that happened on the day of accident.'

163

Marie shook her head from side to side. 'I can't remember much, and what I can, I've already told DS Pullman.'

'That's good, but I just wondered if you'd recalled any little details that you maybe didn't feel were important. If not, it's fine. I'll just go through a few things again, and if something comes to mind, please tell me.'

'I will, but don't expect much, because I've gone over and over the events of that day and it's still nothing but a blur.'

'Of course, I understand that' DI Longridge said. 'But you never know, we may just jog your memory. First of all, there were two boys together on the platform, do you remember seeing them?'

'Vaguely,' Marie sighed, 'I thought they were acting a bit silly, but they were only boys.'

'How old would you say they were?'

'One was about twelve, I guess. The other one looked a couple of years older, but later when he was close up, he was older than I'd first thought.'

'Thank-you Marie,' DI Longridge said, 'that is very helpful. Can you tell me if either of them came to speak to you?'

Marie didn't reply for a moment, a look of deep concentration on her face. Until today she'd had no recollection of speaking with the boys, but earlier, an image of one of them had appeared unexpectedly for a short time.

'I'm not sure, but I think he might have done. She was beginning to get flustered and exclaimed, 'Oh, I don't know, it's all muddled up.'

'Don't worry, you are doing very well. I have a couple more questions, then we're finished. Is that alright with you?'

Marie agreed with the detective's suggestion that the eldest boy had spoken to her on platform four, but denied he had handed her parcel at the same time.

'When he approached me at the top of the steps, I had a sense I did recognise him. That was all. I know he didn't give me anything.'

'Marie,' he said gently, 'we've got some security camera pictures, which show him passing something to you, and then you are seen putting something in your bag. The pictures, are not very clear, but please think again, can you remember that happening?'

'No,' Marie said emphatically, 'I definitely have no recollection of that.'

'Just a minute,' Stuart cut in, 'what are you suggesting? Are you trying to say Marie took drugs from him?'

'I'm just trying to eliminate the possibility.' DI Longridge replied. 'But it's the boy we are interested in at this stage, not Marie. It's possible he asked her to carry a package over to the next platform, and not knowing what it was, and trying to be helpful, she may have agreed. It's all supposition at the moment, but I just need to know how much Marie can remember.'

He turned to the back of the pad he'd been writing his notes on and pulled out an envelope.

'I've got some photographs here I'd like you to look at,' he said, and tell me if you recognise who is on them.' He pulled one out and handed it to her. When she gasped, Stuart jumped from his chair, but she looked at him and shook her head.

'I'm alright Stuart,' she said to him gently, and he reluctantly returned to his seat, but he was very watchful.

'That's me, obviously,' she said without looking up, 'and that's the boy.' She peered at it, but it was a very indistinct image.

'Here,' said Stuart, handing her his reading glasses, these might help.'

'Ah, yes, that's better. It does look as though he's giving me something, but what is it?' She handed it to Stuart, as DI Longridge passed her the second photograph. 'Oh dear,' she whispered, 'this isn't very clear either, but it does look as if I'm taking something from him.' Passing it to Stuart, she turned to DI Longridge. 'I'm sorry, but I can't remember any of this.'

'Now, hang on a minute,' Stuart said, his voice rising, 'this doesn't prove you were putting whatever he gave you in your bag, it could have been anything, you can't even make out what it is.'

'That's exactly right,' DI Longridge said, 'but I'll explain the situation to you, so you will understand what I'm getting at. Firstly, I need to ask you both to keep what I'm going to tell you, safely within these walls.'

Bewildered, they looked at each other and shrugged.

'Yes?' Stuart replied, and Marie nodded.

'Of course.'

'Do either of you know anything about county lines?' he asked, and for a few moments, neither of them spoke. 'Yes' Marie replied, but I've been asked this before. It's drug dealers using young people to carry drugs on trains throughout the country.'

'Ah, yes, I've got it,' Stuart joined in, 'it was on the local news the other week. But what has this got to do with...? Oh, my God. You really do think Marie is a drug dealer.'

'No,' she exclaimed, 'that's ridiculous.'

'Let me explain how it works,' DI Longridge said patiently. 'The term county lines refer to a network of mobile phones which criss-cross the country. They connect small towns and villages to larger towns and cities. The organised criminals force existing dealers to recruit children and vulnerable people to carry and sell their drugs. We believe the two boys who you met, are part of this criminal activity.'

Marie was looking closely at one of the photographs, willing herself to remember the events of that day, but the harder she tried, the worse it got.

'So where does that leave me?' she asked.

'We've been aware of these two boys for some time,' DI Longridge told her, and if we can prove they were trying to coerce you into handling drugs, it strengthens our case against them. Of course, there is also the matter of the attack on you. It suggests they were desperate, but about what we can only speculate at this stage. Violence isn't the norm at this level of the organisation.'

Stuart was peering at one of the photographs.

'This is ridiculous' he exclaimed. 'They're just lads.'

'Lads they may be, but the drugs they help to spread around the country ruin people's lives, and we have to try and stop them reaching previously drug free towns and villages.

'Don't forget what he was prepared to do to protect his drugs.' DI Longridge said to Stuart. Your wife could have been even more seriously injured than she was.'

'What do you believe happened that day?' Stuart asked, 'tell me honestly.'

'We believe they found out we were closing in on them, and living in fear of their lives from their bosses, they needed to offload their package to somewhere they could pick it up later. But they needed to be on that train. The bosses can track their movements using their mobile phones and woe betide anyone who doesn't follow instructions to the letter. Knowing Marie was catching the train to the airport, they seized the opportunity to put their drugs in her case when she left it unattended. They are swift and very light-fingered and would have been confident of retrieving them once they were on the train.'

Stuart listened in disbelief. To think that Marie had been somehow involved in something so sinister was unbelievable.

'What I don't understand,' he said, 'if they'd got everything covered, why did one of them attack Marie? It doesn't make sense.'

'We believe, they panicked, when they saw Marie opening her case. She could have found the package, or alternatively, they may have thought she was going to miss the train. In which case, the drugs wouldn't have reached their destination on time.'

Stuart, was listening intently.

'Do these lads really live in such fear?' he asked.

DI Longridge nodded.

'They do, and not without just cause. Some live in fear for their lives.'

Marie was half listening while she examined the security camera images.

'I can't believe it,' she said. 'They are about the same age as our grandson, Ben. No, I should say our adopted grandson. He's fourteen,' she said, before handing the photographs to Stuart. 'It brings it so close to home. Just imagine. Preston. I can't believe it.'

'It's ripe for drugs,' DI Longridge said, 'all those students at the university, but I'm afraid it's closer than that. The latest places to be targeted are along this coast, and the train service to the airport has proved very convenient for the dealers. Crewe to Manchester and Stockport, and the Styal line travelling to the airport via Wilmslow are making places like Merebank very accessible.'

Marie's head was reeling with all she'd learned, but somehow it made her feel better. Now, she knew it could have been anyone. To the drug dealers, she was a middle-aged woman with a case, in the right place at the right time. 'How convenient,' she said wryly, 'I can live with that, but what about me now?'

'If we pick our suspect up, you may be asked to identify him, but that's unlikely, as we've already got plenty of evidence to pin on him. It would help if you remembered what he handed to you. But thanks anyway, you've been very helpful.'

'There's one thing that puzzles me,' Stuart said, 'you seem to know all about these boys, and what they're doing. Why don't you arrest them and take them out of circulation?'

'Because they wouldn't be able to help us much, and they are easily replaced. What we need to do is find the top dogs, and we're on the verge of doing just that.'

'I don't know why you keep saying they attacked me,' she said suddenly, 'I can't remember, but I don't believe I was attacked. He tried to take the case and I just fell.'

'But you don't remember that?' he asked.

'Not very clearly. I'm just getting a sensation of slipping and falling, but not what caused it.'

'You've got my card, let me know if it comes back to you.'

'I will,' she replied' sneaking another look at the pictures.

'There is just one thing,' Stuart said. 'Why are you now in charge of things?'

He paused, and glanced at Marie.

'Your wife could have died Stuart. We could be looking at a serious charge, and I'm in charge of that investigation. It's nothing for you to worry about. Oh, I nearly forgot to remind you that you are still under security protection, so you will be quite safe.'

'Nothing for us to worry about,' Stuart repeated, under his breath.

Chapter 25

Bryony was buzzing. The weekend had been a complete success and her future with Ross as good as secure. He'd shown her the papers relating to the purchase of the hotel, and the valuation of his business, which had been arranged to back up his request for a loan. For the first time in her life, money wasn't the most important issue, not least because she was certain they would make a huge success of the Regal Hotel, and hopefully expand the business in the future. The imposing building, set on a hillside in acres of land, was a godsend.

She was suddenly weary of all the niggling, and seemingly trivial altercations surrounding the Portland Arms, and she longed to take up the exciting challenges of her new empire. The Portland Arms would be in safe hands, although she doubted the it would continue to be as successful as it currently was under her management.

She would officially leave Hugh and Lucy in charge, with Justin and Ellie dealing with the day to day running of the hotel. She had to admit, Justin and Ellie were capable of managing the hotel, but in her opinion, they needed to move on and gain more experience in hotel management. That of course left Ralph, who'd always held a special place in her heart, but she couldn't put her life on hold for him, especially as he was getting frailer.

After Ross had told her The Regal Hotel would soon be theirs, she'd walked around, her head full of ideas and her imagination running riot, while picturing herself as the wife of Ross Holmes and a partner in his company, Homes from Holmes Holidays. There were so many things she wished to do, but first of all they must finalise the purchase of the hotel and arrange a wedding. Regal, had a certain ring to it, and she could hardly wait for it to become hers.

She had never been so deliriously ecstatic in all her life, and she wanted to share her happiness, but Ross had urged her to show caution.

'It won't be very long before we can tell the whole world, but until then, the less anyone knows the better,' he'd said.

'She agreed with him, partly because it wasn't in her own interest to reveal her plans just yet as it might disclose any irregularities in the finances at the hotel, but she was desperate to tell someone, and she knew the very person who would be happy for her.

Marie's voice was cautious as she answered the phone, and only marginally relaxed when she heard Bryony's voice.

'I just thought I'd give you a ring, to see how you are,' Bryony said.

Marie tried to keep the surprise out of her voice. It was unusual for Bryony to ring her at home, and especially in the evening when Stuart was likely to be around.

'I'm doing alright, but I still get very tired, and my memory still keeps playing tricks with me. How are you?'

'Very well, thanks. Actually,' she said quietly, 'I've got something to tell you, but not over the phone. Do you feel up to going out for a drink somewhere?'

Marie hesitated. Either Bryony had got herself into another fix and wanted Marie's help, or she was up to something a bit iffy. Judging by the tingle of excitement in her voice, which she couldn't hide, it was the latter.

'I don't really feel like going out, but you could come here. We won't be disturbed because Stuart has gone to the golf club. It's become the regular meeting place for the old gang, and he enjoys going for a drink with his mates. We can have a drink here if you like.'

'That's good with me,' Bryony replied. 'Should I come now?'

'Yes, that's fine. See you soon.' With her good hand, Marie dragged the small coffee table within easy reach of the two chairs. Fortunately, Bryony had lost interest in Greg, a mutual friend who had become Bryony's lover. Bryony had involved Marie in her deceitful behaviour until it threatened to end their friendship. It was all in the past, with Greg happily married to someone else and Marie could relax, confident she wouldn't get embroiled in any more schemes designed to get them together again.

When Bryony arrived, she was bubbling over with an excitement which put a bloom on her face, and a distinct sparkle in her eyes.

'Well,' Marie exclaimed, 'there is no mistaking I'm going to hear some good news. Do you want to tell me now, or do I pour the drinks first?'

'I've brought this,' Bryony replied, pulling out a bottle of champagne from her capacious handbag. It's chilled and ready for drinking. What do you think?'

'I think,' replied Marie with a grin, 'I would love a glass, if we have something to celebrate at last, but that is all I can have. I'm on painkillers,' she explained, pulling her face. 'Obviously, you will have to open it though.'

'That's no problem, I'm an expert.' She quickly demonstrated the truth of that, by showing the open bottle with cork safely in her hand, and they were soon taking a sip of a very expensive and exhilarating champagne.

For a few seconds, Marie stared thoughtfully at the bubbles rising up the glass. She and Bryony had had a very rocky friendship, with many gaps when they had no contact at all, but despite that, they always enjoyed celebrating the good times. This had all the hallmarks of one of those times, and Marie was ready for a bit of good news after everything she'd been through, so she took another small sip of the posh bubbly and asked Bryony to 'spill the beans.'

'I'm getting married,' Bryony said, 'to a wonderful man. I can't wait for you to meet him; you'll love him I know.'

Marie put her glass down and went to kiss Bryony. She'd been alone since her divorce from Colin, and although, as Stuart was fond of saying, 'it's her own fault,' Marie couldn't help feeling sorry for her.

'Tell me all about him,' she demanded, 'age, looks, name, rich or poor. No, eliminate the last one, you would never love a poor man.'

'Now where was I?' Bryony said, with a smile lifting her lips, and Marie relaxed and grinned back. Bryony picked up her handbag and took out her mobile. 'Here are a couple of pictures, but they don't really do him justice. So that's about it, now you know everything.'

'It's a bit like a fairy-tale,' Marie said. 'Except in stories, lovers are never middle-aged. Does it bother you, that he's younger than you?'

'It's only a couple of years, and I never think about it when we're together. He doesn't care in the least.'

'Well, that's all that matters.'

'Anyway, that's enough about me. How are you after your accident? You look a lot better than when I saw you last.'

'I am,' she agreed, 'I've almost got my memory back, except for…' she hesitated, 'apart from the important part at the station.'

'Did you tell me you were involved in drugs or something?' said Bryony, 'I honestly can't think of anyone less likely to be involved in that sort of thing.'

'Don't say that,' Marie replied, 'I'm not involved. At least not knowingly. Oh, but it's very complicated, and I'm not supposed to talk about it with anyone.'

'Well, let's forget it then.' Bryony shrugged her shoulders dismissively. 'After all, if you can't remember anything it can't be very interesting.'

'Well, it is, I suppose. The police have pictures of me taking a parcel off someone and putting it in my bag.'

Bryony laughed in disbelief. 'I don't understand. If they suspected everyone who received a parcel from someone on a station platform, they'd be kept very busy.'

'He was a drug dealer.'

'Oh my God, Marie. What are you going to do?'

'There is very little I can do. The police say I am not suspected of being part of the gang, that I was in the wrong place at the wrong time. But all the same, at some point drugs were carried in my luggage. How can I explain that away? I'm scared Bryony, really scared. I can't tell Stuart how I feel. In fact, I'm trying to pretend I'm alright to all the family because they are already worried about me.'

'I thought my life was complicated,' Bryony said, filling her glass, 'but it's a doddle compared to yours.'

'Bryony, I'm not supposed to tell anyone about this, you won't say anything will you?'

'Who would I tell? Don't worry, your secret's safe with me. Come on, let's have another drink.'

'Not for me,' Marie said, 'I'm in enough trouble as it is.'

Later, having finished the bottle of champagne, Bryony walked unsteadily along the promenade and up the steps leading to the hotel, where she found the revolving door an unexpected challenge. Having circled twice without making a successful exit, she accepted the assistance of one of the regular guests who offered to guide her out of the correct side of the doorway. He politely turned down the invitation to join her in a drink at the bar. In a way she wished she didn't know all this new information about Marie, but surely it wouldn't do any harm to let Bill Jackson know a few innocent details? It would probably fix the Portland Arms at the forefront of the supplements and secure her name in the history of Merebank Bay, and that was too good an opportunity to miss.

Chapter 26

Marie and Stuart went their separate ways when they reached the fountain where children were leaning over to dabble their fingers in the water. Stuart was reluctant to leave Marie to make her own way to the gift shop, but she was insistent she was more than capable of going the short distance alone.

'You can see it from here, what can possibly go wrong? Claire is expecting me, so get off with you, and enjoy your game of bowls.' She gave him a quick peck on the lips and laughed as he self-consciously rubbed it off with the back of his hand.

I'm going,' she said before he could find another reason for him to stay with her.

It was an important bowling competition today and she didn't want him to miss it. He'd had a miserable time of it recently, all down to her, and he was badly in need of some relaxation. But she consoled herself with the knowledge that she was recovering most of her memory. If only she could remember what had happened at the station with that boy it would all be resolved, or at least she hoped it would. She was beginning to dread hearing what the police were going to tell her next.

The beach was alive with families enjoying the warmth of the sun, and a never-ending queue of excited children waited their turn for a ride on a donkey. Easing her way through the cluster of people waiting for ice-creams, she found the spring coming back into her step as she neared the lifeboat gift shop, but she still had to protect her wrist and shoulder as the slightest knock was very painful.

Despite what she'd said to Stuart, she did have reservations about what she was doing, because when her memory had disappeared, her confidence had gone as well. But she wasn't going to be beaten, so she pulled back her good shoulder and set off with a look of determination on her face. She was looking forward to meeting up with Claire and other members from the group of volunteers who'd stepped up to take her place while she was ill. Touched by the welcoming greetings from the staff who were there and a few of the regular visitors, she spent a happy hour carrying out very light tasks, but in her determination to familiarise herself with some of the new stock which had been added in her absence, she laboriously scribbled a short list with the intention of testing her memory at home later.

It was pleasant to get back into the rhythm of things and for a short time at least, forget the worries of the past weeks.

'Come on daydreamer, let's get a move on,' Claire said, jiggling the keys, and Marie was surprised to see her locking the door as the last customers left.

'My goodness, is it that time already?' she exclaimed. 'Our husbands will be wondering where we are. 'I'm surprised they haven't come looking for us.'

'Mine has been in touch' Claire said with a smile.

'And what did Russell have to say?'

'They are only just reaching the end of the competition, which it's going to be a very close finish.' Claire fastened Marie's cardigan over her painful arm and tucked the empty sleeve underneath. 'I only hope they win, otherwise we'll be in for a very miserable time at the Sands.

Marie turned the sign on the door to 'closed' and linked her good arm through Claire's as they set off walking towards the café. Despite taking care to protect her injuries, the extra effort of the afternoon had put a strain on them, blurring the edges until she couldn't tell which part hurt the most.

They didn't have far to walk before their destination came into view and as soon as they sat down, she took the painkillers provided by the hospital, and waited for the pain to subside. The café was busy as normal, but instead of the usual background music, a small player on the counter was set to the local radio station airing a programme which was causing an animated discussion between a group of local residents sitting close by. Claire went to the counter to place their order and Marie saw the look of concern cloud her face as she edged her way in to hear what was being said. Claire returned with the napkins and cutlery for the four of them, and placed them in the centre of the table. They knew Russell and Stuart would soon be joining them, so Claire had already placed their regular order of two homemade steak pies for the men and two homemade cheese and onion pies for themselves.

Claire was visibly upset, so Marie waited until she was ready to tell her what was going on. 'I can't believe this is happening,' she said, shaking her head. 'The fracking is going to start again.'

'What? But that's impossible. The government promised to listen to the views of the local people, and we voted against it. They promised,' repeated Marie firmly.

'Apparently, that counts for nothing. I just can't believe it.' She looked for Russell, but there was no sign of either him or Stuart, and Marie wondered aloud if they may have been diverted by the news which would be spreading like wildfire through the town. If it was true, it was bad news The question of drilling for fossil fuel near to the town was bad enough, but the people living close to the site were the worst affected by the earthquakes. And Claire and Russell were one of those couples.

'You know what this means, don't you,' Claire said, and Marie nodded.

She couldn't bear the thought of all the in-fighting and divisions between families it would probably entail. When Stuart and Russell arrived, there was no denying they had heard the news they were dreading.

'The first thing we must do is form a committee,' Russell said. and Marie listened with sadness. When the Russell's children had followed careers in different parts of the country, Claire and Russell had moved to a small development of exclusive houses on the outskirts of Merebank Bay. Out of the blue, a fracking company was given permission to drill on the land close by and very soon the earthquakes began to shake the ground and the price of houses in that area, began to plummet. After a bitter campaign the plan was pulled, but ultimately it was the increasing strength of the earthquakes which was the deciding factor and not the residents' objections.

'The trouble is,' Russell said angrily. 'Every property on the estate will suffer blight, so we'll never be able to sell the house, not for a decent price anyway.'

'They are offering compensation,' Stuart said tentatively. 'Whatever that might be.' Russell's face went crimson.

'You know what they can do with their compensation. They can…'

Claire grabbed his arm. 'Russell', she admonished, 'that's enough. You'll get us thrown out.'

'Sorry love. I just can't believe this is happening.'

A knowing look passed between Marie and Claire. They'd been in a similar situation to this before and they knew what it meant.

Chapter 27

Bryony put the case on the bed, and methodically looked through the pile of clothes until she was satisfied, she had everything she needed. After placing them carefully in the case, she closed the lid and pushed it in the bottom of the wardrobe. The risk of Ralph venturing into her room was low, but she had to be certain he didn't see anything. All she had to do now was make sure everything ran smoothly while she was away.

It was only a long weekend, but she was getting the vibe that her absences were being noticed. Previously she had never taken so much time off work, and if she was to avoid having to give some kind of explanation, their time together would have to be curtailed. All the more reason to hasten the fruition of their plans, so she was hoping this visit would give them the opportunity to finalise the wedding arrangements.

She still had doubts about Hugh's ability to be in complete charge of the business, although Ralph did not share her opinion. If only he would concentrate on the important things, but it was too late to worry about that now. She would have to work on him before she left, but time was running out. Lucy was a quick learner, but with the new baby on the way she would find it difficult to return to work for some time.

Under Justin and Ellie's management, the day to day running of the hotel was secure, but to make certain nothing went wrong, she'd asked Sharon to pop in, even though it was her week-end off. She had an idea to promote Sharon before she announced her own departure, but the only problem was, to which position? If everything else failed, she would have to create a role for her. For the moment, she needed to see Hugh, but he was probably with Colin at the golf club, no doubt discussing the forthcoming wedding which seemed to be the topic on everyone's lips.

She was still annoyed with Colin for not inviting her, but she had her own wedding to look forward to, which would be a far grander affair than a knees-up at the golf club. Although she'd agreed with Ross to keep the plans to themselves, a small part of her regretted the secrecy. She knew Marie would be upset at not being invited to Bryony's wedding, but she intended to soften the blow by sending her some exclusive photographs, followed by a few copies of the glossy magazines which were featuring the event in their society columns. She was anxious not to spoil their friendship again, even though she had to accept she would not be returning to Merebank in the foreseeable future. They would have to keep it secret for a little while longer, but she would put the time to good use by planning everything in advance, so it could then be arranged at short notice when the Regal Hotel would be theirs. Ross had shown her the documents for the purchase of the building, which had been agreed between the two parties, and everything seemed to be in order. He was so excited she had to try and curb his enthusiasm to prevent him making all his friends and family suspicious. His ex-wife was very much a part of his extended family and Bryony knew it wouldn't be easy to win them over to her side, but she had all the time in the world, and she didn't want to jeopardise her own chance of being welcomed into the family simply by rushing things now.

Hearing voices in Ralph's room, she leaned towards the door and was surprised to hear Colin speaking to his father. She couldn't quite make out what he was saying, but the words 'money' and 'wedding' were quite distinct, so she tapped lightly and waited for Ralph to invite her in.

'I thought I heard your voice,' she said to Colin, 'are you well?'

'Couldn't be better,' he replied, 'and you?'

'Yes,' she said with a smile, 'very well thank-you.' Determined to be the one to mention the subject uppermost in all of their minds, she asked him how the wedding plans were going. 'It's not long now I believe,' she said airily.

'No, but everything's going according to plan. I've sorted the venue,' he said, his face lighting up like a child on its birthday. 'Obviously, that didn't take much doing, as we're having it at the club, but Janet's doing everything else, flowers, cake, etc. etc. Look Bryony, I'm sorry you didn't get an invitation. Janet wanted to send you one, but I stopped her, because I knew you wouldn't accept.'

He looked across to his father.

'Dad tells me I was wrong, that I should have given you the opportunity to make your own mind up, so I'm sorry.' He looked so abject she began to feel sorry for him, and she didn't want to take advantage of his discomfort in front of Ralph, so she smiled brightly.

'Weddings always seem to throw up these difficult situations, but please don't worry about this on my account, I haven't given it a second thought.' Without thinking, she crossed the room and kissed him briefly on his cheek.

'I hope you have a wonderful day,' she said, 'and a very happy marriage.' Colin was disconcerted by the unusual turn of events, but Ralph walked over to his fridge and took out a bottle of champagne, which Colin uncorked, and put it on a tray with three glasses.

'This calls for a celebratory drink,' Ralph said, 'Let's toast families, which take all shapes and forms.' They lifted their glasses. 'To families,' they said in unison, and to her surprise, Bryony found herself holding back a tear. She'd never really loved Colin, but she didn't wish him any harm.

Chapter 28

The moment Stuart entered the room, Marie knew something was wrong. He went to hang his coat in the hall and came back carrying the newspaper under his arm.

'Are you going to tell me what's wrong?' she asked, 'you seem very upset about something.'

Stuart sat in his favourite chair and fished his glasses out of his pocket. Holding them up to the light, he meticulously began to clean the lenses.

'Do you remember that policeman stressing the need to keep everything under wraps; that we weren't to say anything about what's going on?'

'Of course, I do. Why, what's happened?'

'This is what's happened, and he's coming to see you about it.'

He handed her the paper and she stared at it and gasped. The headlines on the front page were in bold print which no one could mistake; 'DRUGS IN MEREBANK. MARIE FOWLER SUSPECT. 'See page five for the full story'. Cautiously, she turned to page five and saw the whole page splashed with photographs and stories about her. She was too upset to read it, but she got the gist of it easily enough. To make matters worse, if that was possible, they'd used an archive photograph of her, taken during a previous Carnival, when she was caught pointing her finger at Bryony, the

186

then Lady Mayoress. 'Who's the naughty girl now?' read the caption beneath the picture.

Marie froze, her hands slowing releasing the paper, until one by one the sheets slipped through her fingers and lay scattered around her feet. She looked at Stuart, who remained rigidly in his chair, making no move to pick them up.

'How has this happened?' she asked him.

His face was drawn and weary.

'There's only one way it could have happened. You must have told someone.'

'But I haven't,' she said, 'I'm sure I haven't.' Rubbing her forehead with her fingers, she vainly tried to recall a conversation when she might have mentioned the drugs, but her mind was a blank. 'How can I be sure, when I can't remember half the things I say and do. Shakily, she stood up, almost losing her balance, and Stuart jumped up quickly to hold her as she steadied herself. Pulling away, she went to the window where she stood looking out. 'I'm tired of all this,' she said. 'I'm tired of all the questions, and being made to feel I've done something wrong, when all I did was to go to my daughter when she needed me. And worst of all, is seeing the change in you.'

'What are you talking about?' he asked wearily, 'I haven't changed.'

'You're blaming me when things happen. No don't deny it,' she said when he tried to interject. 'I can hear it in your voice. For instance, just now when you gave me the paper, you implied it was all my fault, when I probably wouldn't have the faintest idea what Sergeant Pullman or the Inspector, whatever his name is, I've forgotten, had said to me. Let alone if I'd repeated it or not. Sometimes I wonder who's side you're on' All the pent-up emotions of previous weeks flooded out of her, in gulping sobs, and Stuart rushed over and took her in his arms and held her until her body stilled and she was calm again.

'Oh, love, that's a terrible thing to say. I don't blame you for anything, and of course I'm on your side. How can you say such a thing?' He led her to the sofa where they both sat down, and he pulled a handkerchief out of his pocket. 'Who's going first?' he asked, turning his tear-stained face towards hers, but without a word she took a tissue from the box on the coffee table, and they both dried their eyes.

All her fears spilled out and for the first time, Marie told Stuart how frightening and confusing it had been to find herself in hospital with no idea of who she was. And now, when she expected to feel safe in her own home, she was suspected of handling drugs.

Stuart broke down again when he tried to describe being in the grip of fear when he was told she was missing, not knowing whether she was dead or alive. He feared she'd been murdered when he learned she'd set off on a journey without telling a single person where she was going, which was so out of character for her. Before they'd had the chance to celebrate finding her, they'd been told she'd lost her memory and possibly wouldn't know them. 'And then last but not least,' he turned to look at the newspaper littering the floor and dramatically threw his arms up in the air. 'You are a drug dealer.' He'd flipped when he saw the paper and thought she'd been talking about it.

'I'm just worried you could be putting yourself in danger' he said to her.

'I'm sorry,' Marie said, 'I've been so wrapped up in myself, I haven't thought about how you must be feeling.'

'We've both been a bit guilty of that, so let's forget it now. Can you think of anyone you might have told? You know you do sometimes open your mouth before putting it into gear.' He gave a wry smile, 'that's not a criticism, it's just you.'

Marie frowned. 'I don't know who 'just me' is at the moment. I can't even think of anyone I've talked to about all this, which is frightening, to say the least. I'm just hoping it might come back to me. If it doesn't, I think I'll go mad.'

Chapter 29

DI Longridge was asking her the same question half an hour later, but Marie was still shaking her head.

'Why is it so important?' she asked, 'I wish I wasn't plastered all over the papers, but why are you so concerned about it?'

'We are not too worried about the average reader', he told her, but it's different if anyone trying to get hold of drugs sees this. It is almost like an open invitation to come and get them, and it could put you in danger.'

Marie's face blanched. 'Oh my God,' she said, 'I never thought of that. Will they come to the house to try and find them?' she asked fearfully.

'They might,' he replied, 'but if they do, they'll walk straight into our trap. Our biggest concern is that the last transaction on record will be when the drugs were passed from the boys to you. As far as the criminals are concerned, the drugs are still in your possession, or have been moved to another territory, without their knowledge. Which won't make them happy.'

'What about the two boys,' Marie asked, 'are they safe?'

'They've gone to ground, but we know where they are, so we're keeping an eye on them.

Before he left, he gave Stuart a direct phone number to call, if Marie remembered giving information to anyone, as she seemed to believe she had.

'I have a vague inkling I might have told someone, something,' she repeated.

'If it comes back to you, please let me know who it is, and I'll remind them that anything you told them is to be treated with confidence. I will also have a word with the editor of the paper; the journalist I spoke to was very evasive.'

DI Longridge shook Stuart's hand, but when he turned to Marie, she was slumped into her chair with her eyes closed

'Tell her not to worry,' the detective said, 'I'm sure we'll be able to resolve it very soon.'

'I hope so,' replied Stuart. 'It's taking its toll on her. On all of us in fact.'

Not long after the detective left, Lydia arrived. Marie had found her a reassuring presence in hospital when she was floundering through the mist of memory loss, and even now was benefitting from her calm reassuring manner.

'I suppose you already know what's happened,' she said, and Lydia nodded in acknowledgment.

'It gets more and more complicated,' Lydia replied, 'but I don't think it will be very long now before you'll be able to put it all behind you. Try not to worry.'

She repeated the words of advice later, as they walked down the path together towards the gate.

'I will,' Marie replied. 'All the neighbours will have seen the paper by now, but I don't think they will be judging me. We're a tight little community, so I have nothing to fear from them.'

'Friends are invaluable at a time like this,' Lydia said.

Marie looked doubtful, as she walked into the house and sank back into her chair.

'You look shattered,' Stuart said, 'What's the matter love? Don't get upset again.'

'I think I've remembered who I told,' she replied hesitantly, and Stuart waited anxiously.

'Sharon, it was Sharon. I told her when they were here for lunch, while you were all playing croquet. I'd been thinking about it and I must have confided in her.'

'But it doesn't make any sense. She's your friend, why would she tell the local rag?' Shaking his head in disbelief he paced the room. 'I don't know Marie, there's something about this that just doesn't seem right.'

'I know, it doesn't feel right, it feels very wrong. One of my best friends letting me down like this makes me wonder who I can trust.'

Stuart knew he had to approach things very carefully at the moment, but he was anxious about the way Marie was jumping to conclusions, especially when it concerned one of her closest friends.

'I just don't think you should blame Sharon out of hand,' he suggested, 'after all, your memory isn't what it should be.'

'Maybe not, but now I clearly remember telling her about this.'

Chapter 30

She was positively skittish as she entered Ralph's room with his morning coffee. Things were proceeding satisfactorily and she wanted everyone to know about her good fortune. If pressed, she couldn't have pinpointed exactly what had changed in the last few days, but her mood had been buoyant and she was feeling very happy. Ralph was dressed casually, but as always, he looked immaculate, and she told him so.

'Is that new?' she asked, indicating the light green cashmere sweater he was wearing. Her mood was infectious and he grinned as he told her he'd entered the men's shop in town on the spur of the moment, simply because he felt like wearing something new.

Bryony walked over to the expanse of window and looked out. 'It suits you' she said, without turning to look at him, and then completely changing the subject she commented on the lovely spell of weather they were enjoying. 'We've been very lucky with the weather until now, I hope it continues, it's good for trade.'

'Indeed,' he replied, 'how has business been this year?'

'Quite good, it's been very steady, but we can't rest on our laurels these days, we have to be constantly thinking of new offers or enticements to get the people here.' Without thinking, she'd allowed the conversation to turn towards the financial position of the hotel, and that was something she wanted to avoid, so she excused herself to keep an engagement with Hugh which he had asked for.

'He does seem to have settled down well,' Ralph said, 'and we do need to listen to the ideas of these young people, as they are more up to date with current trends.'

'Indeed, but we also need to keep an eye on the finances.'

To change the subject, she asked him how the wedding arrangements were progressing, and it had the desired effect and brought a smile to his face.

'They are going well, as far as I know. I'm so glad Colin's found happiness with someone. I sometimes feared he would be alone, and as much as I would have loved him to take over the business, I knew that would never happen without a partner. As it is, he's found something new he loves doing with his bride-to-be, so I'll settle for that. I wish the same for you,' he said unexpectedly. 'Is there any-one special?'

She longed to tell him, but it was too soon. Business deals had to be finalised before they could announce the date of the wedding, and they weren't quite there yet. Especially in relation to the money she was borrowing.

So, she crossed her fingers tightly and lied.

'No, unfortunately I haven't been as lucky as Colin, although,' she said, giving him the full force of her smile, 'it's early days yet, but I have met someone I quite like, so you never know.' Her face gave her away at the thought of Ross, but Ralph didn't comment on it, so after giving him a parting kiss, she left the apartment.

Justin and Ellie were both busy behind the desk, so she went in search of Hugh. She had no idea what he wanted to see her about, but wondered if it might be to remind her that the accommodation they were currently living in, wouldn't be adequate when the new baby arrived. This could prove tricky to discuss without telling them of her impending departure, but soon she would be making him the head of the business. It would bring with it a substantial pay rise, which should enable them to buy a property of their own.

She found him sitting alone in the small meeting room. He looked so young and vulnerable, she wanted to take him in her arms, but that was something she'd rarely done since he was a baby. The modern way of hugging and air kissing everyone you meet, wasn't in her nature, so she walked casually into the room and greeted him. He appeared slightly agitated and apprehensive, which she presumed didn't bode well for the discussion ahead.

'You were very deep in thought; I didn't want to interrupt you.'

'Yes, I was,' he replied. She could read his moods and whatever he wished to talk about was obviously something more serious than needing an extra room to live in.

'You'd better tell me what's on your mind.' she said, and in a vain attempt to be light-hearted, she added, 'are you going to give me an ultimatum, it's either a gym and you stay, or no gym and you go?'

'No, Mum. There's no ultimatum, but you won't like what I'm going to say.'

'It can't be that bad surely?' She was beginning to feel nervous, but she had no idea what was coming next. 'For heaven's sake Hugh, look at me and put me out of my misery.'

He took a deep breath. 'I'm leaving, I've got another job.' The room was very quiet, and his words seemed to resonate around it.

'What do you mean?' she asked. He seemed lost for words, but when he didn't reply she realised he was serious. 'You can't,' she said quietly, 'Tell me it isn't true.'

He shook his head slowly, and she stood up, gripping the side of the table.

'Why,' she asked. 'Why are you going now, when you are doing so well. In heaven's name, Hugh, what are you thinking of?'

'Sit down Mum, I know it's a shock, but we can't discuss it with you standing over me like that.'

'Tell me.' She said, as she sat down.

'It's quite simple really. I'm not allowed to use my initiative here. Everything I suggest gets booted out before it's even been discussed properly. Even grandad thinks some of my ideas are worth thinking about, but you just won't consider any of them. When I came back, I didn't expect any favours, but I thought you'd take my experience into account, but you haven't. I realise it's been hard for you, after you've been in charge all these years. No hard feelings mum, but I've made up my mind.'

Bryony recoiled as she listened to him criticising her behaviour. She felt betrayed by her own son and her initial reaction was to tell him to pack his bags and leave now, but he had a wife and child, and another one on the way, so she couldn't just throw him out. Suddenly, she saw her own plans falling apart, he was pivotal to it all.

'Look, I'm sorry,' she said, 'I'm just not used to other people making decisions here, but I will listen from now on. I promise you, I will.'

Hugh had rarely seen his mother cry, and the sight of her practically begging him to stay made him uneasy, but he knew it was something he had to do. They'd agreed at the beginning of his time in the business that it was a trial run, but it patently hadn't been a success. He couldn't lay all the blame on his mother's doorstep. He'd made the initial mistake of believing he was willing to start at the bottom of the ladder, but his experiences abroad where he'd overseen setting up large projects, had left him wanting more than just being a cog in a well-oiled machine.

'I'm really sorry, I don't want to hurt you, but it's too late to change my mind.'

'Please Hugh, give it another chance, just one more try. What will you do anyway? You've got a wife and family now, you can't just up and leave a job, you've got to have security.'

'I've already got another job,' he said, 'I'm going to be the man in charge of the new Sundown Complex, the one that's just been built. The senior manager of the whole thing. Cinema, bowling alley, soft play area, crown green bowling, ice-skating, you name it, they've got it, the whole lot. It's a very exciting project, and I can't wait to start.'

'You can't leave me now,' she wept. She felt as though he'd punched her in the chest. Of all the different scenarios she could have envisaged, this hadn't entered her mind. 'I can't believe it,' she said. 'You've obviously been looking for a way to leave me while living under my roof. That's another thing. Where will you live?'

'That's not true mum, I was approached by the owner of the Sundown Complex, who invited me to apply for the position. He was aware of my past experience and considered me to be a likely contender for the job. I had to go for a formal interview, but I went on my free day, so I didn't have to take any time off work. The best part is, it also comes with accommodation, a three-bedroom apartment over the offices. It's at the back, where it's quiet. It's too good an offer to turn down.'

Bryony recognised the futility of trying to change his mind. He'd be a fool to turn it down, and she told him so. He was struggling to hide his excitement and enthusiasm, but he almost passed out with relief when she congratulated him.

'I'm devastated, but so proud of you' she said, holding back her tears. She recognised the truth in what he was saying. She had never given him credit for all the things he achieved while working abroad, and deep in her heart, she knew she'd underestimated his abilities while he'd been here. It had jeopardised his ability to develop, and it was too late now. The least she could do was to give him her blessing, whatever it cost her. Well, it's our loss, and I do wish you well. You deserve it,' she gulped.

'Thanks Mum.'

'Does your father know?' she asked, checking her cheeks were dry and her mascara intact.

'No, I wanted to tell you first. I owe you that.'

'Thank-you,' she said, 'I appreciate it.'

Chapter 31

Lily was in a very co-operative mood, which owed a lot to the fact they were leaving early to go to Cora's, from where Lily and Zoe would be taken to school together. Ben, who had no such incentive, was moving at his usual snail's pace, but Sharon left the house, confident he would finish his breakfast and make sure the door was securely locked behind him.

Rusty had been taken for a hasty walk around the block, which Sharon hoped would suffice until she came home at lunch time to take him out again. He was getting slower now, and showing his age, but the vet had assured her at the last check-up that he was basically a very fit specimen. She dreaded the time when he was no longer with them; he was such an integral part of the family, but families changed, whether you liked it or not.

Zoe and Cora were waiting in the front garden when they arrived, and Lily and Zoe greeted each other enthusiastically.

'You would think they hadn't seen each other for months,' Cora said with a smile, and Sharon agreed, but her unusually, serious demeanour didn't pass unnoticed by her friend. After a glance at the girls Cora commented that Sharon seemed a little down and asked if she wanted to call in for a chat after the girls were safely dropped off at school.

There was nothing she would have liked better, but Bryony had asked Sharon to attend a meeting which was scheduled for this morning, even though she wasn't due to work today. Hopefully, it wouldn't last too long, and she could enjoy the rest of her day off.

'Thanks for the offer, but I'd better go and get this meeting over as soon as possible. I have absolutely no idea who else is going to be there or what it's about, and Bryony didn't say whether it's just me she wants to see, or if it's a general staff meeting. She just said it's urgent.'

'You'd better get on then,' Cora said, 'good luck.'

'Thanks, and thanks again for having Lily.'

'No problem, she's no trouble at all.'

It was only a short walk to the promenade, so Sharon took her favourite route to work. Checking the time, she decided to sit for a few moments on one of the benches to enjoy the changing view of the bay. The lovely spell of sunny weather was still holding, and although there was a breeze, it already held the promise of a lovely summer's day.

Cora was right, she did feel low, but although Sharon had allowed her to believe it was apprehension about this hurriedly arranged meeting, in fact she'd hardly given it a thought. Her mind had been completely taken up by the worry of what was happening to her marriage. Marie's conviction that she'd seen Tom in Wilmslow was grinding away at her, but she was afraid to confront him because she didn't feel able to face the truth.

There was a lot of activity around the lifeboat station, and she watched while the crew assembled and, in no time at all, the lifeboat was on its way to being launched. She recognised Damian, who was giving orders to some of the men, but his gaze never came her way; he was focused on the job in hand. As they set off over the estuary, Sharon wondered who could be in trouble on such seemingly calm water. Glancing at her watch, she saw that time was running away from her, and she set off at a brisk pace to discover what problems lay ahead.

Because she'd automatically assumed Justin would also be present at the hastily convened meeting, she was surprised to see him in his usual place behind the desk, and his expression of surprise when he saw Sharon brought a smile to her face.

'I wasn't expecting to see you this morning,' he said brightly, 'can't you keep away from work?'

'Bryony wants to see me,' Sharon replied. 'She rang me last night and asked if I could come in for a meeting. You don't know where she is, do you?'

'I'm here,' a voice behind Sharon informed them, and as she turned to acknowledge Bryony, Sharon threw Justin a surreptitious smile. Bryony Portland had never lost her ability to appear from nowhere, but it no longer had the ability to surprise the senior staff. 'Shall we go in the small conference room? I don't think its booked.' Bryony said, and she groaned inwardly when Justin commented on the fact it was rarely booked.

As Bryony walked away, she turned and asked Justin to send coffee in for them, in about half an hour. This perplexed Sharon even more, because a one-to-one meeting rarely lasted half an hour.

When Bryony was satisfied with their seating arrangement, she arranged some papers in order and then, without preamble, began by asking Sharon to give her honest opinion of the way the hotel was currently being run. As far as Sharon was aware, there were no serious issues waiting to be addressed, so she was able to assure Bryony that everything was running smoothly, but of course there was always room for improvement.

'I occasionally get the impression you would do things differently if you were in charge,' Bryony replied. 'Is that true?'

'Yes, sometimes I would, but I believe there is rarely only one good way of doing things, just different ways,' she said, wondering where this was leading. They chatted about some of the more conventional ideas put forward by Justin, compared with the far more adventurous schemes proposed by Hugh, until Sharon began to feel uneasy about the way the conversation was going.

They talked about Marie and her accident, and their shared opinion concerning the suggestion she may be involved in handling heroin. 'I don't know where the local paper is getting their information, or if they're making it up,' Sharon said heatedly, 'but it's causing Marie a lot of heartache.' Bryony shifted uncomfortably.

'Hugh is leaving the business,' she said suddenly, and Sharon gasped, lost for words. 'Yes, that was my reaction exactly. It was as big a shock to me, I'm sorry to say.'

'Why?' Sharon asked. Have you had an argument?'

'No, nothing like that. To be honest with you, he feels I've held him back here, and he wants to move on to bigger things. Before he came home, he'd gained lots of experience, but of course there just isn't enough scope to expand on that here. The Portland Arms has its own kind of challenges, but on the whole, it runs very smoothly.'

Sharon frowned. 'Surely, he knew enough about the family business when he decided to come back.

He's always talking about his ideas for improving the hotel, so why not give himself a chance? Or,' she added thoughtfully, 'has he already got something else lined up?'

'Yes,' Bryony said, 'he certainly has. He's going to be in charge of the new Sundown Complex.'

'Wow,' Sharon said, 'I can understand why he's been tempted.' Despite herself, Bryony felt herself smiling.

'There is also the added bonus of lavish living accommodation, which goes with the post. So, you see, there is nothing I can do to persuade him to stay.'

Sharon took a moment to digest the news.

'I know it must be a shock to you, but I don't understand why you are telling me. What has all this got to do with me?'

'I'm asking you to take over the running of the hotel. I'm offering you the position of Manager of the Portland Arms Hotel.'

Sharon was stunned. Of all the issues that had been running through her brain since she'd been summoned to this meeting, this certainly wasn't one of them. It took a few moments before she could even begin to reply.

'But what about Justin?' she asked. 'Surely, he's next in line for the job?'

'Justin and Ellie are both invaluable members of staff, but they are not senior management material. You are Sharon, that's why I'm offering it to you.'

Eventually, when she managed to find her voice, Sharon took a deep breath and replied. 'I'm pleased you think I can do it, but I've had no training for anything like that.'

'You've got the experience, but anyway, I've got that covered.' Bryony pulled out a brochure from the pile of papers in front of her. 'There's a course on Hotel Management at Lancaster University and although it has already started, a lot of it can be done online, supplemented by the printed material they'll supply you with. They've agreed to interview you, but the offer here still stands even if you don't get on the course. The business will pay the fees, so that's no problem. So, what do you think? Will you give it a go?'

'I'm overwhelmed and flattered. I don't know what to say, but there are so many things to think about, childcare to name but one.'

'I was going to pay Hugh some extra childcare money, so I don't see why we can't do it for you. But don't forget, you will be earning considerably more than you do at present. When we've discussed your new salary maybe it will help you to decide.'

'I said I would keep all this to myself, but I'll have to tell Tom.'

'Of course, you will, I know that. Now I suggest you go home, have some time on your own to think about it, and go out for a meal with Tom tonight to discuss everything. Don't forget to put it on expenses.'

'Oh, thanks.' She took the brochure Bryony handed to her and flicked through some of the pages. Apart from the University brochure, there was a detailed job description and she gasped when her eyes saw the salary. 'That's more than five times my current earnings.'

'Yes,' said Bryony, 'but don't forget, you'll have five times the responsibility.'

Fortunately, Justin was busy with a guest when she passed through reception, so she was able to leave without speaking to anyone. It would have been difficult to hide her shock and complete surprise, and she needed time to consider how to handle the tricky problem of his disappointment and possible resentment towards her.

Although the house would be empty, she was too unsettled to go home so she decided to take advantage of the unexpected freedom, and take a leisurely look around the shops. She was in the process of paying for a hand tied posy of flowers, to give to Marie, when she caught sight of her passing by the window, with her friend Claire. When Sharon waved, Marie tugged Claire and they carried on walking without even a sign of acknowledgement, even though Sharon was certain they must have seen her.

There was nothing Sharon could do, so she went to find a secluded seat, where she could relax and think about everything Bryony had said to her. With a pounding heart, she opened the brochure and began to read. It was a long time since she'd done any serious studying, but instead of finding it intimidating, she became increasingly intrigued by what she saw. The first chapters of the curriculum were everyday procedures which she was already familiar with, and she almost felt she could take a test on them already.

If she took this on, she would be fulfilling a dream. She'd never regretted the decision to stay at home to look after the children when they were small, but she'd always hoped to further her education sometime. To subsidise their income when Tom was made redundant, she'd worked in a bar, but when they moved to Merebank and she got the job at the Portland Arms, it was the beginning of a satisfying career. And now this; she couldn't believe it. She was absorbed by all the information she was holding; she didn't see Oliver approaching her.

'I'm sorry to disturb you,' but I just wanted to say hello and ask if everything was alright for you after the carnival high jinks.'

Sharon looked up into his smiling face.

'Hi,' she said, with mixed feelings, not wishing to be disturbed, but at the same time, welcoming his company. 'Everything was fine, thank-you.'

'I won't intrude, but you were so upset the other night, I couldn't resist checking.'

'You're not intruding, you are welcome to join me.'

'That would be a real pleasure. I was hoping you'd ask.'

Sharon began to collect the papers and brochure to put them back into the folder, when impulsively she kept the brochure back.

'I'm in a bit of a quandary,' she told him, 'I've received an offer which is almost too good to be true, but I don't know what to do.'

'If it's so good, what's the problem?'

Sharon was aware there was a question of trust if she told him the details, he was after all a client of the hotel, and although not on close terms with Bryony, they did enjoy having chats when they met.

'It's very confidential at the moment, so I'm not supposed to tell anyone.'

'Then don't,' he replied, 'let's talk about something else. I've been enjoying my trips into the Lake District so much; I'm even going to buy some walking boots so I can explore on foot. I won't attempt anything too adventurous because I haven't done hill climbing since I was a lad.' Sharon was only half listening to what he was saying, her mind was on the papers in the folder, but unable to contain herself any longer, she blurted out the reason for her excitement. Sharon told him she'd been offered a job which was a promotion, but heeding Bryony's advice, she didn't give any more details. When she appeared to be undecided about accepting the offer, he was puzzled.

'I still don't understand what the problem is'

'Oh, where do I begin?' she answered with a smile, as she began to list the many obstacles. 'Child care, afterschool club, being a taxi driver to all activities, dancing, drama, hockey, Guides, to name but a few, but then of course that's just Lily, there's also Ben with football.' She hesitated. 'It is even worse now Tom is working all hours.'

'Sharon,' he said with a grin, 'stop looking for negatives. You sound as if you are searching for reasons not to do it. Go for it. It's your life, live it.'

Despite her misgivings, his words echoed in her head, long after they'd parted.

When she arrived home, she rang school to arrange for Lily to attend after school club. She wanted some time to herself before she was caught up in the chaos of the family mealtime and persuading Lily to get herself off to bed, which currently she was determined to stretch out as long as she possibly could.

She took Rusty for a walk in the dunes and while he chased rabbits down holes in the banks of sand, she tried to concentrate on the decision she would soon have to make. She had made no headway when the time came for picking up Lily from the afterschool club. Lily in a mood was a nightmare, and today she was very moody.

She made it very plain she didn't like being made to stay to 'Afters' on Tuesday, as none of her friends were there. She had no interest in showing Sharon the artwork she'd done, and Rusty waited in vain for her usual enthusiastic greeting, as she gave him a cursory pat on his back with hardly a glance in his direction. Today, her incessant chatter and complaining was getting on Sharon's nerves and she had to stop herself from screaming at her to be quiet. Since when had puberty started kicking in at the age of nine?

The lasagne was prepared, while Ben regaled her with details of a science experiment, he'd completed successfully that afternoon. Realising his mother was focussed on the food in the oven which was about to start burning, he went upstairs to put his music on. Tom arrived home in a bad mood, which until recently was very unusual, and she wondered if it was because he wanted to be somewhere else or more importantly, with someone else.

She felt her enthusiasm for the new job slowly seep away, and later, when Lily was asleep and Ben had been placated by his father's interest in his work, Sharon mentioned to Tom she'd seen an item on the northern news about a proposed development of luxury houses in Wilmslow.

'There's no point just telling me that,' he said unreasonably. 'What exactly did it say?'

'Something about bad practice and the remainder of the development possibly not going ahead. Tom, is it the one you're involved in?'

'Yes,' he replied, 'I'm going to Wilmslow tomorrow, it'll be sorted then. I'm sorry I reacted like that, but it's been a nightmare.'

She hoped that was the only thing he'd been worried about, but it seemed as if whatever was wrong would soon be over. It wasn't the ideal time to tell him about her good news, but obviously Bryony was going to need an answer soon, and that wouldn't be possible without talking it through with Tom. Tom yawned and sank back into the sofa.

'There's a good documentary on I think you'll like. Is that okay with you?'

'Yes,' she sighed, snuggling up to him as he put his arm around her, 'but Tom, before we do, there's something I want to tell you. Bryony has offered me a promotion with lots more money. It would mean more hours and a bit of studying though.'

He flicked through the channels and found what he was looking for.

'She's on another planet, how can you take on more responsibilities when you've got a family to look after? It's bad enough now.'

'I'd earn a lot more money,' she said, trying to be heard above the television. 'Tom, will you please turn the television down? This is important to me.'

'Sorry Sharon. That would be nice for you, but we don't need you to work.'

'What if I want to?'

'Then, you must do what you want. I won't try to stop you, but don't forget, you've been asking me to cut my hours so we can have more family time. If you do this, we'll have even less time together.'

'I guess so,' she sighed, and he hugged her.

'But, if you really want to do it, it's your choice, I'll back you all the way.'

She turned and kissed him.

'Thanks Tom,' she said, 'that means a lot to me. I'll think about it.'

Chapter 32

Her mind was in a quandary. Oliver's words kept spinning around in her head. 'Go for it. it's your life, live it.' But it wasn't as simple as that, she shared her life with a husband and three children, and that had been her choice. Tom had said he'd help and support her, but like Oliver, he hadn't really given any consideration to what it would entail.

Marrying when she was young, meant she'd had to forfeit the opportunity of going to university, but she'd always intended to resume her education when their family was complete. Maybe that time was now. Reading the brochure from cover to cover again, with growing excitement, it began to feel real and best of all, possible. She dared to hope, and her heart beat faster at the thought of it. Desperate to share her news with someone, and needing to take the flowers, she found herself walking briskly towards Marie's front door. She rang the bell, and reminded herself to avoid giving the impression she was looking for help with child-minding. The smile on her face died, when Stuart answered the door and hesitated, making no move to invite her in.

'Oh,' he said flatly, 'it's you.'

Shocked, she began to back away. 'It's alright, if it isn't convenient, I'll come back later.' She had never known Stuart look so uncomfortable and unwelcoming, and she couldn't wait to get away, but he took hold of her arm and ushered her into the hallway.

'No, don't. I mean…'

'Stuart, what do you mean?' She asked. 'What's wrong?'

'I don't think she wants to see you, but still, you'd better come in, this needs to be sorted out.'

Making way for her to pass, he spoke in a whisper.

'Just come in for a minute or two. I think there has been a misunderstanding and I don't believe for a moment you've done what she thinks you've done. Neither would Marie if this accident hadn't fuddled her brain.'

'You are talking in riddles,' Sharon said, 'but I need to know what has happened.' Marie was sitting in a chair with her feet resting on a pouffe and she invited Sharon to take a seat beside her. 'Marie, what is wrong?' Sharon asked gently.

Marie sighed. 'I've probably got my knickers in a twist over nothing.'

'Well, I wouldn't say it's nothing.' Stuart said, hovering near the door. 'Not when the police are involved.'

'Oh, God,' Sharon, exclaimed, 'what on earth am I supposed to have done?'

'It isn't you, it's me that's in trouble' Marie said sadly. 'It's all about the boy I saw on the platform. Do you remember me telling you about him?'

'You told me a young man gave you a parcel, but you can't remember taking it, and the police believe it contained heroin.'

Stuart groaned. 'So, you did know,' he mumbled, 'I've been hoping you didn't.'

'Why, what's wrong?' Sharon asked, 'I only know what Marie told me.'

'The trouble is,' Stuart began to explain, 'the police categorically asked Marie to keep the information to herself. There is a big undercover operation going on and secrecy is essential.' Unfortunately, Marie discussed some of the details with you, which means DS Pullman will be asking you a few questions to try and find out if it's you who told the newspapers.'

'The newspapers,' Sharon repeated, looking from one anxious face to the other. 'Do you honestly believe I've talked to them?'

'Of course not,' Stuart said, 'but we can't think who else it could be?'

'Well, I can put your minds at rest on one point. I promise you I haven't said a word to anyone, and that even includes Tom. He's had so much to sort out at work we've hardly had a moment to discuss anything. Whoever informed the papers, it wasn't me, or anyone in our family.'

'I'm sorry love, I knew in my heart it wasn't you, but something's playing with my head.' Marie looked over to Stuart who was nodding his head vigorously.

'The only person I can think of,' he said. Who's capable of doing such a thing, is Bryony Portland. It's stooping a bit low even for her. Marie's right though, our heads are all of a jumble with what's going on.'

'Don't give it another thought, I think you're both coping remarkably well', Sharon said. 'Actually, I came to ask your advice about something.'

Stuart laughed. 'I'm not sure we're the right people to be giving advice, but if there's any way we can help you, we will. Come on love,' Stuart said, 'it can't be that difficult surely.'

'It's Bryony,'

'Oh, it is that difficult,' laughed Stuart. 'Bryony Portland up to her tricks again.'

'Stuart, be quiet and listen to what Sharon has to say'. He settled back in his chair muttering a mock apology which broke the tension, making it easier for Sharon to tell them what was on her mind.

They both listened carefully to what she said and neither of them spoke until she'd told them everything. Sharon felt a sense of relief at having been able to discuss her problem with level headed people like Marie and Stuart, since Bryony had agreed that Sharon could share her news with them as well as Tom. Marie was delighted for her and said it was no more than she deserved, and Stuart congratulated her, but looked slightly unsure.

'It's just that I'm a bit puzzled about the other senior members of staff,' he explained, in reply to Marie's questioning look. 'Have they been told, and if so, how have they responded. 'I'm thinking about Hugh and Justin, I can't imagine they are going to be pleased about it, and that can make working together very difficult.'

She told them how Hugh had pre-empted the whole thing by accepting a position elsewhere, Stuart whistled through his teeth. 'That partnership made in heaven didn't last long,' he said, 'she must be cut up about that'.

He polished his glasses thoughtfully, and holding one of the arms he swung them from side to side before replacing them on his nose.

'I don't suppose,' he said, looking at Sharon, 'he was as biddable as she hoped he'd be. That still leaves Justin of course, and he's been a loyal member of staff for longer than anyone else, I should imagine.'

'I know,' Sharon replied, 'I've thought of him, and Ellie. Bryony did say something about giving him more responsibility, but I was trying to take so much in, I've forgotten the details.'

'Oh, join the club,' laughed Marie.

'As a matter of interest,' Stuart said, 'where exactly does Bryony fit into this proposed arrangement? If you're the boss, what is she?'

'I honestly don't know; I presume she'll be just the same as she is now. I'm just taking Hugh's place.'

'And he's leaving because he wasn't allowed to make any decisions. Don't forget that. Ask her,' Stuart said, 'It's something you need to know. Are you the boss or not? It may all be in your contract of course, but if I were you, I'd clarify it as soon as possible, because it may help you to decide whether or not to go ahead.'

'You're so right,' Sharon said, 'I remember how pleased I was when she made me responsible for promoting and organising weddings, but she just couldn't help interfering. For a long time, she queried everything I did, until I began to wish I hadn't taken it on. But eventually we both adapted to the change.'

Sharon glanced at the clock and began gathering everything together. It wouldn't make a good impression if she started to be lax about time-keeping, and as nothing was set in stone, Bryony was still liable to change her mind. They all walked to the gate together and Stuart took Sharon's hand to congratulate her again, but Marie was very thoughtful as she returned Sharon's embrace.

'What's the matter love?' Stuart asked, and she turned to look at him.

'It's just come to me, the other person I confided in. You were right Stuart, it was Bryony. The night she came round to tell me her own exciting news. Something just jogged my memory and I am almost certain it was her I told. She had quite a lot of bubbly that night,' she added ruefully, 'because she had something to celebrate, and I couldn't drink much.'

Sharon was shocked. She could forgive Bryony most things, but to put her friend's life in danger by informing the newspaper of the police investigations, was unforgivable. The memory of the day when Marie and Claire snubbed her in the square still had the capacity to hurt, but she pushed it to the back of her mind. She was beginning to suspect Stuart was correct in thinking Bryony didn't hold friendship with much regard.

'She could have ruined our friendship,' she said sadly.

'She will never do that.' Marie replied firmly. 'It's up to us to make sure she doesn't.'

Marie and Stuart stood at the gate and watched Sharon hurry down the street in an effort to get to work on time.

'Oh dear,' Marie said to herself, 'I am foolish sometimes, and I never learn by my mistakes.'

'And who does? I'd like to know. How about a nice cup of tea?'

'The cure for all ills,' she replied.

Chapter 33

A quick check on the bank accounts confirmed her fears. The money still hadn't been transferred and she didn't know what to do. On her first approach to the bank, she'd deliberately given the impression there was no urgency in the request, but now she was recognising her mistake. If she started chasing them up too soon, it may generate questions she was desperate to avoid.

Having little choice in the matter, she decided to leave it a few more days, but Ross was becoming impatient, so she had to think of a way to persuade him everything was progressing satisfactorily. They both needed to know their money was available before they could go ahead with the purchase of the property, and to add to her worries, Sharon seemed to be taking a long time to accept the post she'd been offered. Although, under no obligation to appoint her successor before she left, she was reluctant to leave the hotel in a difficult position, for Ralph's sake. Obviously, Sharon still had a lot to learn, but Bryony had confidence in her potential, so there was no reason to think she wouldn't make a success of it. The situation was similar to the one she'd found herself in following her marriage, when it quickly became obvious that Colin had very little business expertise. She'd stepped into the role and with the help of Ralph had learned quickly and she was convinced Sharon had the ability to do the same.

Justin, was the next and most difficult issue to be dealt with. In the normal scheme of things, he would be in line for promotion, but she had no confidence in his management skills, and she was hoping he would be satisfied with a small step up the managerial ladder. In lots of ways, he was excellent at his job, but he lacked the flair to be a top manager. Despite that, it was essential to persuade him to stay as he would leave a big hole to fill, which would create a serious problem for Sharon, and ultimately Ralph.

Trying to control her nerves, she reluctantly decided to ring the lifeboat gift shop, hoping it wouldn't be Claire who answered. For some reason, Claire always succeeded in getting under Bryony's skin, no matter what she said or did, and today was no different.

'Marie's already left,' Claire told Bryony. 'I can give her a message when I see her tomorrow, if you like.'

'No thank you,' Bryony replied, 'I can contact her myself.'

Marie's response when she answered the phone, was cool, but they quickly established a time for Bryony to visit later that afternoon when Stuart would be out.

The police had already told Bryony, they were aware of the part she'd played in the passing of information to the paper, leaving her no choice but to apologise to Marie for what she'd done. The reporter had also been more co-operative, and admitted his part in trying to obtain information from Bryony Portland.

Marie was very edgy, due to a visit she'd made that day to the police station, to identify her case and handbag, and the items contained in them. She was unable to say if anything was missing, because she couldn't remember what she had put in them in the first place, which simply confirmed her feeling of inadequacy. The thought of her personal belongings being rifled by some unscrupulous men was more than she could bear, and the idea of her bags being used to transport drugs made her feel physically sick.

DS Pullman had been able to reassure her that some of the contents of her purse were still in place, including her store cards, but unsurprisingly, there was no cash. If Marie was correct in thinking she'd been carrying a large amount of money, there was no sign of it now. She had no desire to claim any of her belongings except the purse and mobile phone, she was convinced she would have had. They would have contained the personal details she was desperate for, but she knew there was little chance of them, or the money being recovered. DI Pullman had explained how the sim card would have been separated from the phone long ago. To her relief, the discovery of her handbag in the case solved the mystery of why she didn't have it in her possession when she fell down the steps.

Stuart was in total agreement with her regarding the contents of the case. He was adamant Marie wasn't going to touch any of the clothes which had been found.

'The sooner we can get rid of anything that scum have handled, the better it will be,' he said firmly, 'but there's no reason why we have to wait for that before we have a shopping spree to replace it.'

Marie related all this to Bryony, who went over it all in her head as she walked home. She had a distinct feeling Marie had been deliberately vague, which could only mean she still didn't trust her, despite her apology.

Meanwhile, Ralph had stood at the window and watched Bryony leaving the hotel. It saddened him to consider what he was about to do, but unfortunately, since the bank had alerted him to what was happening, he had no choice, so he took a key and let himself into her flat. After a quick glance around the room, he walked towards the bureau where Bryony kept her personal papers, and in the first drawer he opened, and lying on the top of everything else, was a folder, with a photograph of a very large, imposing hotel set in extensive grounds. It only took him a few moments to find what he was looking for, and after skimming a few of the papers he realised his worst fears. Bryony was taking his money to fund an elaborate undertaking, and despite what she had told him to the contrary, she was heavily involved in a relationship with a man. Fortunately, the money was safe in the bank.

When the bank had initially contacted him, he'd hoped the money was intended for one of Hugh's schemes, but now he knew that wasn't the truth. The bank manager had checked the account meticulously before contacting Ralph, and the evidence was there, including the application for all the money to be transferred out of the business account into Bryony's personal account. Bryony was taking Ralph's money to invest in her lover's business.

She would have to be stopped and stopped quickly.

Not knowing how long she would be out, he hurried to the office and printed off copies of all the papers in the folder, and after he'd returned the originals to her room, he picked up the phone and rang the bank.

Never in his life had he felt so betrayed.

Chapter 34

It was Saturday, and Sharon had the morning to herself. Tom had taken Lily to her dance class before going to meet Colin at the golf club to discuss the proposed erection of a marquee for the forthcoming wedding. The firm Colin had originally booked to provide and construct it, had let him down, and Tom, in his usual friendly way had spontaneously offered to help him out.

Hiring a marquee had proved no problem, but after electing to put it up themselves, Tom enlisted the cooperation of a few friends, who'd answered his call for help. When Sharon pointed out how the appeal of a promised round of golf followed by a drink in the bar must have helped, Tom laughed but didn't deny it. As Damian was one of the team, Sharon and Louisa had arranged to have an afternoon on the beach with Lily and Pearl, leaving Sharon's morning completely free.

Resisting the urge to settle down with a book, she picked up the small pile of prospectuses downloaded from the internet, and spread them across the table, before placing them in order of preference.

The online courses would be more practical for her, but even those required occasional attendance at the college. Fortunately, several of the colleges were close enough to Merebank to make them feasible, so she concentrated on those. It didn't take long to narrow the list down to the best choice for her, and she was so engrossed in reading all the information she'd amassed, she didn't hear Tom come into the room.

Swooping down over the table, she gathered all the leaflets together and put them back into the file she'd bought. 'My goodness,' she exclaimed, 'look at the time. I'll have to rush and pick Lily up from dance class.'

'Don't worry, I'll get her.' Tom said, 'we decided to have a break for lunch, so I'll go.'

Sharon took advantage of his offer by gathering Lily's things together for their trip to the beach. 'I thought you were going to have a liquid lunch in the golf club. Not that I'm complaining,' she added hastily.

Whistling a lively tune, Tom picked up his car keys. 'No, we decided against it, as we've just reached the point of putting it up. I suppose we'll be quenching our thirst later when we've nearly finished.'

Still whistling, he strode out of the room and down the path to the car, with the jauntiness of a man who didn't have a care in the world.

She walked to the window and watched him go. He seemed to be more his old self, relaxed and happy, and when he turned and waved to her, she was overcome with emotion. If only they could capture this moment and keep it. She hoped with all her heart that Fiona wasn't responsible for his change of mood.

Lunch was ready by the time the family arrived home, and apart from Sharon chiding Lily about the small mountain of ketchup she piled onto her chicken salad, everything passed smoothly.

Sharon was surprised they were planning to erect the marquee so early, but Tom told her if it was erected according to the instructions, and barring a storm, it was quite safe for much longer than a week.

Ben, who was just about to leave the table, was following the conversation closely. He looked questioningly at Tom, before turning to look at Sharon.

'Are we invited to the wedding?' he asked. 'Yes,' she replied, but before she could finish, he swung round to face Tom again.

'But how can we...ouch. What's that for?'

Sharon looked crossly in Lily's direction.

'Did you just kick your brother?'

'No,' she replied, equally grumpily, 'it must have been Dad.'

Sharon looked from one to the other of the guilty faces around the table,

'I don't know what's going on between you, but let's settle it once and for all. We are going to the evening reception, but not the afternoon ceremony. I have accepted the invitations on behalf of you all, and your plus ones, so don't start changing your minds. You'll have the whole day free to do what you want.'

'Ah, now I understand,' Ben spluttered with his hand covering his mouth. 'Can I leave the table.'

'With pleasure,' Tom said.

'I didn't do anything,' Lily complained, 'and I'm getting into trouble again. It's not fair.'

'No, you're not in trouble.' Sharon said. 'I've got a feeling these two are up to something, but I have no idea what.'

Leaving the clearing up to Tom and Ben, she checked the small rucksack, to make sure she had everything she needed for the trip to the beach, and as they were leaving Tom gave Lily and Sharon a hug. Lily wriggled free but Sharon hugged him back.

'Can we have an early meal this evening?' Tom asked. Sharon's heart sank as she dared to ask him if it was for any particular reason.

'In a way yes. I need to talk to you, but it's too complicated to explain now.'

'My goodness, how intriguing,' she said lightly, but as she turned to leave, he took her arm and pulled her back. 'I love you,' he said, 'whatever happens, never forget that.'

Louisa and Pearl were already on the beach when they arrived, and Lily ran down the slope and across the sand to where Louisa had spread two beach towels. Sharon kicked off her flipflops and took the small rucksack off her shoulders.

'I don't know why we need all this baggage just for an afternoon, but it all seemed necessary when I was packing.'

'You should see what I've got,' Louisa groaned, 'I thought it would get easier after the baby stage, but it doesn't seem to make any difference! You should have let me give you a lift.'

'It's ok, I really didn't know what time I could get away. I wouldn't say no to one going home though, if that's alright with you?'

'Of course, no problem,' Louisa said.

Lily had already taken her dress off, and as she'd put her swimming costume on at home, she was ready to go. She was soon busily digging a hole and piling the sand up to build a castle. Under Lily's guidance, Pearl was doing the same, and her lack of expertise was made up for by her enthusiasm and excitement. When sand sometimes flew through the air, Louisa and Sharon agreed to hire a wind-break to protect them from the breeze and shield the two families close by, who were in the direct line of flying sand. Louisa walked across to where two boys were walking donkeys, supervised by their older brother, who was hiring out the windbreaks and sunbeds.

'Damian told me the same family has kept donkeys for generations,' Louisa said, as they searched for a large pebble to hammer in the wind-break.

'I know,' Sharon said wistfully. 'It must be lovely growing up in a place like this. We came here nearly every year, for our holiday, and as I grew up, I used to envy the people who were lucky enough to live here. And now, look at me; I'm one of the lucky ones.'

'You don't give the impression of feeling lucky.' Louisa peered at her with a frown. 'Is there something wrong?' Sharon shrugged her shoulders. Telling Louisa would somehow make her fears turn into reality, but she desperately needed someone to confide in, and she knew she could trust Louisa. With her eyes on the girls, she spoke quietly.

'I suppose I'm being silly, but I think Tom is having an affair.'

'What on earth has prompted this?' Louisa asked, and by the time Sharon had voiced her reasons for suspecting Tom, Louisa had formed the conclusion Sharon was over reacting. She did agree that the incident in Wilmslow, when Marie believed she'd seen Tom, was very puzzling, but in no way did it suggest he was having an affair.

'Why would he do that, if he had nothing to hide?' Sharon asked.

Louisa shrugged. 'I've got no idea, but everything surrounding Marie's disappearance is odd. At the same time, I don't believe the fact he is meeting this Fiona person in Wilmslow, is necessarily suspicious. After all, it is where the housing development they're involved with is being built, isn't it?'

'Yes,' conceded Sharon, 'but I can't explain how I'm feeling. Tom always discusses what's going on at work, and this time he's changed. The more he's seeing of her, the less he talks to me, and I get the feeling he enjoys her company more than mine.'

Louisa gave a little laugh.

'Now you are getting into fantasy land, I think your imagination is getting the better of you. Honestly Sharon, I think you need to talk to him.'

'That's what I'm worried about,' she replied, 'he wants us to talk tonight.'

'There you are then. You'll get it all sorted out.'

'Yes,' Sharon agreed, 'but what will be the outcome? That's what I'm worried about.'

'I can't think how to say this,' Louisa said to Sharon, 'but you must trust me when I tell you that Tom loves you very much. Obviously, I don't know if he is having an affair, but what I do know, makes such a suggestion very unlikely.'

'You're talking in riddles,' Sharon replied, 'and how can you be sure he loves me very much?'

'You just have to take my word for it for the moment, but all will be revealed quite soon. In the meantime, please don't say anything you might regret.'

'How will I recognise this revelation when it comes? Sharon asked.'

'You will, believe me,' Louisa replied, with a very knowing look on her face. 'That is all I'm going to say on the matter.' Sharon realised she would have to be patient, but for what, she had no idea.

The two girls had built an impressive, though wonky castle, and Lily was trying to demonstrate the difference between patting the pile of sand, to make it firm, and Pearl's heavy-handed bashing with her spade. Louisa jumped up and intervened just in time to save it from instant demolition, and suggested they put the flags on it instead.

Ice creams all round brought a little peace to the proceedings, and watching Lily and Pearl brought Sharon's emotions to the surface. As if reading her thoughts Louisa asked if Sharon ever regretted what she'd done for her and Damian.

'Whatever makes you ask that?'

'It was such a massive thing to do, carrying a baby for nine months, and then giving it up.'

'I suppose it was, in a way, but what you said was right. I carried a baby, not *my* baby, so it wasn't a case of giving her up. Pearl was always yours and Damian's.' She smiled at Louisa. 'So, to answer your question, no, I've never regretted it, in fact it's just the opposite. If I hadn't done it, that gorgeous little girl probably wouldn't exist, and that doesn't bear thinking about. But as cute as she is, I'm quite happy with the three children I've got, thank you.'

'You've made such a difference to our lives. Damian and I can't thank you enough.'

'Seeing how happy you are is all the thanks I need. Now, I think we'd better take the girls for the donkey ride we promised them, or we'll never hear the end of it.

As they joined the queue, Lily saw a group of school friends walking on the promenade above them, but as she returned their greetings and enthusiastic waving of hands, she turned away in embarrassment. 'I don't want to go on a donkey,' she whispered, 'I'm too old.'

'Okay,' Sharon replied, 'I'll ask if you can lead Pearl's donkey instead, she'll like that.'

'Thanks mum,' Lily replied.

'Sometimes, I forget how grown-up you are,' Sharon replied, making a mental note to stop concentrating on her own problems to the detriment of her children.

Chapter 35

It was a rare occurrence, opening the small, private safe in the office, as Bryony and Ralph were the only two people who knew the code. There was nothing except her guilty conscience to prevent her from doing it, and it was too late to pay any heed to that. Justin would be in charge for the rest of the day, and Bryony was impatient. The longer she waited for the bank to respond, the more uptight she became, checking and double checking the wording on the documents in the safe. There was no margin for error. Even the slightest discrepancy had the potential to raise Ralph's awareness to what she was doing.

'I'm just going to make an important call in the office,' she said to Justin, 'please make sure I'm not disturbed.'

'Of course,' he replied with a smile, but as she entered the office and closed the door, his expression changed. Ellie was badgering him yet again, about asking Bryony for an increase in his salary. He knew she was right; he hadn't had a rise in three years and his responsibilities were steadily growing, but it was becoming increasingly difficult to choose a suitable time to approach Bryony. In a way which was most unlike her, Bryony was becoming more reluctant to record her appointments on the staff time-sheet, something she'd done meticulously in the past.

Before their divorce, she and Colin had often travelled abroad, but she always kept a line of communication open and remained in regular contact with the hotel. But recently, in stark contrast, she was taking a few hours off and even an occasional long weekend, without saying where she was, or how they could get in touch with her.

He would like to think it was due to an increased trust in his ability to manage the business, but he was more inclined to suspect there was a man involved, and although he wished her luck in her private life, he hoped she wouldn't take her eye off the ball in her professional capacity.

He didn't mind the extra work, in fact he welcomed it, but he had a growing family now and they needed all the money they could get. He was so deep in thought he didn't see Ralph pass the desk until he'd almost reached the office.

'Oh, I'm sorry, sir.' he called out, 'Bryony is in the office, and she doesn't wish to be disturbed.'

Ralph inclined his head.

'It's quite alright Justin, I'm aware of Bryony's whereabouts.' His voice was so low, Justin strained to hear him, but he got the gist of the words and relaxed. Mr Portland was the owner of the hotel after all. 'What he says, goes,' he told himself, as he watched him open the door.

Bryony stood perfectly still. She could hear voices nearby, but she had given Justin clear instructions she didn't wish to be disturbed, and she could rely on him to carry them out. But this time, she knew he'd let her down when the door began to open causing her to swing round angrily to face the person who was standing there. Her feelings changed the instant she saw Ralph, and she began to tremble with trepidation when he glanced down towards the papers in her hand. After a few seconds he raised his head and looked directly into her eyes.

Her mind was racing. 'Oh, hello Ralph,' she gasped, 'I'm just…'

Ralph raised his eyebrows questioningly. 'Yes, Bryony, you were just what?'

Desperately trying to think of a legitimate reason for standing in front of the open safe with its contents in her hand, she was lost for words.

'It's alright,' Ralph said, 'there's no need to explain, I know what you're doing, so I'd be grateful if you don't start making up a pack of lies. We obviously need to talk, but we must find somewhere we won't be disturbed and we can have the privacy we need.'

She hesitated, unsure what to do, but Ralph looked towards the safe and said coldly.

'You'd better put those back in there, I'll change the code when we've had our discussion.' The barb pierced her heart as she replaced the documents in the safe and tapped in the code. That he didn't trust her was obvious, but with his customary, impeccably good manners, he led the way out of the office and through the reception area. She didn't look in Justin's direction, but even so she was aware of him watching her with interest as they passed the desk.

'You will explain what this is all about?' Ralph said, when they were alone, in the small meeting room. Please keep to the truth. I have no desire to hear any of your complicated machinations.' He sat passively, listening to her explanations of why she'd tried to access the money, of her love for Ross, and her desire to help them both achieve their ambitions to form the basis of a working relationship. When she'd finished, she looked at Ralph, hoping for some kind of understanding, but his expression was unchanged, cold and dispassionate

'I'm so sorry,' she said, breaking the silence. 'It was a loan, which I'd hoped to pay back quickly, before you even knew it was missing.'

His voice was cold. 'My idea of a loan is obviously very different from yours. To me it is something agreed between the lender and the borrower, while you obviously perceive it as taking something you want, without the owner knowing. In my book, that is known as stealing and should be reported to the police and dealt with as such.'

Bryony gasped, horrified at the suggestion that he was even considering involving the police.

'Please Ralph, don't report me, I never meant you to know about it. We would have paid it back, I swear.'

'I don't know how you can be so sure of that; it sounds like a very risky venture. Do you trust this man?'

'With all my heart,' she said, 'but I don't know how he'll react if I'm arrested for theft. He doesn't know I'm taking it without your knowledge.' Her head dropped as she said, 'I'll probably lose him.'

'Oh, Bryony,' Ralph sighed, 'how has it come to this? If you'd approached me and asked to borrow some money, I would have least looked into the viability of the project and asked for legal advice. That way, you would have had an independent opinion which would have helped you to decide whether it was worth risking so much money on.' His normally bright eyes were clouded with sadness, and seeing what she'd done to him, she had a pang of conscience. 'We have been very close,' he said, 'and your care for me when I was ill was exemplary. I will never forget it, and I can never thank you enough for that.' He shook his head sadly. 'I deeply regret our friendship has come to this sad end.'

'Does it have to?' she cried. 'Surely this doesn't mean we can't come to an arrangement of some kind?' He made no move to offer comfort.

'Yes, I'm afraid it does, both as a member of my family and a previously valued business partner. I am going to have to speak to Hugh, and maybe some of the other members of staff, to decide a way forward.'

'Are you going to tell them everything?'

'No. If I had intended to punish you, and involve the police, I would have waited until you'd taken the money. As it stands now, you haven't actually stolen anything, but of course you've made an application to the bank to transfer it to your account without my knowledge. You must agree with my proposals, otherwise I may not be so lenient with you. I will tell the staff, and close friends, that you are resigning from your position here, to get married and join your husband's family business. There will be no need for you to enlarge on that, but if you feel the need to go into more detail, that is your decision.'

He stood up, ready to leave, but turned away when she moved towards him. All her dreams were crashing down and she wasn't even sure if Ross would still want to marry her. Their plans were built on promises of money and support, and she was no longer in a position to provide them. She had got it all so wrong, and this time she knew it would mark the end. This time, there would be no way back.

Raising her head, she turned to look at Ralph. She was aware of the effect the mascara-stained tears would be having on her appearance, but she didn't care, and made no attempt to wipe the smudges away.

'How did you find out?' she whispered.

'It's quite simple.' Ralph replied. 'You obviously didn't read the small print on the documents. When you tried to access the money, you told the bank that only one signature was required, which was true if one of the persons involved was mentally incapacitated. Unfortunately for you, I am in full control of my faculties, which I made perfectly clear when the bank rang up to check if I was in agreement with what you were doing.'

My solicitor is already drawing up an agreement between us, which states your reason for leaving and the money owing to you. We will both sign it tomorrow and I expect you to have moved off the premises by Friday.'

She gasped with shock. It was Monday morning and he expected her to leave by Friday.

'I have nowhere to live,' she whispered.

Sadly, he raised he eyes to her. 'This is no longer your home. Please do as I say, or I might change my mind concerning the police.'

She watched him walk dejectedly out of the room, his shoulders drooping and his head leaning forward. For the first time, he looked like an old man, and she hated being the one who was responsible for doing this to him.

Keeping her eyes averted, she walked towards the lift, and although she couldn't see Justin, she could feel his eyes watching her. When she reached her room, she threw herself onto the bed and wept. For Ralph, for herself, and most of all for Ross and the future they'd planned together with such love and hope. Where would she go now? She would live anywhere, in anything if Ross was with her, but she knew he wouldn't be able to accept that. When she thought of how close they'd come to owning their own hotel, she sank into despair. Later, she nervously picked up the phone and rang his number.

Chapter 36

A few days had passed since Bryony's offer, and still Sharon hadn't made a final decision. For some unknown reason, Bryony was keeping a very low profile and could hardly bring herself to speak to anyone. Even Justin, was beginning to comment on her behaviour, and voiced his opinion that something must be seriously wrong.

Sharon's self-confidence had grown when she'd looked at the course work and sample past papers, but for her, the biggest stumbling block, was how to fit it into the challenges of bringing up a family.

She would never forget the night Sam was caught up in the terrorist attack at the Cotton Hall in Manchester. She and Tom had no idea he was there, and they'd vowed they would never again allow themselves to be too busy to have time for their children. So, this was a big decision, with so much at stake, and Sharon was determined she wasn't going to be rushed.

Whenever she tried to broach the subject with Tom, his mind seemed to be elsewhere, but when she forced the issue, he insisted it was her choice, and she alone should make it. He was also adamant that he would be willing to help in the home whenever necessary, and she must not use the family as an excuse to turn it down. He seemed to be genuinely supportive, but with the spectre of Fiona Campbell hanging over them she couldn't rid herself of the fear that he might leave her.

Lily had developed an upset tummy, which had put paid to the discussion they'd planned for Saturday evening, and whenever Sharon suggested an alternative time Tom brushed it off and said he also had urgent decisions to make. Hearing this, did nothing to allay her fears, and she was terrified of finding herself abandoned and alone. She had never before doubted his love, and she hated herself for it now, especially as her suspicions were based on trivial incidents, usually concerning his trips to Wilmslow. The more she thought about it, the more ridiculous it became; but the green-eyed monster was digging in.

It was Monday, and Sharon was rushing to get through the school run on time. Fortunately, Lily had made a speedy recovery from the tummy bug which had ruined their chance to talk on Saturday evening, and she was back to her usual happy self.

'I won't be a minute, I'm just doing my hair,' Lily shouted from her bedroom and Sharon couldn't stop herself from pointing out this must be at least the fourth time she'd changed her hairstyle that morning. Finally, Lily was satisfied with the latest attempt at getting it right and they were soon on their way to school.

'Do you think Rusty gets lonely when we leave him alone?' Lily asked, after giving him numerous hugs before they left the house.

'I don't think so, he's used to it,' Sharon replied with as much patience as she could muster. He is getting old and probably enjoys a bit of peace and quiet.'

'I don't think I'd like that,' Lily responded thoughtfully.

'What wouldn't you like?' Sharon asked, her mind already elsewhere. 'Peace and quiet,' replied Lily.

'I don't think you need to worry about that,' Sharon said, 'there is very little peace or quiet where you are. You're a chatterbox.'

'I don't know why you call me that. I've never heard boxes chattering, have you?'

'That's true,' Sharon replied with a smile.

As soon as they reached the school gates, Lily gave Sharon a quick hug before running to catch up with her friends, and Sharon started walking in the direction of Marie's house. Marie had rung Sharon with a garbled message which Sharon couldn't fully understand and she'd arranged to make a quick visit on the way to work to find out what it was all about.

When she arrived, Sharon told them about her little exchange with Lily, and they both found it hilarious given Lily's non-stop chattering.

'She's as sharp as a knife, that one,' Stuart said. He apologised for leaving, but he'd been persuaded by Marie to join his friends at the bowling club, for a friendly competition with the team from just along the coast.

He was still chuckling as he went down the path, and Marie smiled as she watched him go, and commented on how relaxed he was. She told Sharon how much more confident she felt, especially as she gained her mobility, so there was no reason why Stuart couldn't take up his interests again. Sharon could understand both sides of the argument, but after she'd told Marie her opinion, she asked her to explain the telephone conversation.

'It sounded very secretive on the phone.' Sharon said, with a frown.

'It is,' Marie told her. Bryony had given information about Marie's disappearance and rumours of drug trafficking, to the local paper in exchange for favourable cover of herself and the Portland Arms hotel in the town's forthcoming three hundred years anniversary publicity. Under normal circumstances it would have been viewed as a harmless piece of journalistic gossip, but the involvement of ruthless thugs automatically raised the bar to a potentially dangerous level.

By the time she reached the hotel, Sharon had decided what she was going to do. Bryony had put Marie at risk for the sake of her own vanity, and almost caused a rift between Sharon and Marie, regardless of the hurt it might cause. She didn't want to be involved with her any more than was absolutely necessary, so it was pointless to entertain the idea of working even closer together.

But as she worried, Marie's parting words, came back to her.

'Don't allow the things Bryony has done, cloud your judgement' she'd said wisely. Make your own decision.'

Chapter 37

Tom had left for work this morning, smartly dressed in suit and tie, looking for all the world like a successful businessman on his way to close a big deal. The problem was, as far as Sharon was concerned, the deal was most probably a personal one between two people, and the other one involved certainly wasn't her.

'Have a nice time in Wilmslow,' she'd called to him as he left, but he didn't rise to the bait, and as she couldn't make out his muttered response, the crockery being put in the dishwasher did well to stay in one piece.

'Dad did answer you, mum' a small voice said and Sharon turned to see Lily standing looking at her with a look of consternation on her face. 'I think he said he'd ring you later.' Sharon held her breath to compose herself. She couldn't repeat the words spinning round her head to Lily, but the children had been taught to reply when they were spoken to, so she would believe Sharon was annoyed with Tom simply because he hadn't answered her call.

'Oh, thank you sweetheart,' she said, giving her a hug and a kiss, but Lily rubbed her face with the back of her hand.

'Ugh, no kisses,' she squealed, wriggling out of Sharon's arms.

Ben came running down the stairs, his feet heavy on every step.

'Mum, I can't find my kit and there's a game after school. Do you know where it is? I'm going to be late.'

'Where did you leave it? It will be in your drawer if you put it to be washed. Otherwise, it will still be where you left it, in your sports bag.'

'Can you help me mum? I don't know where it's gone.'

'It hasn't got legs, so it hasn't gone anywhere, it's probably where you left it. You must learn to be responsible for your own football kit, I've already told you where it will be.'

Hiding the smile creeping over her face she listened to the drawers being opened and closed, until Ben's voice called out with a note of satisfaction.

'I've found it,' followed by his footsteps running down the stairs. 'It was in a different drawer.'

'Oh, I'm sorry about that; maybe the others were full because you jam everything in, instead of folding them properly. Are you ready for school?'

'Yes, I'm going now.'

Lily was gathering her bits and bobs together and urging Sharon to hurry. 'Come on mum, it's time to go.'

'Okay, okay. I just need these for work, but I'm ready now. Right, we are off. Don't worry, you won't be late.'

Sharon lingered a while, looking across at the cordoned off area where the children attending breakfast club were being supervised. She watched the mums who were rushing off to get to work on time. Here in the playground, stay-at-home mums, were making plans to meet later, some with their younger children, and with the chaos of the morning still fresh in her mind, she came to the conclusion, she would appreciate a slice from both cakes, if they were on offer.

The light showers forecast for later in the day were making an early appearance, so she postponed her planned visit to the bakers and walked quickly towards the hotel where she joined some of the residents who were returning from an early stroll and hurrying up the steps to avoid the rain. Going into the office, she tried unsuccessfully to tame the curls which had sprung up in the damp air and she was surprised when Ralph Portland walked in and asked her to join him in the small meeting room when she was ready. She called at the desk and asked Justin if he had any idea what it might be about, but he made himself busy and suggested she asked Ralph himself. After arranging for them to take the phone calls she was expecting in the next hour, she made her way to the room where Ralph Portland was waiting for her.

'I'm afraid you are going to be very disappointed and probably saddened, when you hear what I have to tell you,' he said ruefully, 'but unfortunately I've been left with a very difficult situation and I hope you are going to be able to help me.' Opening a folder, he glanced at the first page before turning to face Sharon. 'The first and probably most important thing, is to tell you that Bryony is leaving the business.'

Sharon gasped. She stared at him in disbelief, but any thoughts she'd misunderstood him were wiped away by the unhappiness etched on his face.

'I know,' he said kindly, 'I understand how you are feeling, it was as much a shock to me as it is to you.'

'But why? The hotel is her life.'

'Not any longer it seems, but that in itself is no bad thing. She is getting married and joining her future husband in his business.'

Sharon sank back into her seat with relief.

'Oh well, that's a shock but I'm pleased for her. At least we know she won't be rushing off and leaving you in the lurch.'

'I'm afraid Bryony will be leaving the premises on Friday and won't be returning, I have given you the official reason for her leaving, but there will be a lot of speculation about her swift departure and as you will be in the frontline for dealing with it, I feel it's only fair to give you some background detail, which I trust you to keep to yourself.'

Sharon braced herself and murmured. 'Of course.'

Ralph gave a little cough and began to explain what had brought Bryony's time at the hotel to an end. His face was pinched and his body tense as he outlined the events as they'd happened.

'I believe she intended to return it sometime, but in the meantime, it could have potentially put the future of the hotel at risk.'

'But why?' Sharon asked again. 'This place means the world to her, why would she jeopardise everything she's worked for?'

'It seems someone is more important to her than anything else now. If she'd come to me for advice, I might have considered investing in her enterprise. You see I respect her business acumen so much, but now I have no choice but to cut all ties with her.'

Moments passed, while Sharon tried to make sense of what she'd heard. Her first reaction was one of shock that Bryony was leaving, but Bryony Portland as a thief was beyond comprehension. She was constantly emphasising to the staff the importance of loyalty and trustworthiness in whatever role they played in the hotel. What Mr. Portland was telling her bore no relation to the woman and boss she knew.

'Have you reported her to the police?' she asked, and despite everything she'd heard she held her breath until Mr. Portland shook his head and told her he'd decided against it. He explained his reluctance was based on everything she'd been as a member of the family, and all she'd achieved as the head of the business.

'I just wanted you to be aware of my reason for cutting all ties and asking her to leave at once. This sort of thing doesn't come easily to me and I know the tongues will wag.'

Dejection hung over him, and she longed to share some of the burden, but how could she do it? He had been betrayed by the one person he really trusted, and by not taking legal action, he was losing the opportunity to explain his reasons for her instant dismissal. Ralph's weak smile didn't reach his eyes when he told her he was aware of the position Bryony had offered her, and she felt nauseous with the realisation that her hopes were about to be dashed.

'So where does this leave me now?' she asked apprehensively.

'We're having this discussion, because I value your opinion and I know Bryony shared my hopes for your future here. But, before we discuss that, I would appreciate your honest opinion of Justin's ability and future potential?'

For a few seconds, Sharon was shocked into silence. Her future was hanging in the balance, and yet she was being asked for her opinion on the member of staff who would potentially be her rival. With a sinking heart, she told him she was very impressed with Justin.

Ralph didn't immediately reply, but began to search through the pile of papers on the table in front of him, until he found what he was looking for. Sharon recognised Bryony's writing and saw her own name at the top of the page. Nervously she waited for him to speak, but her heart was pounding in her chest. Now, she realised how much she'd wanted the job, but as her opportunity gradually slipped away, she wished it had never been promised.

Ralph's expression was thoughtful, but as he raised his head to look at her, he was smiling. 'Thank you, Sharon,' he said 'I appreciate your honesty. As you are probably aware, for some reason Bryony didn't share our opinion, and believing he'd reached his level of competency long ago, she never saw him as senior level management material. I, like you, believe through his dedication and ability, he has earned the position of General Manager of the hotel.'

'I'm sure you won't be disappointed,' Sharon said, wanting the meeting to end so she could escape and shed the necessity of keeping her feelings hidden.

'Now, we come to you.' Ralph said with a smile, but this time Sharon couldn't conjure up even a weak response, as she waited to hear what he had in mind for her. Bryony told me she'd made a tentative offer to promote you to General Manager, but I believe you had the impression it was a definite offer?'

'It was, although I can see now that is totally irrelevant, as she is no longer in charge. I must be honest I couldn't see how it would work, as Justin would justifiably be very upset.' She took a breath 'And would have probably moved on,' she added.

'I think you're right,' he replied. 'But now, you can see I have already decided Justin has taken the place you thought was yours.' Sharon nodded.

'Justin will in some respects fill Bryony's place, doing the day to day running of the hotel, but I'm changing the job description slightly to give me the opportunity of appointing a Senior Manager. This person will need to be someone who has vision and can move the hotel forwards. With the new Sundown Complex coming, we don't want to compete with them on their level, but we must offer our clients something which will keep them coming back.' He leaned back into his chair, his face suddenly more animated and filled with enthusiasm.

'What Bryony's behaviour has done,' he said with a smile, 'is draw my attention to the reason why that money was moved to a separate account. I decided to set it up when I was ill, to make it accessible for emergencies and give Bryony access to it. Now, I have decided it is doing no good just lying there, so we are going to utilise some of it to give the hotel a complete refurbishment. No longer having the capability or energy to oversee it myself, and recognising it would be asking too much of Justin when he's already taking on a new position, I'm offering you the new position of Hospitality Manager, who will be responsible for implementing the changes and keeping us abreast of times in the future. In a way it would have been the role Hugh would have wished for, but it is too late for that now and I have every confidence in your ability to take it on.'

Ralph smiled broadly as he waited for Sharon's response, but it took her a few seconds to understand what he was saying, and she couldn't believe it. Afraid of further disappointment, she tentatively asked him if it was a permanent job, and when he confirmed it was, she gasped.

'Of course, we will have to have contracts drawn up,' he said, 'but that isn't a problem.'

'But I don't understand, won't Justin resent it just the same?' she asked. Ralph assured her Justin was aware of what was being proposed and he was delighted. He would be running the business, with Ellie as his deputy, and they were more than happy with that.

'When all the changes are in place, you will be in charge of promoting the hotel and making sure our resources are put to good use. Will you be interested, do you think?' he asked, 'if not, there will always be a job for you here. I don't want to lose you Sharon.'

Relief and excitement coursed through her veins. 'Yes, oh yes,' she said. 'I'd love to accept the offer.'

'You can if you wish, work flexible hours. By virtue of the job description, it may occasionally require you to work outside your normal hours, but it will be at your discretion.'

'This just gets better and better,' she said, beaming at him.

'Oh, and one last thing, before we finish,' he smiled, 'I want you to hire someone to help you choose the new furnishings throughout the building. This will be a temporary position obviously, but we need a person with a flair for design and colour.'

'I know the perfect person,' Sharon exclaimed, 'Louisa. She has a degree in that very subject, and has a perfect eye for co-ordinating furnishings.'

'Perhaps you can have a word with her, and if she's interested, and you are confident she would be suitable, we will put her name on the short list and interview her. Before that of course, I'll get your contract drawn up as soon as possible.'

After he'd congratulated her and told her to take the rest of the day off, she almost floated out of the hotel. The enormity of what she was taking on hadn't really sunk in, but she was confident she had the ability to do the job well. She couldn't wait to tell Tom, but she was almost home when she received a text from him, telling her he had something important to discuss. He'd arranged a babysitter for the evening and had booked a table at a restaurant where it would be quiet enough for them to talk. Her heart sank but she tried to dismiss it from her mind as she hurried to pick Lily up from school.

Chapter 38

Bryony paced the room, panicking and fretting. Countless times, she'd gone over in her mind the only options left open to her, and for the first time in her life, she felt devoid of control, and it unsettled and frightened her. Ralph's deadline of Friday was unreasonable and unkind, and she was finding it impossible to find somewhere decent to live within that timescale. She was forced to rule out Merebank Bay, knowing it would be unbearably humiliating for her to face people, when the news spread about her being thrown out of both the Portland family and the business.

Time and time again, she'd started to ring Ross's number, but courage had failed her at the last moment and now, she was running out of time. She didn't doubt his love for her, but would chasing his dream mean more to him than their relationship?'

She'd vaguely considered asking Hugh if he could offer her a job, and hopefully accommodation to go with it, but the Sundown Complex would be a popular destination for local people as well as attracting visitors from miles around, and it would be impossible to stay out of sight from people who knew her.

If only she hadn't decided to have the large extension built onto the house on the promenade, she would at least have been able to stay there for a few days, but the foreman had burst out laughing when she rang to see if it was habitable. Thankfully he'd thought she was joking and didn't take the question seriously.

Her heart beat faster when the hotel extension rang, and a man who identified himself as a policeman asked if he could have a few words with her. His assurance that she had nothing to worry about did nothing to calm a rising sense of panic.

'I'll wait here, take as much time as you need,' he said, and as soon as he'd rung off, she contacted Sharon to ask her to show him to somewhere quiet to wait.

It took a few minutes to freshen her face, touch up her lipstick, and run a brush through her hair, before she was satisfied with her appearance. By the time she exited the lift in reception, the image in the mirrors lining the wall reflected a confident, sophisticated woman, but her heart was hammering in her chest as she tried to accept the awful truth, that Ralph had broken his promise and reported her to the police, despite all his reassurances. The temptation to run was very strong, but where would she run to?

The officer introduced himself as DS Pullman, the detective involved in the case of Marie Fowler, and he explained his reason for being here. To her surprise, she realised his visit was unconnected to her borrowing the money, but she was being questioned for passing on information about Marie and her whereabouts. Struggling to disguise her immense sense of relief, she acknowledged her guilt in committing that offence, and DS Pullman accepted her explanation that she'd had no idea of the repercussions of what she was doing.

'I'll briefly explain the situation,' he said. 'This is more serious than harmless gossip, it could put your friend's life at risk. Marie has inadvertently become involved with the county lines network and the drug dealers may think she has some drugs belonging to them. They will stop at nothing to recover what they believe is theirs, so although Marie is under police protection, she has been put at more risk.

There was nothing to be gained by denying anything, because Bill Jackson had already told her he'd cooperated with the police and explained to them, that he was the one who'd teased the information out of Bryony Portland.

Before he left, DS Pullman told her the main reason for his visit, was to enlist her assistance.

'There is a chance, that Marie will remember what had happened that day at the railway station, and she will very possibly want to share it with someone. If that person happens to be you, please come to me, not The Merebank Gazette,' he said.

It was a mild rebuke, but she was still quaking when she passed under the inquisitive gaze of Justin and Ellie as she walked slowly and deliberately back towards the lift.

She longed to talk to someone, and in the past Ralph had been her confidante and friend, but she was nothing to him now, he just couldn't wait to be rid of her. She threw herself onto her bed and wallowed in self-pity.

Later, exhausted and despondent, she replied to the text from Ross asking her to meet him at the Windmill Inn. There was an urgency about the message, so she simply replied and told him that she also had something important to tell him. Although she still longed to see him, her reply was curt. With the fear of how Ross would react to her news, she set off to drive at speed to the Windmill Inn.

The scenery flew past the windows unnoticed, as with the words of the policeman ringing in her ears, she sped towards their regular meeting place. She arrived early and remained sitting in the car but when the time for meeting came and went, she began to get anxious and doubts began to creep in. He hadn't given any reason for wanting to see her, but he had sounded as though it was urgent. She tried to keep calm, telling herself they were engaged to be married, but she couldn't get rid of the fear that he'd somehow discovered about the money and decided to call off the wedding. To pass the time, she walked across the car park to the hotel and went to the ladies' room, and when she returned, she saw him parking in the space next to hers.

In contrast to his usual exuberance, he sat, shoulders slumped and head down, but when he caught sight of her, he left the car and ran to take her in his arms.

'We need to talk,' he said gruffly.

'I know, let's go into the bar. It should be quiet at this time.'

There were a few locals seated around the bar, who momentarily broke their animated conversation to nod their greeting. Ross and Bryony were now familiar figures and very quickly, the men returned to their discussion, leaving Ross and Bryony to make themselves comfortable in one of the booths which gave them the privacy they needed.

Without a word, Ross went to the bar and ordered a gin and tonic for her and a pint of beer for himself. When she raised her eyebrows, he told her they would have a meal before leaving, so one drink was okay. He knew she didn't approve of his cavalier attitude towards drinking and driving, and when they were together, he respected her wishes, but there were times like this, when he felt justified in breaking the rule.

He drank deeply from the glass before he spoke.

'I'm so sorry,' he began, 'I don't know how to say this.' He clasped his hands together and squeezed them tightly between his knees. 'My father has changed his mind,' he blurted out, 'there will be no more money available to me to invest in the business. I've tried everything but he's adamant he won't change his mind.'

Bryony stared at him. There had been no talk of money from his father, it was Ross's business, and his investment. She'd invested her own money in his enterprise, believing they were buying the hotel with their joint finances, so she had no idea what he meant by saying his father had changed his mind. The unpalatable possibility of her having chosen a weak man again, who was utterly dependent on his father, was too much to bear and she shuddered with distaste. She lifted her head and looked directly at him.

'I don't understand, are you telling me you haven't got the capital to buy the hotel, even with my input?' His face was creased into a frown, showing up lines she'd never noticed before, but his thwarted little boy attitude incensed her until she felt like slapping him.

'I'm so sorry,' he repeated forlornly, 'but that is exactly what I'm saying, my father has pulled the plug.'

'But it's your own money you're investing, what has it got to do with your father?'

'It's money which will be mine in a few years, and he led me to believe he would release it early to enable me to develop the business. Now, for some reason he's changed his mind.' Something inside her flipped, and she looked at him angrily, unable to accept their plans were completely ruined. She told him he must talk to his father again, but he insisted there was nothing else he could do.

'You don't know my father, like I do,' he explained. 'Oh, I know he's all sweetness and light when he's with you, but it's all show and it doesn't stop him from blaming you for the divorce, even though it happened before we even met. Now, he's decided there is no more money available for me to invest. So that's it. No Regal Hotel for me, sorry, I mean for us.'

In the silence which followed, Bryony tried to consider the situation she found herself in. Once again, she'd placed her future in the hands of a man she trusted, and once again she'd been let down, but she was determined to salvage something out of this situation. This time, there was no going back cap-in-hand to Ralph, she was somehow going to make a success of their plans, however long it took them. There was one more hurdle to cross, and she decided to give some thought to it before telling Ross.

He still believed she was bringing another considerable contribution to their venture, but now with the purchase of the hotel falling through, it took away the need for her to tell him that she couldn't keep her side of the bargain either. This would give her time to speed up the completion of her house in Merebank, which would provide the money in the future for whatever they decided to do. The funds she'd already given him were safe, but this way he would never need to know how near she'd come to being accused of taking the money without Ralph's agreement. Her anger subsided, allowing her to turn to him with a smile. He sat slumped in his chair, but at the sight of her face he pulled himself upright.

'Dare I hope you will still marry me?' he asked, taking her hand and stroking the diamond in her ring with his thumb. 'Will you marry me, now you know the truth about me; a man with some money, but not the wealth you thought?'

She smiled and told him it made no difference to her feelings for him. Ross grinned, and to celebrate he bought two more drinks, but under Bryony's instructions he also ordered food for them both. Although he was obviously relieved, there was a tenseness in him, so after they'd eaten, she asked him to tell her what was causing him to be so uptight.

Apprehensively, he told her he'd been head-hunted for a job, but before he could make a decision, he would run it past her. He asked Bryony to listen to what he had to say, with an open mind.

'Well, you'd better tell me what it is,' she said curtly, 'otherwise I can't form an opinion.'

He told her about his friends, Luke and Sarah, who owned two hotels in Greece and were in the process of buying a third. The couple were looking for experienced managers to take over the one they were currently running, to leave them free to get the new business off the ground. As they'd been let down already, there was no time to waste. Ross had had a word with Luke, who said he was willing to offer Ross and Bryony the positions, and encouraged Ross to run the idea past Bryony. Anxiously, Ross waited for her reaction.

When the silence lengthened, he told her the couple were going from strength to strength, and started to persuade her what a fantastic opportunity it would be for them to start again.

She asked him how much he knew about the hotel in question, and he put the small case he'd carried into the pub, on the table.

'It's all here,' he said, 'financial accounts, staff, turnover of restaurant, and casino, you name it, I've got it.'

'Casino? Did you say there's a casino?'

'Oh, sorry, I thought I'd mentioned it, but yes, there is a very successful casino in the grounds.' Bryony was very thoughtful.

'There's an awful lot to consider, not least, what about me? Am I to be the little wife who simply follows on?'

Ross smiled. 'I can't quite see you in that role. No, darling, our roles will be equal.'

'We need to go into it, very carefully,' she said, thoughtfully flicking through the file.

'I know, but it's all in there, I think you'll find most of the answers to your questions in the file somewhere. I have visited it, and it is everything it shows in the brochure.' Ross sensed a slight quickening of interest, and could hardly speak as he found himself holding his breath in anticipation. The contracts are already drawn up for the post, Luke doesn't want to waste any time after what happened with the other couple.

Bryony raised her eyebrow.

'Post?' she asked.

'Sorry, sweetheart. A slip of the tongue. Posts.'

'It is certainly food for thought. If the offer is as good as it sounds, it's definitely worth considering, but how do they know we're suitable.

'They know me and my work, well, and trust my judgement. A Zoom interview with you, was mentioned.'

'Excellent, 'Bryony replied, that's more professional, and reassuring.'

'Bryony Portland, I love you,' he said, and then he frowned. 'I'm sorry. When you rang me, you said there was a problem and we needed to talk. How did you know?'

Raucous laughter from the men at the bar almost drowned out his words, giving her time to think of an answer.

'I didn't.'

'So, what's your problem?'

It's nothing to worry about, its sorted'

'Let's do a recap. Bryony Portland, I love you.' This time he kissed her.

Chapter 39

Sinking deeper into the froth of bubbles, Sharon luxuriated in the extravagance of her favourite perfumed toiletries. She'd kept the gift from Tom for a special occasion, but tonight she'd given in, and was pleased she had. She needed all the help she could get to face whatever he was going to tell her.

Despite the relaxing qualities of the jasmine and sandalwood, and the silkiness of the water, it took time to ease the tension in her body, but gradually she could feel it ebbing away. Running through the list of things he'd done or not done which had led her to suspect him, crystallised how flimsy her concerns were. Ignoring some, which she was willing to accept might be figments of her imagination, it all came down to a few dubious meetings or evening get-togethers which had stretched late into the night and necessitated an overnight stay in a hotel.

The one occasion, she knew he'd lied, was when he denied being in Wilmslow, when Marie was convinced, she'd seen him. There was no sense in denying he'd been there if his reason was an innocent one, and by keeping his silence he'd prolonged Marie's and Stuart's agony, to say nothing of their family and friends.

It was so out of character for Tom to behave in such a thoughtless way, she could only surmise his involvement with Fiona Campbell had clouded his judgement. In a divorce court, it would sound ridiculously unsubstantial, but in reality, it was heart-breaking.

Wrapped in her fluffiest bathrobe, she vacillated over which dress to wear. The cream wraparound was without doubt the sexiest dress she owned, but she'd worn it the evening Oliver had taken her out, and she didn't think it was appropriate. She held it up and looked at herself in the long mirror. Memories of the occasion came flooding back, but she pushed them to the back of her mind where they belonged. She was still undecided about whether to wear the cream dress or not, when Tom walked into the room.

'I like that,' he said, looking at her reflection.' Are you wearing it tonight?'

'I don't think so, the neck's a bit low; I keep meaning to put a stitch in it, but then I forget.'

'Well, you don't need to cover up for me. Just the opposite in fact.'

She looked up and their eyes met, reflected in the mirror. She was afraid there was a hidden meaning behind his words, that he knew when she'd worn it, but he said nothing. Flustered, she quickly put the dress back and held up another. 'What do you think of this one?'

His eyes skimmed the dress, but he seemed to have lost interest.

'Yes, it's nice,' he said, as he left the room. Choosing a completely different outfit, she dressed and went downstairs as Paula the babysitter was arriving.

'You know where everything is,' Sharon said to her, 'just help yourself as usual.' Turning to Lily, she began to tell her what time she had to go to bed, but Lily stopped her.

'I already know Mum, it's a school night so in bed for eight o-clock, read for half an hour and settle down at eight thirty.'

'You've got it,' Tom said, as he walked into the room. He bent down to give her a hug, but she wriggled herself free.

'She's growing up fast, that one,' he said, as they walked to the car, 'if you blink long enough, she's changed in every way.'

'I suppose I don't notice it as much as you do, with seeing more of her.' She replied without thinking. She wished she could snatch the words back as soon as they were out of her mouth, but Tom didn't even seem to hear what she'd said. At the restaurant, they ordered a sharing platter of appetizers, but Sharon found she had no appetite and she idly pushed an olive around her plate.

'I've got something to tell you,' Tom said. 'Please don't interrupt, until I'm finished.'

'Very well, but make it brief.' Her hands were gripped so tightly, she could feel her nails digging into her hands and she could hardly breathe.

His eyes followed hers around the room until they were both satisfied, there was no-one they knew within hearing distance. He was surprised to see her face looking ready to crumble before he even began to speak. It was so unlike her to react like this at any time. Even in the past, when he'd been passing on his problems and worries concerning the business, she'd been strong and supportive. He decided to get it over with as quickly as possible so they could enjoy their meal.

'It mainly involves Fiona Campbell,' he began, but she stopped him.

'Oh, you do surprise me,' she said and he was about to ignore her and continue when he saw she was struggling to compose herself.

'Come on Sharon,' he said. 'It's bad I know, but it's not that bad.'

She picked up her bag and stood, ready to leave.

'If our marriage isn't important to you Tom, you needn't bother to explain. I'm going.'

'Sit down Sharon, please', he begged, 'I've been dreading telling you what I've done, but even so, I honestly had no idea you'd take it so badly. Will you just give me the chance to explain?'

Reluctantly, she sat down and shook her head slowly from side to side.

'You've got a cheek Tom Lester,' she said in disbelief. Tom's eyebrow lifted a fraction.

'I'm a bit confused,' he said slowly, 'are you annoyed because you found out before I told you? Is that it. And, just out of interest, how did you find out?'

'I'm not stupid,' she replied, 'and I didn't find out, about specific things, but you weren't careful enough hiding your tracks. There were lots of little clues along the way, late meetings with Fiona, overnight stays booked by Fiona, clubbing, oh let me see now, yes, of course, organised by Fiona. To tell you the truth Tom, I'm sick and tired of hearing about Fiona Campbell.'

A frown deepened as he tried to make sense of what she was saying.

'You are not half as fed up of her as I am,' he said, 'but if she's getting on your nerves as much as that, why don't you feel sorry for me?

'Sorry for you? I won't be laughed at Tom. You should know me better than that.'

He took her hand. 'I'm not laughing at you. I'm smiling because I love you, and I'm smiling because I think you've got the wrong end of the stick, and you couldn't be more wrong. Hear me out Sharon, please.'

Cautiously, she sat back and prepared herself for what he had to say, hoping against hope she was wrong. When he began to talk about budgets, and building regulations, she believed it was a delaying tactic, and she urged him to get to the point. Then she realised his smile had been replaced by a serious look of concern, and she began to listen intently.

There was no mention of infidelity, and the name Fiona Campbell never passed Tom's lips, except to say how devious and scheming she was. All he talked about were houses, building decisions and the quality of fixtures and fittings.

He even sounded sorry for multi-millionaire footballers, and then he finished off by apologising to Sharon for walking away from making a substantial amount of money.

'There you have it in a nutshell. I've pulled out of the Wilmslow project.'

'So, you're not building exclusive houses for very rich people?'

'That's right,' he replied, 'and I'm really sorry Sharon, I've blown it because of a few probably misguided principles.'

'I'm a bit confused, tell me again, what were they?'

He took a deep breath, before explaining how the developers had insisted on using inferior products provided by their cronies, despite the price of the luxury houses they were building. Only the thought of the money he would earn kept him there for a while, but there were endless arguments and delays, especially with the head of procurement Fiona Campbell. He hadn't been happy from the start of negotiations, but when he discovered substandard insulation had been ordered, he told them he wouldn't be associated with it. He was bound by a contract and couldn't just walk away, so he decided to get legal advice.

Sharon listened intently. 'Why didn't you tell me? We've always shared our problems.'

'I know, but I wanted to wait until I knew how I stood legally before involving you. Then, to make matters worse, you told me you were thinking of going to college, and I didn't want your decision to be decided by how expensive it is. I wanted to be able to tell you all the childcare, and well literally all your expenses, would be taken care of.'

'You know I would have supported your decision.'

'Yeah, but it still doesn't make it easier,' he sighed.

'Is the dodgy insulation dangerous?'

'For sure. Obviously, it will be okay as long as there are no fires, but it doesn't meet building regs.'

Her smile was warm, as she asked what the lawyer had advised him to do.

'I think you can guess,' he replied ruefully. 'Don't touch it with a barge pole, and maybe I drop a few hints to the powers that be, about the cause of the delays to completion. Fiona bloody Campbell was trying to save her own skin, even to the point of tendering other places for the insulation materials, but it was too late for me. I don't want anything more to do with it. She's been a nightmare. I think she is so jealous of people with money, it eats her up. She's definitely jealous of the footballers' wives.' He gave a little laugh. 'I think she'd like to be one of them.'

'So, she doesn't fancy you then?'

'Me? God no. She can't stand me, because I've been trying to block all her shifty deals, and anyway I don't have enough money for her. As a matter of fact, she's left the business.' Seeing Sharon's expression his face cracked into a broad smile. 'Don't ask me why, because I don't know and I don't care.'

All the anxiety of the last months melted away, but one crucial question still remained, and despite her reluctance to spoil the mood, she needed to know the answer. Tom was watching her closely and sensed something was wrong. 'What is it, Sharon, don't you believe me?'

'I do believe you,' she replied, 'but there's something I still don't understand. It's about the day Marie says she saw you in Wilmslow with a woman. I want you to tell me the truth. It was you, wasn't it?'

She waited patiently, as he took time to choose his words carefully, but when he started to grin, she couldn't hold back and told him crossly she didn't find it funny.

'Neither did I, at the time, in fact I had a few sleepless nights worrying about what I'd seen, because it was obvious to me, Marie was having an affair. I was convinced she wasn't a missing person, because here she was, enjoying the company of another man. She definitely didn't look as if she wanted to be rescued. Honestly, Sharon, I didn't know what to do'

'You could have saved Stuart a few sleepless nights if you'd told him, and we would have found Marie sooner.'

'You didn't see what I saw,' he insisted. 'They were like a couple of love-birds. He even cut up her food and fed it to her at one stage. For God's sake Sharon, I really believed they were having an affair, and you would have done too, if you'd seen them. She certainly didn't look as if she was there against her will, and I wasn't going to be the one to tell Stuart. It would have killed him.'

'What about telling me?'

'You wouldn't have been able to keep it secret. You'd have felt too sorry for him.'

She smiled, and agreed. 'You're right of course.'

'What's so funny, are you laughing at me?'

Now it was her turn to see the humour in the situation, and she couldn't stop smiling. 'It's so funny, I thought you were having an affair with Fiona Campbell.'

'And I thought Marie was having it off with a policeman.'

'He was helping her to eat a meal because one arm was strapped up.'

'Okay, have it your way, but I still say if you'd seen them, you would have thought the same. Now here comes our meal, let's forget two-faced Fiona Campbell, and enjoy it.'

Leaning across table, he told her again there had never been anything between him and Fiona, and he expressed his surprise that Sharon had believed him capable of deceiving her. She couldn't explain why she'd doubted Tom's integrity on such flimsy evidence, but it was becoming obvious, they would both need time to build up the trust they'd previously shared. Although she felt as though her face was lit up like a beacon, for the moment, she didn't care who saw it. At last, Sharon knew the truth.

Chapter 40

Bryony had been staying at the Windmill Inn, ever since she'd moved out of her accommodation at the Portland Arms. She'd secretly hoped Ralph would weaken and let her stay longer, to give her the opportunity to sort her life out, but he was implacable, and insisted all her belongings were to be removed in the time-scale he'd set out. Luckily, all of her valuable furniture and furnishings were in storage, waiting for her property to be finished, so it was mainly clothes which had to be removed from the hotel. Unfortunately, some of them were still stored in the room occupied by Hugh and Lucy, which caused embarrassment on both sides.

The house, which was nearing completion, was now her main source of financial security, but there were several legal arrangements to be finalised. She had already employed an agent to take care of them, until she decided what to she was going to do in the future. Ross favoured selling it to realise the investment while the property market was buoyant, but although she would never live in the house now, she couldn't bring herself to part with it. What saddened her even more, was the realisation that she would never be welcome in Merebank again. She could only hope that the details of what she'd planned to do, never slipped out.

She and Ross were due to fly to Greece the following week and despite her reservations about what the future in Greece may hold, her enthusiasm for their new life was steadily growing. The internet had proved helpful in giving her an insight into the intricate running of a casino, until one day Hugh had found her immersed in a page devoted to the role of a croupier in a casino. Intrigued by her new found interest, he at first thought his mother might be entertaining the idea of applying for a job at the Sunshine Complex. She was put in a difficult position, but when he was sworn to secrecy, she explained to him about the new venture. He wished his mother well, and told her he admired her spirit.

She was delighted, when Ross told her he'd secured a room for them at the Windmill Inn, which was theirs until the day of their departure. The only shadow cast over everything had been the lack of interest shown by his mother, who went out of her way to extol the virtues of Ross's ex-wife Mandy. Bryony lost no time in coercing Ross to accompany her to visit his parents, laden with flowers and chocolates. His father, who due to ill health, was on enforced rest, received them with an unexpected show of affection, and his mother gradually seemed to warm towards Bryony, who was putting on her best display of devotion.

None of this augured well for their Registry Office wedding, which would be very sparsely attended, and she was slowly coming round to Ross's suggestion for it to be held in Crete. Her wedding dress, which she'd bought weeks ago, was far more suitable for a warm climate, and holding their wedding in Knossos could prove beneficial. It would be an ideal way to introduce themselves to the staff and the local people, who they would be relying on to support the business they would be running.

Although she'd almost made up her mind to change the venue from the Registry Office to Greece, she decided to keep Ross guessing a little while longer. She was becoming quite adept at bringing out the softer side of him when she was trying to get her own way over something. She could envisage a happy partnership in the future, for both of them.

Looking again, at the brochures which featured their hotel and casino, she shuddered with apprehension. It had fifty bedrooms, so it was well within her capabilities to manage it herself. From the video Sarah had sent her, it all looked immaculate and tastefully furnished and the grounds were beautiful. She could very easily picture herself and Ross living there. The casino was an unknown quantity, but she was confident in her own ability to learn the tricks of the trade very quickly, and hopefully Ross would play his part.

'I've got an idea,' Ross said one day, 'Let's go to The Regal for a couple of days. It's getting boring just hanging around here.' Time was passing slowly, she had to admit that, but she wasn't sure about going to the place they'd been hoping to buy.

'I'd love to go to the Lakes for a few days, but must it be The Regal?'

'I don't see why not,' he said. 'It won't be easy finding one as good on the spur of the moment, and we know we'll get excellent service and food. Let's throw a few things in a case and we can be off before lunch time.

I'll just dash back home to pick up a few things, and I'll be with you about twelve.'

Bryony put her hand on his arm, and despite his impatience, he came to a stop and listened to her. She explained how difficult it would be for her to visit The Regal so soon after they'd lost the chance to buy it and she would much prefer to stay somewhere else.

Ross was surprised at the depth of her feeling, but he suggested another hotel he knew which was much smaller.

'It is a fascinating boutique hotel, and what it lacks in size, it makes up for in excellence,' he said.

That afternoon, when she was sitting in the hotel garden overlooking a lake, she found herself agreeing with him. It was the perfect place to relax and unwind from all the tensions of the last few weeks.

Spending the following day visiting some of the less touristy places in the Lake District, her pleasure was real, and the combination of hills and lakes lifted her spirits once again. This was her favourite part of the country and she'd always felt she would spend her retirement here. Well maybe she still would, although somehow, she doubted it.

Chapter 41

Lily had stayed the night at Marie's, but she was up bright and early, so to soften the blow, Stuart took Marie's breakfast to the bedroom and switched on the television, in the hope she would get involved in her favourite breakfast news programme. He was constantly reminding her she was still recuperating and needed more rest, but his words often fell on deaf ears. Today was different.

First of all, they had to get ready for a secret, but very happy event taking place at the beach huts this morning. That was to be followed by the really important part; Colin's marriage to Janet in the church ceremony in the afternoon. The reception at the golf club in the evening, would leave no opportunity for rest, so Stuart urged her to take advantage of this golden opportunity to grab some precious moments of peace and quiet.

Marie was tucking into the grapefruit segments, when her attention was caught by an item on the local news. It was covering the growth of drug addiction in children and the effects on both them and their families. The issue of the county line growing and spreading across the country was of great concern, especially to the small towns and villages where there currently was no known problem.

There were several interviews, but one was particularly interesting to Marie as it touched on her current experience. A boy, who was a designated carer for his mother, had experienced problems at school and dropped out of the education system. He'd been targeted by drug dealers and was now a dealer and an addict.

Most of the members of the public when asked for their opinions, were almost entirely critical of the boys and blamed them for the influx of drugs into their local environment, which until recently had been drug free.

Marie quickly switched the television off when she heard Lily coming up the stairs, but she was devastated by what she'd seen and heard.

'Grandad says there's a policeman on the phone and he wants to come to see you today.' Lily said, importantly.

Marie's heart sank. Was there to be no let up?

Lily watched intently as Marie crossed the bedroom and called out that it certainly wasn't convenient today. Stuart responded, by saying she must take the call herself, as DI Longridge wanted to speak specifically to her. He climbed the stairs and handed her the phone, with a whispered.

'Sorry, love, but he says it's important.'

Trembling, she listened carefully as DI Longridge explained there'd been an unexpected and important development since he'd seen her last. He needed to have a word with her in person, that day. At first, she adamantly refused, saying there wouldn't be any possibility of fitting it in, and when she explained what they had planned, he agreed it did pose a problem. Nevertheless, he still insisted he was coming, and advised her to choose the least inconvenient time, in the tight schedule.

Suddenly, she saw a way to utilise the visit. It was imperative she told him what she'd remembered about

Adam, as soon as possible, and what better way than for DI Longridge to come here immediately, before the news item became common knowledge.

'Actually,' she told him, 'I've got some news for you. If you come as soon as possible, that would be best.' As soon as possible it is,' he confirmed. This gave Marie a short time to work on her version of what had really happened, just before she fell down the steps at the station.

At first, after hearing about the change of plans, Lily was unhappy, pointing out they wouldn't have enough time to get ready, but Marie convinced her it wouldn't be a problem as she was quite prepared to throw the detective out if necessary. After a quick chat with Stuart, Marie agreed it was now safe to tell Lily what the surprise was, but only when she'd promised to keep the secret to herself. Lily's quizzical expression turned to squeals of delight as she listened to Marie's description of what they were planning to do, and the important part Lily was going to take in it.

'We'll have to hide the telephone, so Lily can't phone Sharon, because there is no way she will be able to keep it to herself,' Marie whispered to Stuart. He agreed, and suggested he could help, by keeping Lily occupied between now and the start of the celebration.

Marie sat and watched Stuart and Lily pottering in the garden, while casually flicking through a magazine Bryony had bought her. Suddenly, her attention was caught by a headline. 'Homes from Holmes, Is it a two-way split?' There was a family photograph of the parents and two siblings, including Ross Holmes, with his ex-wife Mandy. The article went on to describe the acrimonious divorce the couple had just been through, and the fall-out repercussions which had been the cause of the successful family business being put at risk. Ross was reported to be leaving the business and possibly the country, to begin another venture, which at the moment he was refusing to reveal.

'Well, well,' Marie sighed. 'Bryony, what are you getting yourself into?' There was no denying he was a very handsome man with possibly a substantial amount of money, but was he everything he professed to be? Only time would tell, but the inference from the article hinted at him being cut off from his family business, and possibly the members of his family. When she began to tell Stuart what she'd read, he stopped her, saying he wasn't interested in anything Bryony was doing.

'She's a trouble-maker and doesn't care who gets hurt, including you. No, especially you, so don't give her the time of day in future, is my advice.'

'I suppose you're right,' she replied.

'You know I am,' he said firmly. 'I'd concentrate on the day ahead, not Bryony. Or DI Longridge, for that matter,' he added under his breath.

Chapter 42

In the newly built extension to the golf club, preparations for his wedding were proceeding very well and Colin was very pleased with everything. The tables and chairs had been set out in rows for the actual ceremony, but they would be moved to the perimeter of the room for the evening celebrations. The D.J had been given a list of the couple's choice of music, although they had said he was welcome to intersperse it with familiar party songs.

A large net full of balloons was hung from the ceiling and fairy lights twinkled everywhere.

Ralph, who'd called in to see how things were progressing, remembered Bryony's aversion to balloons, calling them common, but he couldn't help feeling it was going to be a very jolly affair tonight and he was looking forward to it, even though he wouldn't be staying until the end. His nights of festivities into the early hours were over.

'Hi, Dad,' called Colin from the top of a ladder, 'I'll be down in a minute.'

'I'm alright,' Ralph replied, 'don't worry about me.'

Moments later, Colin was by his side. 'Have you seen the marquee?' he asked, and when Ralph told him that was his next port of call, Colin insisted on taking him.

The two men walked out of the building towards the marquee which was to act as an overflow area when the numbers were swelled by the guests who were invited for the evening celebrations. 'In here we're having a jazz band alternating with a rock and roll group,' Colin told his father, with more than a hint of pride in his voice.

Ralph was filled with admiration. This was certainly going to be a very well organised event, and he was genuinely looking forward to it.

'It was Janet's idea to have this,' Colin told his father. 'She was adamant we held our wedding here, but we didn't want to compromise on numbers, so she came up with this suggestion. To tell you the truth, dad, I never knew we had so many friends.'

Ralph put his arm round his son's shoulder. 'I'm pleased to see you so happy; you and Janet seem to get on very well.'

Colin was silent for a moment, thinking about what his father had said. 'I am happy,' he said,

'And yes, we do get on well. Bryony and I should never have married, because I knew from the outset, she didn't love me. It was always Greg she wanted, but I was flattered when she accepted my proposal. We were both miserable in the marriage and it was the best thing for both of us when we separated.'

Ralph agreed, but added. 'I'm so pleased that Janet came into your life when she did, now you can look forward to the happiness you deserve. I've never told you how proud you make me feel, and especially of everything you've achieved here, but I want you to know now, I think you've done a great job. It's no exaggeration when people say it's becoming the hub of the community.'

'Thanks Dad,' Colin replied, I appreciate that.'

They watched a group of friends putting up the temporary bar and Colin suggested they shared a bottle of beer. 'I can't drink too much before the wedding,' he said, but I'll be having a bit of lunch soon, do you want to join me?' Ralph accepted the drink but declined lunch. 'I'd better get back and check everything is alright. We're a bit short staffed with all this going on, it's been almost like a mass exodus'

Grimacing, Colin apologised, but his grin belied his words, 'That won't please Bryony and I'm sorry if I've put her in a bad mood. What's happening with her anyway? I heard she's not been around much recently. 'Is she on holiday?'

'No, not exactly, but I'll explain when you come back from your honeymoon.'

'Oh dear, has she been up to her tricks again?'

'You could say that,' Ralph replied as he walked away.

Chapter 43

DI Longridge was on time as usual, and knowing they were on a tight schedule, he lost no time in explaining to Marie the reason for his visit.

'There has been a massive breakthrough in our investigation,' he said, 'a witness has come forward with information which has changed the whole line of investigation.

'Is it going to help me?' she asked?'

'Very much so,' he replied with a broad smile.

'The man has to remain anonymous at the moment, so for the sake of what I'm going to tell you, I'll call him, the witness, and this is in his own words.'

The witness had been on platform four, where the lady was waiting to catch the train to the airport. The lady had first come to his attention when she was trying to see the message informing passengers of a change of platforms and he'd read it out to her. A few minutes later, he became aware of two boys standing close to the lady as she was trying to put something into her suitcase, and before walking down the platform to make a call on his mobile, he glanced up once or twice to make sure they weren't harassing her. The witness saw one of the boys handing her an envelope. The witness knew it was an envelope, because in the handover, the boy dropped it, and it fell between them. The lady watched as it was blown away, caught in a blast of air from a train travelling through the station. The lady left without it, so when the witness retrieved the envelope, he took it with him, with the intention of returning it to her on platform five. But, by the time he finished his call and reached the platform where his train was waiting, there was no sign of her. The witness, remembers passing a group of people surrounding a person lying on the ground near the bottom of the steps. He considered stopping, but after hearing one of them saying they'd phoned for an ambulance, he decided against it. There were already too many people crowding around someone who was in need of medical attention, and he assumed the person had been taken ill or fallen. As he walked towards the train, which had been delayed until the ambulance arrived, he saw the two boys again and one of them carried the lady's case onto the train, making him think they must be travelling together. Anxious about the possibility of missing his flight, and subsequent meeting, he forgot all about them, until the train made a brief stop at Wilmslow, when he saw the boys jump off and run towards the exit of the station. He recalls being slightly puzzled about the absence of the lady and her luggage.

Marie was silent. There was so much to take in. DI Longridge waited patiently.

That explains, Stuart said, 'why this man has only just come forward.'

'Yes, DI Longridge replied. 'He was out of the country until this week, and it was only on his return when he saw some of the publicity about the incident, that he realised he'd witnessed something important.

'Where does it leave me?' Maries voice was hardly more than a whisper.

'In the clear,' DI Longridge told her. We had already taken the two boys into custody and taken statements which tied in very well with that of the witness. Your case had already been found, as you know, and Adam has admitted putting the drugs in your case when you walked over to the litter bin, and also taking the cash out of your handbag. By taking a taxi, probably using some of your money I'm afraid,' he added, looking at Marie, 'they made it to their pre-arranged drop, just in time. You are completely exonerated of any involvement in drug dealing, no matter how tenuous.'

'What about the boys?' she asked.

'We are trying to get them on a rehab course, but it also depends on whether you press charges against Adam.'

'It's all coming back to me now, even the incident on the steps. Adam did offer to help, but made a grab for the handle at the same time. I was already off balance and I slipped and fell. He didn't deliberately push me, and I'm sure he didn't intend to make me fall, so I won't press charges.'

Stuart had remained very quiet since he'd entered the room, but there were some questions he needed answers to. 'Even if he didn't push her, they were still doing wrong. Will they be punished?' he wanted to know.

'I can't answer that, it's out of our hands now, but hopefully, they will be rehabilitated. The young one, Christy, has only just been recruited, so will probably get off with a caution, but I don't know if Adam will take the offer of rehab again. You have to feel sorry for some of them. For whatever reason, these kids drop out of the educational system and no matter how much help they are offered, they can't get back into the mainstream of society. For instance, if those boys had lost the drugs they were handling, it would be classed as a debt which they'd be expected to pay back. They would have to trade more to make more. It is a vicious circle they can't escape from.

DI Longridge saw the apprehension on Marie's face and he paused, and asked if she would prefer to continue to make the decision about Adam, at a later day.

'No,' she said.

'Are you sure, love?' Stuart asked, 'maybe you should think on it. There's no hurry.'

'How many times do I have to say it, Marie snapped. 'It was an accident.'

'Oh, I nearly forgot to give you this,' DI Longridge said, as he pulled an envelope from his pocket. 'A well-travelled milk bill and twenty-pound note.'

'Oh, we are well and truly in his debt,' Marie said with a smile on her face, we must find a way to thank him.'

'Have a good day,' DI Longridge said.

Marie assured him she fully intended to, and thanks to his news, she was certain she would have a fantastic day.'

'Oh no, where is Lily?' she exclaimed, looking round.

'Don't panic, Stuart laughed, 'she's next door playing with Nancy's kitten.'

'Oh, heaven preserve us,' Marie said, collapsing onto the nearest chair.

Chapter 44

'For the umpteenth time Sharon, I can't give you a clue,' Tom said, 'it's a secret and clues do tend to give secrets away.'

'But I have no idea what to wear. Is it a jeans and T shirt charity coffee morning, or are smart trousers and silk blouse a better choice? Just give me an idea, Tom, please.'

He walked over to her wardrobe and searched through the collection of dresses hanging there.

'Ah well, I can help you on that score,' he said slowly. 'It's posher than that. I think maybe this would do nicely.' With a flourish, he lifted out a dress and held it up.

'Yes,' he said, this will do very nicely indeed.'

'I'm not wearing that,' she exclaimed, 'it's my new dress for the wedding reception tonight.'

'Fair enough,' he said with a grin, obviously enjoying teasing her, 'I'm not wearing my best suit, and new shirt and tie, so I think you should consider your second-best dress. I'm diving in the shower now, so make your mind up quickly, we've got less than an hour before we leave.'

Intrigued, and a little irritated, she began to get ready. Tom had assured her it wouldn't matter if the odd person caught sight of her dress during the morning, but even so, she wanted it to feel fresh for Colin and Janet's evening celebration. But she'd taken on board what he'd said about his suit, and decided to go along with it. It was obviously something to do with the wedding, maybe a pre-wedding breakfast, and if everyone else turned up in their finery, so must she, but not the dress she'd bought for the wedding.

Hearing Ben in his room, she called to ask if he'd taken Rusty for a walk, and assured that he had, she took a sip of the champagne Tom had opened. 'Oh, someone's in a hurry,' Tom said, with a knowing smile, when the front door was slammed shut, and footsteps could be heard running down the path.

'I haven't a clue, what you've been planning,' she said, holding up her flute, 'but I'm feeling very happy.'

'Thank-goodness for that,' Tom said to himself, followed by a robust, 'Right, it is time to be going.'

Sharon began to fix her lipstick, but he urged her to move towards where the car was parked. 'We're not going very far, but we will drive there I think,' Tom said as he opened the passenger door with a flourish.

When they reached the car park close to the beach huts, there were groups of people making their way to the beach, but there was no sign of anyone she knew, until suddenly she heard the unmistakable sound of Lily's voice.

Sharon came to a sudden halt. 'Tom, you've got to tell me what's going on, or I refuse to take another step.'

'Okay,' he replied, 'but it will have to be quick or Lily will explode with excitement. It's something I arranged ages ago, to celebrate our anniversary. I wanted to book a full section of beach huts and today was the nearest available date with enough huts free. Stupidly, I didn't realise it was Colin's wedding when I arranged it, but everyone invited is coming here before going onto to the real wedding.

Sharon put her hand over his mouth to stop him speaking and told him to explain in a few simple words what was happening. Taking a deep breath, he told her they were about to renew their wedding vows in a mock ceremony, with the family playing the main roles, and friends as guests. It's our pretend wedding, with Lily and Jodie as your bridesmaids, Ben is my best man, and presiding over everything is Sam. Celebrations will be held in the huts and activities on the beach.

Sharon was speechless as she listened to Tom and gazed around looking for signs of the proposed celebrations. Tom, mistaking her silence for reluctance, urged her to go along with the plans he'd made.

'Please Sharon,' he urged, 'I realise now, I should have warned you, but everyone's waiting.'

'Then what are *we* waiting for? she laughed. 'We don't want to be late for our own wedding.'

Pulling her towards the first hut, he explained the need to get dressed up, and as they went in, she was met by an incongruous sight. Sam was playing the part of a very serious vicar; Ben was the best man with an oversized ring on an even larger cushion. Jodie, as a bridesmaid, was resplendent in a fluorescent outfit, obviously borrowed from one of the ugly sisters in a pantomime, and Lily was also a bridesmaid, dressed in a party dress with a startlingly garish posy and headdress. Within seconds of arriving, Tom was in top hat and tails, and Sharon had a long skirt tied around her waist and a posy and headdress identical to Lily's.

As they walked the short distance along the promenade, the music began to play and, on cue, their friends spilled out from the row of beach huts which were festooned with balloons and banners, and enthusiastically clapped the arrival of the wedding party. The 'service' proceeded in chaos, and when it was time for them to exchange rings, Sharon froze as Tom began to slide her wedding ring towards the end of her finger. She rarely took her ring off and she didn't want to start now. To her relief, he repeated the words said by Sam, the acting vicar, before pushing the ring firmly back to its original position, without it leaving her finger.

The food was plentiful, so Tom threw out an open invitation for spectators, especially children, to help themselves to a slice of pizza or a hot dog and join in the fun of the games. There were prizes for winners and losers, making the whole thing a great success. When it was opened, the towering, cardboard wedding cake, revealed a variety of tiny cup-cakes with strawberries and fresh cream, which prompted Sharon to say she would have to sample a few of them before the day was out.

'How on earth has Tom organised this, without my knowing?' she asked Louisa who had joined her.

'It can't have been easy,' Louisa replied, 'but he's had a lot of helpers.'

The guests who were attending the real wedding, were beginning to leave, and Sharon was busy saying goodbye to them all. Marie and Stuart had left earlier, whispering to Sharon they were going home to snatch a little catnap before going on to Colin's wedding. Sharon saw the tiredness beneath their lovely smiles, and she was overcome with gratitude for what they'd done.

'I would never have asked you to have Lily overnight if I'd known,' she told them, but they waved her concerns away, and told her that as usual Lily had been no trouble and they wouldn't have missed it for anything. But, they admitted, relentless excitement at that level, was tiring.

By the time Sharon arrived home to prepare for the evening disco, she agreed wholeheartedly with their opinions.

When they were all showered and dressed for the evening disco, they sat around the kitchen table to talk about the highlights of the day. Sharon told them it was one of the happiest days of her life, causing one or two gulps of emotion.

When Lily wondered aloud, about the next family wedding and whose it would be, Sharon didn't miss the look which passed between Sam and Jodie, and she guessed that was already featuring in their plans.

Ralph enjoyed the wedding ceremony and the delicious food served at the wedding breakfast, but the thing which gave him the most pleasure was seeing all his immediate family enjoying themselves together. Even though Hugh had decided to move on, Ralph admired him for his ambition, but he regretted the role Bryony had played in causing him to leave the business. Her desire to be admired by everyone had clouded her vision, and people like Hugh and Colin had suffered. Away from the constrictions of her power, Colin had flourished and was a much happier and successful man

During the lull of activity, between the meal and the evening celebrations, Ralph decided to take his doctor's advice and return home for a short time to rest. As soon as he reached his apartment, he lay on the bed and felt himself drifting off to sleep. When he woke, he felt refreshed and ready for the evening's entertainment. His friend had been invited to the evening celebration, and they were both looking forward to attending one of the jazz sessions in the marquee during the evening. That meant they would both be up and about later than usual and would be glad of a lift home.

On his arrival back at the celebrations, Ralph found himself surrounded by friends and family and soon he was drawn onto the dance floor by his very pregnant grand-daughter Amelia. In consideration of her condition, they were enjoying a slow waltz, when the music changed and the Master of Ceremonies announced the arrival of the bride and groom. Colin and Janet started the evening by performing a very professional first waltz, proving they'd practised their steps at the class they'd attended.

'Who would have guessed it of Colin?' Stuart said to Greg, as they joined in the clapping when the happy couple gave an impressive final swirl.

'Who indeed?' agreed Greg, taking his wife Katy's hand to lead her onto the dance floor. Sharon watched them as they expertly quick-stepped between the other dancers. 'Didn't they meet at Amelia's wedding?' she asked Marie.

'They did indeed. It was a very eventful time for a number of people, including Damian and Louisa of course. He was a groomsman and Louisa was a bridesmaid.'

'And look at them now,' Sharon said with a smile.

'Yes,' Marie replied, 'They are so happy,' In a corner of the dance floor, Lily and Zoe were attracting attention with their elaborate dancing, and some of the dancers on the floor were joining them, trying to follow and learn the intricate moves.

'It is beyond my capability to learn something like that,' Marie said with a smile, 'but Lily never stops trying to teach me.'

'I must pay you for her dress,' Sharon said. 'It's absolutely beautiful, but how did you manage to buy it without having Lily with you to try it on?'

'I didn't, I had it made, Marie explained. 'I got the measurements off Lily's Rosebud Princess dress and bought the material and a pattern, with the intention of making it myself. Then of course this happened.' She lifted her broken arm, and shook her head ruefully, 'I'm useless now, and not fit for anything, but a friend who makes clothes for her grand-children, offered to do it for me. I don't want you to pay anything, it's my gift to Lily.'

Sharon, who's emotions were very close to the surface, began to shed tears of happiness. 'It's been such a perfect day; I can't thank you enough.'

'Hi everyone,' Louisa greeted them, pulling a chair up to the table, 'I'm sorry we're late, but Pearl seemed to sense we were leaving and she just wouldn't settle with the babysitter.' 'You should have brought her, Sharon said.

'No, we fancied a grown-up night for a change,' Louisa looked at Sharon and beamed with pleasure. 'You look beautiful,' she said, and it was a lovely ceremony. Did you really have no idea what was going on?'

'Not a clue,' Sharon replied. 'To be honest if I had, I would probably have said it was a silly idea. But actually, it was lovely.'

'Now, do you understand, when I said I knew Tom loved you?'

'Ahh, yes.'

'What's all this,' demanded Marie.

'It's nothing,' Sharon replied. 'Just my silly imaginings,'

Marie had to be content with that.

Chapter 45

Bryony arrived at the airport and joined the queue winding through customs and security. As time was short, it was a real advantage to have checked in online, giving her time to unwind with a drink in the departure lounge. She was expecting a call from Ross, but there were some places in the hospital with very poor connections, and she was reluctant to ring him at this late stage, when it was so close to departure time. She wasn't sure how he would accept her decision to make the journey without him, but she'd felt she was left with no choice.

It was shortly before they were due to leave for the airport, when Ross received the call from his mother, telling him his father had been admitted to hospital with a suspected heart attack. She expected Ross to go immediately to be with her, but seeing Bryony's obvious disappointment, he made no promises to either of them until he'd seen the doctor who was in charge of his father's care. When Bryony received the call from Ross, telling her they would have to cancel their flight, she was left with a dilemma, so before she decided what to do, she made a call to Ross's friends Luke and Sarah in Greece, to break the news that she and Ross would be unable to make the journey and start running the hotel as arranged.

Luke was disappointed to hear the news and told her he would like to speak with his wife to discuss what the next move would be. Anxiously, Bryony tried to convince him it would be a short delay, but they both knew there was no certainty of the outcome being known.

When he rang back it was to put a proposition to her. The situation would put them under a lot of strain, and obviously they couldn't keep the positions open indefinitely. They needed help now.

Luke told her they'd been very impressed with her Zoom interview, and together with Ross's recommendation, both he and his wife felt confident Bryony would be able, with help, to run the hotel until Ross made it over there. They offered her time to consider it, but time was running out, and without hesitation she accepted the offer and told them she would be on the flight as arranged.

Her next attempt to contact Ross was interrupted by the last call for passengers to Iraklion to go immediately to the departure gate, so she would ring him when she was aboard the plane.

When the aircraft was in the air and mobiles could be switched on, she phoned Ross and was pleased to hear him sounding cheery. 'It's not looking too bad,' he said, 'so don't worry, we'll be able to go soon. I'll ring Luke when I can get my phone charged. Maybe you could bring a charger in, when you visit.'

'I think you'll need one before I can come to see you'

There was a silence on the line. 'What do you mean? Bryony, where are you?'

'I can see Cheshire below me, and I was just thanking one of the cabin crew for my gin and tonic. Let me explain,' she said, grateful for the empty seat beside her as she told him what had happened.

'How did you get there on time?' he asked, 'it must have been one heck of a rush.'

'It was, but I made it.'

She held her breath, waiting for his reaction, and then she heard a roar of laughter.

'I didn't know what to do,' she explained, 'but I didn't want to let them down, especially after they contacted me and said they were confident I could run the ship until you came.

I was afraid they would withdraw the offer to us. I think you'd better tell your parents, but I don't know what you can say.'

'I'm going to tell them exactly what you've done, and also what a feisty, wonderful woman I'm marrying just as soon as I possibly can. I promise you; I'll be on the plane to Iraklion at the very earliest opportunity.'

'Where will you stay until then?' she asked him.

'I haven't thought about it, but I may as well be at home, I suppose.'

'Don't forget to collect my wedding dress, it's in the wardrobe at the Windmill Inn. 'You can't miss it; It's in a travel case.'

'I won't. I promise. Anything else for me to bring?'

'No, just yourself.'

Chapter 46

Sharon and Tom were dancing to the waltz they'd danced to at their own wedding. It was a slow number and when Lily caught sight of them holding each other close, she stood still for just long enough to pull her mouth down on one side to show her disdain for their actions.

'The little madam,' Tom said, holding Sharon even tighter, 'I thought she'd be ready for bed by now.' Sharon rested her head on his shoulder, and their waltz turned into a smooch. It had been a lovely day, from start to finish. She'd had no idea what Tom had been planning and the boys and Jodie had given no clues, so it had been a complete and utter surprise, and a beautiful one.

Colin and Janet's marriage had touched everyone with its heartfelt sincerity, and the subsequent celebrations had catered to everyone's tastes. There had been much laughter amongst some of the guests, who found they had very little time to leave Sharon and Tom's party, to go home and change, and reach the church in time for Colin and Janet's wedding.

A few of the men had walked together along the promenade, giving a spontaneous rendition of 'Get me to the church on time,' so, they were all having a very busy and enjoyable day.

Lost in her thoughts, she hadn't heard what Tom was whispering to her. 'Sorry?' she said, 'what did you say?'

'I was just wondering if you fancy a walk on the prom, there's a fantastic sunset out there.'

'Oh yes,' she replied, 'we haven't done that for ages, I'll just ask Cora if she'll keep an eye on Lily.'

There were a few couples walking on the beach, making the most of the balmy evening and the glorious sunset. One or two families were reluctantly making their way back to their cars and couples strolled along the beach with their arms around each other.

'Do you remember when that was us?' Tom asked, and she nodded. 'We're so lucky to be living here Tom.'

'I know.' They'd almost reached the beach huts which were quiet now, but her heart beat a little faster at the memory of the carnival evening. As if reading her thoughts, Tom said, 'Do you really like him, Sharon?'

'Like who?' she asked, stalling for time.

'Oliver, the man you got all dolled up for, in a sexy dress you wouldn't wear for me.'

She was silent, playing for time. How did he know? A siren screamed as a police car travelled along the promenade, before disappearing into the distance. 'It's true I did wear that dress when I went for the meal, but it didn't mean anything. Don't forget, I bought it for our anniversary celebration and I felt let down. I understand now why you did what you did, but at the time I thought you were seeing Fiona.'

'That isn't answering my question.'

'Yes, I do like him, but that's all. He's a friend, nothing more.'

She turned to face him, and held his hands in hers. 'That's all there was to it. He was kind, and there when I needed someone to talk to, although I never spoke about us,' she told him. 'It was never going to be anything more than that.'

'I was seriously worried you know. I thought I was losing you.'

Sharon was shocked. 'But why?' she asked, 'and how did you even know about him?'

'Just little things, which on their own meant nothing, but added together seemed more important. And I saw you dancing with him on the prom.'

Her heart lurched. 'Why didn't you let me know you were there?'

'You looked happier than I'd seen you look for a long time, and that didn't exactly make me feel good.'

'It was just a bit of fun, but actually I was unhappy. Don't forget, I thought you were having an affair.'

'I take that as an insult,' he snorted, 'at least the bloke I saw you with wasn't bad looking and seems nice enough, but what on earth made you think I was interested in her?'

'You were always having meetings, especially in the evening, and your mind always seemed to be elsewhere. Of course, the episode in Wilmslow didn't help.'

'It seems we were both getting carried away. I was really worried you wouldn't go along with today, and so many people were involved, including Lily, although she didn't know until the last minute.'

'It was a lovely idea,' she said, 'zany but lovely, just the sort of thing you would have done when we were first married. Tom, why were you near the beach huts, that night? I thought you were with your mates.'

'I was looking for you, I wanted to be with you.'

'Then you'll have to catch me if you can.'

Her voice was carried on the breeze as she turned away and ran along the promenade as quickly as she could.

Her heart pounding in her chest, she threw herself down on a bench, panting for breath. Exhilarated by the chase, Tom caught up with her in seconds, and his eyes sparkled as he laughed and sat next to her, pulling her close.

They sat together, breathing deeply, as the sea breeze rolled off the shore and cooled their skin. Something about this moment, the renewal of vows in their heads, and the sound of the sea, epitomised their affection for this place they'd made their home, and they turned to each other. Their love, had always been there, sometimes buried under work and the normal demands that life had thrown at them, but always there. Sharon smiled. As she turned to go, she caught sight of Ralph, standing at his picture window high in the hotel.

'Look Tom,' she said as she waved and he waved back, 'doesn't he look lonely?'

'I don't know how you can tell from this distance.'

'I can, and I think he looks sad.' She took his hand. 'Come on, let's get back to our family and friends, and enjoy the rest of this wonderful day.'

Milton Keynes UK
Ingram Content Group UK Ltd.
UKHW040800291223
435170UK00001B/10

9 781803 816982